ALSO BY DAVID TREUER

Rez Life

The Translation of Dr. Apelles

Native American Fiction: A User's Manual

The Hiawatha: A Novel

Little: A Novel

Praise for *Prudence*

"What does it say about our troubled times—and David Treuer's considerable talents—that his World War II–era novel speaks to the present moment in American history with more eloquence and complexity than the nightly newscast. . . . Tender and devastating. . . . [A] master class on suspense, shifting perspective, and conflicting desire."

—Anthony Marra, *The Washington Post*

"Treuer does a masterful job exploring the multiple stories that culminate in the death of a young woman in small-town Minnesota. . . . One of the most honest, moving novels about America in quite a while."

—*Los Angeles Times*

"Both blunt and hushed in tone, wielding a sledgehammer while walking on tiptoes . . . Treuer doesn't just unravel the plot we might expect; he prompts us to interrogate the assumptions—racial, sexual, and otherwise—that build up those expectations in the first place."

—NPR

"Tightly plotted hybrid fiction that combines elements of a mystery, a literary romance, and a Greek tragedy." —*Chicago Tribune*

"So good that when you get to the end, you'll want to reread the beginning to see how the author set his magic in motion." —*MORE*

"Without judgment, but also without blinking, [Treuer] expertly vivisects characters who can't own up to the truth about themselves, showing how the unaddressed damage only deepens over time. . . . *Prudence* hurts, and that hurt lingers. Very few novels take that much of a risk." —*The New York Times Book Review*

"[A] master craftsman of evocative scenes . . . *Prudence* is evidence that Treuer's literary powers continue to grow. He knows people and goes to places foreign to most American writers, and his stories deeply honor 'the unremembered,' to whom he dedicates this book."

—Minneapolis *Star Tribune*

"Beautifully captures a place and an era. . . . Treuer imbues mundane moments with reverence. . . . And he masterfully weaves into the narrative minor characters who have major resonance." —*Seattle Times*

"Treuer's writing is supple, his story intricate. That it's set against the backdrop of one of the most tumultuous periods in history makes it all the more haunting and powerful." —*Out*

"Compelling . . . [and] arresting . . . Treuer writes as an insider . . . his Ojibwe characters are multifaceted individuals, not mere decorative ciphers. They are, moreover, engaged like everyone else in their country's broader history. . . . [Treuer] brings to life a little-examined corner of America, and shows how it, too, was touched by war."

—*Financial Times*

"Treuer writes beautifully about the dark corners of human nature, and the brief reprieves that come in even the most unhappy lives."

—*Entertainment Weekly*

"The relationships . . . are deep and complex. . . . The language is etched with poetry, the emotions deeply felt." —*Pittsburgh Post-Gazette*

"In succinct, finely tuned prose, Treuer . . . reveal[s] . . . [an] intimacy [that] in this time and place . . . is truly a love that dare not speak its name. Treuer depicts its growth . . . realistically and tenderly."

—*Milwaukee Journal Sentinel*

"Treuer's novel captures in [a] careful, lustrous narrative, a time in which passion was restrained in public yet extravagantly expressed in writing. He not only sets his book in the early twentieth century, he channels authors of that era—the writers he sees as his stylistic cousins." —MinnPost

"So intricately plotted, so filled with strong characters, it should win major awards." —*St. Paul Pioneer Press*

"At its core, [*Prudence*] is a tale of unrequited love and random violence . . . [yet] in Treuer's skillful, multi-vocal telling, neither love nor death appears sensational or simple. . . . Both Native and non-Native people suffer and yearn, and the craft of the novel lies in the ways it enables the reader to traverse the social and emotional distances the characters themselves are unable to." —*Public Books*

"An intricate ensemble piece; exploring themes of loss, desire, race, war, and the secrets we keep, through the point of view of five beautifully realized characters. . . . In clear, uncluttered prose, Treuer guides us through ten years [and] multiple voices . . . gorgeous."

—Portland *Oregonian*

"Treuer creates remarkable depth of emotion with language that is spare, descriptive, and poignant. . . . It's no secret that love is complicated, but rarely have its complications been explored so hauntingly. This is a novel that will stay with you long after you finish reading it."

—everydayebook.com

"Treuer's experience writing about Native American history and culture is apparent in this analysis of race and memory."

—*Huffington Post*

"Acutely emotional . . . mesmerizing [and] beautifully told."

—*BookPage*

"Magnetizing and richly original . . . [with] extraordinarily affecting characters. . . . Treuer's trenchant and compassionate novel glimmers with nature's potent beauty, fresh historical detail, and scrupulous insight." —*Booklist* (starred review)

"Achingly moving . . . speaks volumes about . . . integrity, culpability, and resilience in the face of collective tragedy." —*Publishers Weekly*

"A self-assured, absorbing story . . . [that] explores the darkness at our cores." —*Kirkus Reviews*

"Thoughtful and engaging. . . . [A] well-told tale with realistically portrayed characters . . . [and] a voice that is low-key but forceful . . . [and] elevate[s] this story to a powerful level." —*Library Journal*

PRUDENCE

DAVID TREUER

RIVERHEAD BOOKS
New York

RIVERHEAD BOOKS
An imprint of Penguin Random House LLC
375 Hudson Street
New York, New York 10014

The Library of Congress has catalogued the Riverhead hardcover edition as follows:

Treuer, David.
Prudence : a novel / David Treuer.
p. cm.
ISBN 978-1-59463-308-9
1. World War, 1939–1945—United States—Fiction. 2. Families—Minnesota—Fiction.
3. Leech Lake Indian Reservation (Minn.)—Social life and customs—Fiction.
I. Title.
PS3570.R435P78 2015 2014028541
813'.54—dc23

First Riverhead hardcover edition: February 2015
First Riverhead trade paperback edition: February 2016
Riverhead trade paperback ISBN: 978-1-59463-407-9

Printed in the United States of America
10 9 8 7 6 5 4 3 2 1

Book design by Susan Walsh

PRUDENCE

PROLOGUE

THE VILLAGE—AUGUST 3, 1952

Everyone remembers that day in August 1952 when the Jew arrived on the reservation.

In later years the Indians would sometimes wonder idly at the strange fact of his arrival, and his departure on the first train to Minneapolis the next morning. But the Jew was forgotten that day, until then a day like any other; hot and muggy and filled mostly with the thrum of wind-plucked power lines and the crack of grasshoppers lifting out of the sand and spent grass. The Jew stepped off the train and into the thoughts of the villagers, and he exited the station and their minds just as quickly, because an hour or two after the train groaned to a stop, one of the hotel maids found Prudence's body in the room above the Wigwam Bar. And then there was that. Her poor young body arched and twisted and frozen in the August heat. And Prudence's baby, too, whom no one saw alive, not even Prudence, in its little cathedral of blood. And there was that, too.

Not long after the maid found her, the sheriff had come. After him the coroner. Then Felix and Billy, separately. Soon, everyone in the village, Indian and white and in between, had gathered outside the hotel, and in front of the hardware store, and the grocer's, on the platform that served the depot, and in the Wigwam itself. Since the village didn't consist of more than those small stores and the hundred or so Indians and loggers whose houses clustered around the railroad tracks, the gathering didn't look like much.

It was, as dramatic events go, quiet. There wasn't much fuss when her body was loaded onto a canvas stretcher, covered with a white sheet, and handed down the narrow stairs like a ham in paper. The passage of Prudence's body from the apartment above the Wigwam was performed with the solemnity of the viaticum. No one raised a fuss, even though she was twenty-six and pregnant and alone, and now dead. It just wasn't that kind of village. And northern Minnesota wasn't that kind of place. Besides, it was 1952 and there was a war on. The world was much too big to worry itself about a dead Indian girl. No one wondered, really, what had happened or why, in the way people who aren't accustomed to being wondered about discover they dislike thinking about themselves. It was too hot, in any event, to do more than sit and shake one's head. No. It was much better not to think of Prudence at all.

PART I

THE PINES
AUGUST 1942

ONE

Emma Washburn watched the small figures across the mouth of the river. There was no change. Not that she could see from where she stood in the front room, which served as dining and sitting room for the Pines. She stood with her hands on her hips and then, after a moment, crossed them under her bosom, and then again placed them on her hips, as though her posture could somehow affect the search for the missing prisoner. No change. Across the river the men still milled in the yard of the prison camp formed by the right angles of the unpainted cabins. The camp had gone up quickly. Where there had been nothing the previous August was now a high fence enclosing four bunkhouses, a dining hall, three guard cabins, and a storeroom.

Back when they bought the Pines in 1923 the opposite bank was just a grass-covered bluff with nice, shady trees ringing the edges. The Indians from around the reservation camped there sometimes. They were harmless. Nothing at all like the Indians in the movies. Before the camp Emma heard them singing and saw the lights of small fires on the bluff in late summer. And that's how it had been until the prisoners started coming in February 1942. At first they slept in canvas tents, but by spring they had the camp set up. What an eyesore.

As the heat had built up over the day, and with it the wind, Emma had heard the barking of the dogs and the shouts and whistles of the policemen and volunteers as they formed yet another search party. Why did they have to put the camp right there, where you could see it out of the front windows? And why did that German have to escape, this week of all weeks, just when Frankie was coming back? Why did he have to try and escape at all? His war was over. The cabins weren't bad and they were even paid for their labor, if you could believe it. Surely his people wouldn't treat American prisoners so well. Emma waved the thought away.

Despite her many duties—making sure the girls heated the water up enough to really clean the sheets, seeing that Felix put up the wood for the kitchen stove and finally got around to cleaning up the beach (the smell was getting stronger), counting the lemons and the oranges and weighing out the flour, soda, and sugar because it wouldn't do to send someone off to town for more, what with all the guests and the millions of things that had to be done to make sure it all went smoothly, cleaning the windows inside and out so no one, especially Frankie, had to wake up and see cobwebs and dead mayflies instead of trees (if they were on the backside of the Pines) or the lake (Frankie would get the lake room, of course), and starching the napkins and the tablecloths herself, and in the heat, only because the girls, being Indians, didn't know what proper starching was, and, oh, the bait, too, because the Chris-Craft would go out at least twice a day, assuming that the constable returned it, because the search couldn't possibly go on much longer—Emma could not tear herself away from the window. This could ruin everything. Even with her worry about all the things that had to get done and Frankie's train arriving that afternoon and the whole thrumming enterprise of the Pines, which depended on her, and the search party organizing itself like an anthill that had been stepped on, she felt like a king, yes, a king, not a queen. A king with his castle at his back, gazing out over the scene of a siege, which, God willing, would be lifted soon so they could all breathe and, more than that, so they could all properly welcome home the prince, who was coming all the way from Princeton before heading south for aviation cadet training in Montgomery.

"You could go with them at least once, Jonathan," Emma said without turning around. The rustling of the paper stopped. He always heard everything. "It wouldn't hurt. Everyone is joining in."

"It *would* hurt, dear. It would. You know how hot it is out there. And the woods in August? It's a jungle. Let the locals do it. And the Indians. Let them do it. It's what they're good at."

Of course, even after buying the Pines in 1923, when everyone else was selling or trying to sell, and keeping it running, and hiring Finns to cut and mill timber for new cabins and taking on Indian girls during the season to do the cleaning and washing and even letting old Felix live there as caretaker, year-round, didn't buy them much credit with the locals, as her husband called them. The Washburns would never be locals. They would never really belong up north, not in the minds of those who were there before them. But it was the Washburn place, and Washburns occupied it and kept it from sinking into the ground. A little Chicago spit, she liked to say, a little Chicago spit and a lot of determination, and there wasn't anything a Washburn couldn't keep running. Though she was the one who put in the work. She was the one who came up by train soon after ice-out each year and got the place going again. Every spring she left Chicago the first weekend in May and took the Hiawatha to Saint Paul and then the B&N to Duluth, where she switched again and headed west to Bena, the small town of Indians, mixed-bloods, and loggers in the middle of the reservation. Without fail Felix would be at the station, waiting next to the Chevy Confederate, the bed filled with supplies, and he'd drive her out to the mouth of the river where the Chris-Craft waited, lapping against the dock he had built, shored up with cribs he made from tamarack and filled with river stone, listing, of course, because the ice had pushed it over, but Felix would get to it in due time. Felix parked the truck and then started the boat and ferried her across the river to the Pines. What a sensation! Every time, the first glimpse made her heart rise up and beat faster, without the lessening effect that repeated exposure to a thing usually causes. Like love (but why did she think of that?). All winter she yearned for a glimpse of the white clapboard main house with its fieldstone chimney poking through between the front room and the "lobby." And the smaller cabins huddled around back like children waiting behind a beautiful mother. It filled her with pride to think that it was hers. It had been a grand resort once and she would make it grand again—a place for their family and friends and someday her grandchildren to gather. Of course it was *theirs*, together, but: it had been her idea to buy it and to live there and make it a business. Not that it had become a true business. The visitors were confined to friends and family. But that was just fine—it was a place for them, and as the years passed, her initial fantasy of a real resort, a combination of the domestic and the wild, shifted to an even more pleasing reality of a family that came together again and again in a special place that was theirs alone and grew stronger by coming together. Jonathan didn't care much one way or the other. When she first went to see the Pines and came back to Chicago gushing—*the trees! the lake!*—he had said it was too far away. The Dells would work. Hayward, maybe. You couldn't even drive to the Pines, you had to cross over in a boat, and it was on a reservation, and surely the Indians would break in or set it on fire or something. Jonathan didn't trust anyone. That was his problem. But the Gardners—who owned the mill in the village and three more throughout the state—had a place up the shore and so did the Millers (surely he remembered them from when they stayed at Lyon's Landing the first time they'd gone up, shortly after they were married). And they had children, too. Children Frankie's age.

Each spring, when Felix eased the boat into the dock and tied it to the wooden cleats that he had carved from spruce root, quite nimbly for an Indian with big, clumsy hands, she stepped off the rocking boat and onto the solid dock as though she were stepping into the world she had been waiting for all her life; a world for which she was *intended.* Always, before doing anything else, she stalked the property as if in a dream, touching the weathered boards of the boathouse and toeing the dead grass and weeds to see if the daylilies had begun to poke their spears through the earth. She walked around the main house and looked for shingles on the grass and worried over every fleck of paint that had peeled off the spruce clapboard. After the long winter and the bustle of Oak Park it shook her to realize that some things, even those things far away from her in space and time, and especially those things that she loved, continued to exist, continued to endure. That anxiety and that wonder, mixed as they were, must be what love was. This was love.

Her marriage was something else. It had a different timbre. A different tone. It more closely matched the stateliness of their home in Oak Park than the wildness of the Pines. She and Jonathan had been married twenty-seven years now, and with each passing year the union grew more spacious. It had more echoes. There was more room to move around in it now than there had been at first—in those early years when Jonathan was just starting his practice and she lost Josephine and then after much trying Frankie had been born and Emma had her concerts and recitals, which slowed to a trickle and then to drips and then stopped altogether except for the once-a-year party they held in the second-floor ballroom. The house in Oak Park was a proper house and theirs was a proper marriage. She never worried about the solidity of either, but nor did she exult in them. They just were and always would be.

It was different with Frankie, of course. He was, *still* was, her baby. Not just because he was her only child (there had been Josephine, but she had been with them for just a few weeks before God took her away). He was special. When she thought of him she felt the same combination of dread and wonder, fear and pride, that she felt when she arrived at the Pines every May. Frankie was a special boy. In the months after he was born, his cheeks were flushed red. Rosy. He sweated easily. As he grew older he never turned into the robust boy Jonathan had hoped for. "Anemia," Jonathan pronounced when Frankie, at eight, fainted during gym class. When he turned twelve and gave up athletics altogether, Jonathan said that Frankie had a hormone imbalance. Emma and Frankie accepted this as true; after all, Jonathan would know.

But when Fenwick's let out, and Frankie came to the Pines, he bloomed. His favorite thing was to follow Felix around. Not that the old Indian spoke to him much. But Frankie seemed content just to spend time with him, watching him carefully as he mended the dock or replaced siding or cut back the riot of goldenrod and joe-pye that crowded the cabins abutting the woods. Or he'd go on adventures with Billy, the half-breed who had begun as a dock boy and became, over the years, Frankie's daily companion. Frankie grew tan over those summers, as though the sun's movement were harmonized with his. His skin lost its blush and turned apricot, golden. Not that Jonathan noticed, when he deigned to show up for two or three weeks in August, after much beseeching and urgent letters and even telegrams. But Emma was always thrilled at how robust, how alive, Frankie became in the summertime. "Oh! You're my little Indian, aren't you? My little Indian man. Isn't he, Felix? Isn't he turning into a little brave?" Felix always nodded and said, "Uhhgg. Yes. A little brave."

He was brave now. Princeton had changed him. He had grown taller, his shoulders broader. He'd joined the Nassoons and sung in Blair Arch, his face thrust up to the vaults as though a string ran from his chin through the arch and into God's gentle hand. His voice rang clear and strong. He was, Emma thought, a passable tenor for that kind of music, for glee club music. He would never sing *Die*

Winterreise, nor should he. And opera! No, no, no. But the glee club pleased him and it suited him and it was good to do things that both pleased and suited a person; this was the key to happiness. And, with the whole country in the swing of war, Frankie had decided to join the Air Force. A pilot, he'd written in February. He was to be a pilot on something called a B-17. He had already joined the Reserve Officers' Training Corps in addition to his regular classes, and he found time on the weekends to take flying lessons in Lawrenceville. He was to go to Maxwell Field in Alabama for aviation cadet training, and from there, who knows where?

So everything had to be perfect at the Pines. It wasn't. First they had put that prisoner camp across the river, and now one of them had escaped. She'd wanted one last glorious August, one last innocent holiday before Frankie joined the world and the war. But how could you forget something like the war when you opened the curtains and saw the camp across the way? And with one of them escaped. There was no telling where he was or what he was up to. You couldn't trust them a bit. Germans were awfully clever and they never gave up, even when they were beat.

"They might need a doctor, you know," said Emma, finally, as she turned from the window. "Someone could get hurt. Or maybe the prisoner is injured somewhere out there in the woods."

She approached the French doors that separated the front room from the sitting room. Jonathan sat to the side of the fireplace in the leather chair she'd bought from the sanatorium when it closed, his legs crossed. The paper was open on his lap.

"If you're worried about appearances, send Felix."

"It would just be better if they found him before Frankie gets here. That way we can all relax and enjoy ourselves."

"Send Felix. It's genetics, you know. Some races are better at some things than others. It's as simple as that. He was born to it."

"I know. I mean, I know you're right." She bowed down to the truth of what he said. These things had been proved by science, of course. Jonathan turned back to the newspaper. Men and their papers. She was glad Felix was illiterate. Otherwise he might be just like Jonathan.

"It serves them proper anyway. What brain trust thought it would be good to put a bunch of captured German sailors on the banks of the Mississippi? Of course they are going to try and escape downriver."

"I wonder if Frankie will see any Germans when he is in the Air Force."

"Germans make for good pilots. And they have very good planes."

"Oh."

"It's a shame we have to fight them. Now, the Chinese!" Jonathan wagged his finger at an imaginary debater. "Watch out for them. Them and the Japanese. They can't be trusted."

"Oh, dear."

"Anyway. It's bad enough that the paper is a week old before it gets here. I don't want it to age any more before I finish it."

"Frankie will bring a new batch with him. I asked him to in my telegram."

"Ernest and the others are meeting him?"

"They were supposed to. But now . . ." But now Ernest and David and some of the other boys Frankie had gotten to know over the years might get sucked into the search, and the welcome party would be a bust. And if they did meet the train, who knows what trouble they might get into on the way home? Maybe they would go to the Wigwam. Or someplace else. And then, with the boat being used in the search, how would they cross the river?

Emma brushed past Jonathan, her muslin skirt with the little plaits of straw—they made such a pleasing sound when she walked up the heart-pine steps or deftly set the table in the dining room—brushing against Jonathan's chair and his outstretched and tap-

tapping foot, which dangled in midair over his crossed leg. The parlor, with the fireplace and few stuffed chairs and the couch against the far wall, wasn't all that big. One did need to brush past others sometimes when in such small spaces (this wasn't the Mackinaw Hotel, after all), but she'd done it on purpose, had wanted to show Jonathan that she was taking matters into her own hands, that she was going to make sure that everything was perfect. She wouldn't leave anything to chance, escaped prisoner or no. And what was one escaped German sailor? He wasn't a soldier. He wasn't a killer. He probably had to watch gauges on his U-boat. He was a clerk in uniform sitting at his desk under the sea. Anyway, she hadn't exactly meant to flounce past Jonathan. She wasn't twenty-three anymore. She was forty-one. An old lady.

Jonathan didn't want to help with the search, and that was embarrassing. When everyone was out helping each other, you certainly didn't want your husband sitting at home reading the paper. She would go herself, except that someone had to make sure the Pines was up and running properly. Not just properly, but grandly. And it would just add to their shame for her to put on her khakis and garden boots and one of Jonathan's flannels and walk through the brush with the Indians and the loggers. Jonathan would certainly not let her hear the end of it. But more than that, she had hoped he would show more excitement, more joy, at the prospect of Frankie coming back to the Pines one last time before he joined the Air Force, if only for two weeks. So far the only thing Jonathan seemed to feel was annoyance. He was annoyed (or "put out," as he said the night before) by the hubbub, by the expense (did they really need a bushel of lemons?), by the general activity and disruption. All he wanted to do was read his papers and books on politics and genetics and have a scotch before bed.

He'd always been mildly annoyed by Frankie, this was true. Emma's face was stuck in a frown as she walked the short hallway toward the kitchen, where the girls were preparing the food. Jonathan was not an effusive man, not given to big hugs or romantic gestures or anything of the sort. He was embarrassed by the drama of affection. Embarrassed by affection itself. Or so it seemed. He had always been uncomfortable when Frankie wanted to sit on his lap. Almost as uncomfortable as when he had to fulfill his marital duties. Though thankfully such negotiations were far behind them now, receding in the turn of years. Frankie's nature, his personality, seemed to disappoint Jonathan somehow. His delicate nature. Anemia. Hormones. Whatever it was. Jonathan had consulted colleagues and had put Frankie on a regimen of cold showers and raw liver. And when Frankie protested (the water was cold, the liver was disgusting), Jonathan shook his head and threw his hands up in the air as though in defeat—though it was Frankie, not Jonathan, who had been defeated. It was Frankie who cried. It was Frankie who had failed. Jonathan had emerged from these ordeals unscathed and unmoved, convinced there was something, somehow, wrong with Frankie. Something beyond fixing. There were more tortures in store. Frankie was forced to join the Boy Scouts. He was sent to camp in Michigan. But these weren't opportunities as much as humiliations. He came home, each and every time, with new stories for Emma; stories about his misery and discomfort. Frankie had never been manly. Nothing was going to change that. Under his new Princeton muscles, his shoulders were still as narrow as his hips. His wrists looked, even to Emma, painfully thin. But Jonathan was hardly a strapping man himself. Frankie was built just like his father. Not that the father could see it, or would ever admit it. Oh, no! Ask him and he'd remind you that he boxed for Princeton and had competed in the pentathlon in the 1928 Olympics. Ask him and he'd remind you of the marches he'd undertaken in the Great War. He was full of stories about his own exploits, if you got him going, but he was hardly a big, bruising man, and so his criticism of Frankie rang hollow and all it did was hurt the boy. And so what if Frankie wasn't robust? He was joining the Air Force and was going to England to fight the Germans. He was a brave boy. He didn't have to go but you should see him when he started talking about oppression and aggression and how democracies have to fight the strong to protect the weak. When he got to talking about this at his eating club (Emma imagined) his cheeks went red and he pounded his fist on the table and stood with his shoulders square. Oh, how he *sang* when he talked of justice! When he erupted into those proud speeches at home he looked fiercely at Jonathan, who couldn't even meet Frankie's gaze because he knew, Emma knew, they all knew: Frankie was talking about Jonathan. He was a brave boy. So what if he wasn't a big, strapping man?

Take Felix, for instance. Now, *he* was a big man, a big man with huge hands, hands that could close a steel trap spring without effort. He could work all day bucking firewood and then sit down to dinner without a sigh or a limp. He was a fighting man, too. It was the first thing that Jonathan had asked him when Emma hired him as a caretaker. "Where were you during the Great War?" Felix had nodded slowly in that dumb way of his and said, "In it." "Oh, really, quite right," said Jonathan. "Far back, I imagine?" Felix shook his head. "No. Far front. Ypres." And then he held up two fingers. And Jonathan hadn't pushed any more. It was Jonathan who had been far back in the lines, tending to the wounded, and then not until 1917. That was all Felix had to say about the Great War. He didn't talk much, but he told Frankie stories about the old days of battles between the tribes and the coming of the white man and he showed Frankie animal tracks and brought him things from the woods and even gave him the gift of some bells sewn to leather cuffs, which Frankie explained were spirit bells that had belonged to a medicine man. No wonder Frankie was drawn to him. Every boy should have an Indian to play with. What a childhood!

Emma was still lost in these thoughts when she pushed open the kitchen door. The girls were seated around the table. There were four of them, all Indian, three under the age of twenty. Two were shelling peas they'd picked in the kitchen garden. The other two were peeling potatoes. Emma wished she had more regular work for them. Not that they were very good workers. They tended to dawdle and gossip. If Emma didn't stand over them and direct them they'd talk the day away, giggling at some shared joke in the language Emma would never understand. But they seemed like nice enough girls. And the time they spent at boarding school wasn't entirely wasted. They could sew and mend, cook simple things, and even, if the situation called for it, write. Not that she'd have them keep the books or anything like that! They were Ojibwe girls, round-faced, dark, with kissing-thick lips. Their hair was straight and shiny and black. And they had slow, big, almond-shaped, heavy-lashed eyes. When they laughed in Emma's presence she was always shocked by how white their teeth were and a little disturbed by the darting of their quick pink tongues. They were quick, too, with their hands. Whether picking peas or peeling potatoes, their hands were good at their work—smooth and efficient, the muscles bunching and jumping under the skin of their plump forearms. Their arms were nothing like Emma's, which, she had to admit, suffered in comparison—stringy, pale, with veins coursing dully beneath the skin. It strained her wrists to use the hoe too long or to lift a boiling pot off the stove, things they did with ease. Even the one named Mary. She was the oldest of the four and had a clubfoot and a humpback. The only ugly one, the Quasimodo of the group. The word "ugly" was itself ugly but there was no other word, really, that would do. Mary worked hard though and didn't gossip much with the other girls. Jonathan had diagnosed her with lupus. Emma felt pity for her. She had barely any English and she lived with her family way out in the bush in a wigwam, like a real Indian. Emma had never been out to Mary's family's camp but it was easy enough to imagine. Dirt floors. Dogs everywhere. Filth and hopelessness and lack of comfort. Not that Mary could expect any real comfort, much less love, in the future. Life for the poor girl would probably remain much the same. She would go through it alone, that was certain.

If only the girls understood the joy of cleanliness. That and the iron. They never understood either. Never understood how truly wonderful and comforting a nicely starched napkin was, or cool ironed sheets, so welcoming when you slid under them after a day of hard work. But the girls were pleasant and punctual, even though they had to walk from the village to the dock on the far side of the river, a two-mile hike on trails along the lake. And, say what you will, Mary made the walk with them, humping along on her bad leg like a peasant in some story. If the boat wasn't available they always found a way to get across, and even rowed themselves or paddled, if someone had left a canoe down by the shore. Which, come to think of it, was probably what the German prisoner had done. He'd probably just slipped away in a canoe and was halfway to Mexico. Jonathan was usually right about these things. The sailor was long gone and it was time and energy wasted trudging through the brush all day when there were more important things to do. For instance, she must remember to tell Felix to clean the dead fish from the beach. The stink, which had started the day before, was getting steadily worse.

Emma smiled down at the girls briskly.

"How is everything going? Will we have enough?"

"Yes, ma'am. Heap of peas. Potatoes, heaps." The girls laughed as if the one who spoke had said something hilarious but it was hard to know what was so funny about talking like an idiot.

Betty, she was the one who spoke. Emma prided herself on knowing their names (Betty, Candida, Mary, and the young one, the prettiest one, Stella). Where on earth did their parents find these names? On the back of a box? One Indian from the village was named Ovid.

Ovid, of all things! And he'd probably never even heard of the *Metamorphoses*! Emma had read it twice. Once in secret while she was still at St. Mary's since the nuns wouldn't have allowed it in the classroom, and once again in the open, in a class at Mount Holyoke. She'd been stunned by the violence, the erotic passages, by the language and the raw riot of beauty. Girls like these—from a small logging village on a reservation, raised with hardship and parents who'd never been to school, much less read any poetry at all—wouldn't know anything about the sublime.

"Will you remember to save the potato water? You know you will use that for the ironing? Right?"

"Yes, ma'am. Yes, we will," said Stella. She looked down, and Emma was struck, as the girl averted her gaze, by how long her eyelashes were. Surely the village boys—whites, half-breeds, even full-bloods—would be lining up for her soon, if they weren't in line already. Emma sighed. Such a pretty girl.

Frankie had been raised around these girls, and ones just like them (they did come and go) most of his life. The Washburns had purchased the Pines three years after he was born, and he'd spent part of every summer there until he'd gone away to Princeton. But even though he'd been raised among them, he seemed barely to notice them. He'd never stared after one of them as she set flowers on the tables in the front room or glanced over his book at the haunches of another when she swept out the ashes from the fireplace (it did get cold at night sometimes, especially in May). Several times Emma had caught Jonathan doing just that. His foot would jiggle faster. His paper would droop. And just as quickly it would rise again and he would look no more. It was natural for men to look. But Frankie was nobler than most men, and didn't leer over the girls. Not like Ernie. Ernie was Frankie's age and they had been friends for years. His family was from Rockford, not Oak Park. The family owned a quarry and had done well for itself, and they had purchased land just down the shore from the Pines and built their own summer place, though Ernie stayed at the Pines more often than not. Probably because the Washburns were the only ones with a boat like the Chris-Craft. Ernie liked all the things that Frankie didn't. He liked to fish and drive the boat fast and water-ski and take long hikes into the parcels of forest that hadn't yet been clear-cut. When he came to the Pines he'd stare at the girls. When he was a teenager, he'd drop things and ask the girls to fetch them in order to stare down their blouses, though Emma had had the good sense to make them wear aprons, so there was nothing to see. Once she caught Ernie in one of the empty cabins with Betty. They were drinking whiskey he had brought and they had gotten carried away. Their laughter betrayed them. Frankie was there, too, and Billy. But they were sitting in the corner and had, as far as Emma could tell, taken only a few sips.

Frankie had been interested in more innocent pleasures. She didn't mind that he liked spending time with Felix, even if he was Indian. It would give his youth more color, deeper tints, when he cast his gaze back over it as an adult. And Billy. The girls had such interesting names but the boys . . . Indian boys were all named Billy. They'd take out the canoe and paddle up the river. Or Frankie would help Billy with his chores around the Pines. They were quite close. Frankie had urged Billy to stay in school, at least to finish high school. And he had, the only Indian in his class to do so. The rest had left after the tenth grade. Frankie had asked Emma many times to send Billy books care of the village postmaster throughout the winter months—any and all she found that she thought he might like. Of course she did. Of course. She tried to send him useful books over the years, ones that provided perspective (which those people so desperately needed). Gibbon, of course. He was good for perspective and wit. And Frazer, *The Golden Bough*. And Virgil, Homer, and more ancients that Frankie had recommended but she hadn't heard of. Something by Longus, *Daphnis and Chloe*. Another by Heliodorus,

The Aethiopica. She sent, of her own choosing, Dickinson, Cather, and Shelley. They were romantic things, those collections, but couldn't really, really do a young man harm.

Frankie sent his own books, first from Fenwick's and then from Princeton. Judging from the receipts, Emma saw that Frankie sent him a lot of confusing modern novels, which Emma doubted anyone, much less Billy, actually read: among the titles were two strange ones, *All the Conspirators* and *The Memorial.* Oh, well. Even though he had graduated, Billy would most likely end up working a trade, if he was lucky. A carpenter, perhaps. Or a welder. Lord knows they needed a lot of both because of the war. Emma wondered if sending him such lofty books might set up the poor boy for disappointment down the line. The kind of attention Frankie lavished on him and the books they sent might make Billy dream of things he could never have. But Frankie had wanted to make the gesture, and who were they, the Washburns, to decide what someone like Billy could and couldn't have?

"Billy is here today, isn't he? Billy's coming?"

"Yes, ma'am. He's with the others." Betty pushed her lower lip out in a quick pout, pointing with her lips toward the front of the Pines, the lake, the prison camp, and beyond. Why these people didn't point with their fingers Emma would never understand.

"Is he still a good boy?"

"Yes, ma'am. He a good boy."

Emma felt blessed with a son like Frankie. He would never betray himself or these girls and get one pregnant. Emma looked down at Stella. So pretty. And she'd probably be fat and pregnant in a few years. Emma hoped she'd look back fondly on her time at the Pines.

"Well, finish the food and then the ironing. No wrinkles, okay? Potato water, that's the key."

They murmured overlapping *yes, ma'ams*.

"Is Felix down by the boathouse?"

The girls shrugged.

"Well, if you see him, tell him I am looking for him."

Emma walked out the back door into the bright sunshine of the early afternoon.

Felix wasn't in the kitchen garden. Of course he wouldn't be there now, in the heat of the day. He liked to wake early and do the heavy work between five and seven o'clock. He was quite a find. Emma didn't know what they'd do without him. An Indian, up at five o'clock, hoeing and weeding the garden! Not that she ever knew it. He went about his work quietly. He was never in a rush. Never loud or hurried. He took his slow, deliberate time doing everything. But the work got done, and that's what counted. And if he said he'd be someplace—in the village to meet her train or down at the dock with the Chris-Craft gassed and ready, a metal cooler filled with bait and sandwiches wrapped in wax paper for a fishing party—well, he was there, waiting.

Emma saw that the gardening had been done for the day: the rows had been hoed into shape, the furrows lined with straw. The weeds, which grew so rapidly between the plants, were cut out and piled in the corner with the compost. The hoe, spade, and rake leaned in formation on the low white picket fence to the right of the gate. The kitchen garden was a joy, and it filled Emma with pride of ownership to look out on it on a fine morning; to look out on the even rows of corn, beans, peas, and the delicate fronds of carrots and radishes that belied the strong, woody roots below the loosened earth.

The girls had their work to do—they had the peas going but they had not picked the beans or any fresh carrots. There was no corn to speak of, still too early, which was a shame, because it was doubtful that Frankie would get anything resembling fresh corn in the Air Force.

Felix must be down at the boathouse. It was nearing noon and he would have ceased all the chores that sent him into or near the woods; swiping away at the weeds or stacking wood for the kitchen stove, or cutting up the two spruces brought down by that storm a few weeks earlier. The cabins had been swept out and the screens repaired the week before, in case anyone from the party caught an early train and wanted to come up to do some fishing or just to relax. By tonight, Emma hoped, all the cabins would be full. Frankie was sleeping upstairs in his old room, naturally. Ernest and David would be staying in the cabins with one or two Princeton boys whose names Emma kept forgetting. (It wasn't like her, but if she were honest with herself, she was a little unnerved by the fact that Frankie had a life separate from hers now, and most of the people he knew she did not know; this is a hard fact for any mother to accept.)

Felix must be down at the boathouse. He wasn't around the cabins or the back of the big house, and he was clearly finished with the kitchen garden. Emma didn't need to keep on him like she did the girls. If you told Felix to do something, it was done. Simple as that. She'd had her reservations about him at first. She'd seen him around the depot in the village, where he worked as a handler, but aside from registering his size and strength and the darkness of his skin, she'd stopped thinking about him until Harris over at the Wigwam had suggested to Emma that she hire him as a handyman.

"Good God, the man is strong," Harris had said in approval.

"I don't doubt it. Anyone can see that. But is he dependable? Will he show up more than once? You know how it is."

Harris had looked at her with that amused look locals gave her and Jonathan when they first bought the Pines. And still, sometimes, now.

"No, not really. How is it?"

"You know. Will he whiskey up after we pay him? And then not come back? Things like that."

Emma was still in the phase where she thought being a resort owner, a businesswoman, was a matter of being shrewd with people, of not letting workers "get one over" on her. When she thought back on these early interactions, she actually blushed, not a little ashamed at her lack of trust.

"Well, that depends on you. That depends on how you are with him. He's seen a lot of the world, you know. He's been around. He's something of a big shot around here with the other Indians."

"What skills does he have? Can he read? Or write?"

"You hiring a handyman or a bookkeeper?"

"I suppose that would be a lot to ask."

She hired him to put in the dock. Just to see how he did. If that went well, she'd have him work on the house, but not until he proved himself. She wasn't going to let just anyone work on the Pines. The dock was one thing. The actual house was another.

The dock had gone in beautifully. Felix had worked steadily from start to finish. First he felled tamaracks along the river and boomed them together and dragged them behind the old boat to the beach in front of the Pines. Then he cut them to length and built the cribs, spiking the green tamarack together into box shapes that he filled with river stone. Then—and this was clever, the way he did it—he used ropes and the old boat to pull the long timbers into place. By the end of the week he was all done, and had, as a flourish, carved wooden cleats, which he pegged to the dock boards. Emma, impressed, asked him to fix the cabins. And then the main house. Before she knew it, she had grown to depend on him. Aside from Jonathan's two weeks in August, she was alone for the most part, except for Frankie, and some of their friends who came up once in a while to fish. And back then Frankie was just a child and could offer only the company and protection a child can offer, which isn't much, not much at all. It was nice to have a man about the place. Emma imagined that Felix scared off would-be intruders. He was so tall and broad-shouldered, with such enormous hands. His black hair, even now without a trace of gray (he must have been twenty-seven or twenty-eight in 1925, when she hired him), was cut short. When he sweated, she could see his scalp between the black barbs of his hair. He had a large nose and his eyes were set deep in his head. He was slow to answer when addressed directly and slow to speak, as though he were counting out his words on his fingers. Passingly, Emma had wondered what the world looked like to someone who couldn't read. When Felix accompanied Emma to town and they happened to run into someone from his tribe, he spoke to them in the Indian language, and as far as Emma could tell, he spoke with the same slow deliberation.

Within a couple of years, Emma had come to depend on Felix so much, *trusted* him so much, that she offered him the boathouse as a year-round place for him to live. It was a large cabin, and the back could be set off from the work area in the front. The room in back wasn't big, but it could hold a small stove, cot, table, and two chairs, and that was enough for a bachelor like Felix. Emma didn't wonder whether he might want a bigger place, somewhere he could entertain friends or even a woman. She never wondered whether he had a love life. It was more or less impossible to imagine. Sometimes, though, in the summer, usually in late May and again in September, Felix would disappear for a few days. He would approach Emma with his hat in his hands and say that he had some things to take care of but he wouldn't say what, and Emma didn't ask. He would pack a small backpack and take one of the canoes and paddle out along shore. He was gone, as he said, a few days, but he always came back.

He must be down at the boathouse now. But there was much to be done. They had to get the boat back from the search party. They would need it to get Frankie and the others across the river. And the beach still needed to be cleaned. This time of year was terrible for the beach; it was awash with weeds and broken bulrushes and the large, tuberous roots of lily pads that the beavers pulled up from the river. And the fish often died from the heat and washed up there and it didn't take long for them to rot. Jonathan said that fish begin to decompose the minute they die. It was easy to believe.

There was quite a stink down there now and Emma hoped that Felix had seen to raking the beach and burning the fish in the burn barrel. But then it would be good if someone from the Pines helped with the search, even if it were only Felix. He was dependable, but there were too many things to worry about at once, so Emma would have to make sure, to make *double* sure, that everything, every *last thing*, was in place.

TWO

Felix sat in the folding wooden bridge chair he had salvaged from the big house on the south side of the boathouse, facing the river and the German camp. Two summers earlier Emma had declared the chair too rickety for the big house and exiled it. Felix had taken the chair to the boathouse, and when he was done working for the day he had inspected the joints and tightened the nuts that held the legs on, and finally had soaked some stiff rawhide in boiling water and wound it around the splices below the seat. They dried tight and the chair became his and held his weight without complaint.

He sipped his tea and looked out across the water, remembering a woodworker in his village who, with nothing more than a dull knife and a bent saw and an ax, made the most wondrous things. Cradle-boards of ash bent so far as to form what looked like rabbit ears. Ironwood frozen at right angles. New drum legs, bowed almost in circles near the top, like lacrosse sticks, to replace those burned during a long drunk over an especially hard winter. The woodworker took tobacco and money and did whatever was asked of him, more patient and cunning with the wood than hunters on the game trail. As a child, Felix had been convinced that he used some kind of magic. At seventeen, Felix had asked him to make a cradleboard for his own first baby, due in a matter of months. "Too soon," said the woodworker, "you're asking too soon. Wait till after the baby comes." But Felix was greener than the wood itself, and the baby wouldn't be there until after he and his brothers walked north across the border and joined the Canadian army, and so he had to ask, even though he knew better. In 1919 Felix burned the cradleboard along with the rest of his wife's and child's things. The woodworker had been right.

The camp across the river had come together just as magically. It was on the high ground overlooking the Pines. Felix had come there often as a child with his parents and the others, to rice the edges of the river and to set nets for whitefish in late fall and pike in early spring. But seemingly overnight, cabins and a mess hall and a fence had risen out of the grassy bluff, like mushrooms after a rain. The cabins were made of rough-cut pine and covered with roll roofing. They seemed snug and tight and comfortable. Not like the boathouse. The boards were gappy and the two windows—one facing the river and the other facing the big house—were loose in their sashes and rattled in the wind until Felix, for lack of glazing putty, had soaked rags in paraffin and tucked them in the gaps with a filet knife. The boathouse was small, twelve feet by sixteen. Bigger than the wigwam he had grown up in, bigger than the house he'd built for his wife, but small nonetheless. Just inside the door to the left was a cookstove. To the right was the barrel stove. The left side of the cabin, facing the lake (if there had been a window), held his cot; opposite were a few wooden crates with his clothes and other possessions. He had nailed orange crates to the walls to keep his pants and shirts away from the mice. The small sleeping area was set off from the front of the cabin with wool blankets he'd tacked to the rafters. His parents had done the same thing in their wigwam, and it felt right to do that in the boathouse, though he had no one from whom he had to separate himself, no one for whom he could perform his rites of modesty, which persisted nonetheless.

Felix leaned back and sipped his tea and looked out over the rim of chipped enamel to the camp across the river, to where Frankie would appear soon, with that other boy, the sneering one, Ernie. He could do without Ernie. Felix was agitated. It had been a year since he'd last seen Frankie. And soon, right after his visit, he would be joining the war.

It was very hot. The painted pine was warm against his back. No wind ruffled the surface of the river. There was something soothing in drinking hot tea on a hot day. It was as though he were taking the day into himself. The heat was close and still. The sky was clear. Not a cloud to be seen over the lake or upriver, to the west, where the bad weather usually came from. This was the worst time of year. The swarms of dragonflies were gone. The bats had begun migrating south. There was nothing to stop the flies and mosquitoes, no line of defense. They just came and came and kept coming, like the Germans had over the top of the trenches, like he had done, too.

The camp was alive with activity, but although it was no more than three hundred yards from the Pines, the sounds that came across the river seemed to be muffled by velvet or flannel. There was a lot of movement in the yard and outside the commandant's cabin. Whistles were being blown, and the volunteers from the village and the sheriff and his deputies were organizing themselves into clumps. All for one prisoner who had escaped. When they didn't know what to do, and even when they did know, white people couldn't help themselves, they just buzzed and buzzed and buzzed. The British and Canadians he had served with in the Great War had been like that too, digging, moving, barking orders, moving again, digging again, retreating, advancing; a great hive of activity that did little except create a constant drone, like a mosquito. Mosquitoes couldn't help it, of course, it was just how their wings worked. But that sound, so distinct, was what made it possible to slap them—to reduce them to a tiny little smear where once there had been life.

Emma was like that, buzzing and buzzing around ineffectually—she couldn't help herself. That was just how her wings were made. When Harris had first told him that Emma was looking for a caretaker and Felix raised his eyebrows as a way of asking about her, Harris laughed and shook his head. "*Binekaaz*," he'd said. And he'd been right. More like a partridge than a mosquito, clucking and clucking and drumming her wings, jumping up on logs and down again, circling her chicks (though she had only the one, Frankie, unless you counted in her brood, as well you might, the Pines itself—the big house and the small cabins out back). As though all that activity, all that energy, were some kind of defense against the life that was out there stalking them. But it was always the ones who moved fast and without purpose who were eaten—mosquitoes, partridge, soldiers, too. The ones who stalked, who moved slow through the brush, they were the ones who did the killing.

It was past ten o'clock and Frankie wouldn't be at the Pines till one at the earliest. There was still a lot to do. He closed his eyes.

Emma had been unusually antic for the past week, as anxious for Frankie to return as Felix was. And since the German escaped she had hardly sat down. She was sure it would ruin everything but it was hard to see how that was possible. A man wasn't so dangerous after all. Just one white man alone in the woods. All the same, she had been standing at the front window all morning, retreating to the kitchen to check on the girls, going back to the window, looking out the kitchen window at the garden, as though that would somehow change, and then back to the front window again. As for him, Felix had gotten up before the sun. He had hoed the garden so that when the girls got there they could begin to work on the vegetables. He'd mended the garden gate so it didn't squeak, and after the sun came up and the bugs retreated farther into the woods, he took the scythe and cut back the grass and goldenrod around the edges of the Pines. After that he'd made a slow circle of all the cabins, inspecting the screens for holes. He made sure each cabin had a pail of water near the door, a box of kindling by its small three-dog stove, and a full pitcher of water on the washstand. More kindling had been needed, so he had gone out to the woodpile next to the trail that led to the tote road and, using the felling ax in one hand, had split enough wood for all the cabins and extra for the cookstove, which was sure to be going nonstop for the next two weeks. All the other resorts used bottled propane, which he had mentioned to Emma a few years before but she wasn't so sure propane was safe.

When the sun was high in the sky, around seven thirty, he'd raked the front lawn, clearing it of sticks and pinecones so it would be safe to go around the place barefoot. He'd saved this task for later because it was the kind of thing that Emma and Jonathan wouldn't even notice unless they saw him doing it. He knew white people well enough to know that unless you drew their attention to something it was likely to go unnoticed. And Emma in particular was so worked up about Frankie's arrival that he wanted to assure her that everything was in order and the visit would be a great one. No one would go barefoot, though. He was sure of that. Frankie was too old now for such things.

He used to go barefoot all summer. From the minute he came up in May, his shoes came off and they didn't get put back on till late August. Felix smiled at the thought. Frankie and Billy both ran around that way, even after Frankie had stepped on an old piece of metal during some game of hide-and-seek and Emma had fretted for days about lockjaw. Nothing came of it. Nothing ever did. By the end of the summer, those years back, Frankie's feet were as tough and brown as Billy's.

Every summer, Emma and Frankie had come up on Memorial Day to reopen the Pines. There had been weeks filled with work for Felix before then. He'd opened the shutters and repainted them, hung clotheslines, put up wood, fixed the dock, taken the Chris-

Craft to the marina to make sure it worked. Every three years he sanded it down and re-varnished the wooden hull and deck. Bats had to be cleared out of the chimney. Once a raccoon had made a nest in one of the stoves in the cabins and he'd had to kill it and its pups. And every spring, no matter how hard he worked, Emma stepped off the Chris-Craft with Frankie and looked at the Pines with a grim look and said something like, "There's so much to do! The place is falling apart!" Felix said nothing. Nor did he say anything much when Frankie fell in by his side and they split wood together or drove the Confederate into town to buy supplies for the summer—kerosene, flour, sugar, lard, seed. Without fail, the mosquitoes would already be out. They bothered Emma and she took to wearing long, flowing skirts and blouses with billowy sleeves to keep them off her arms. Frankie slapped at them and scratched his ankles and Emma made a great fuss of pulling him aside and applying calamine to his legs and arms and neck, practically bathing him in the stuff. Frankie let her do it. Felix said nothing. Even when Frankie was in the middle of helping Felix with some chore and Emma called him he came and stood there in the sun, embarrassed, and let her rub him down with the lotion while Felix pretended not to notice. It must have been humiliating for him.

Felix, for his part, helped Frankie in his own way. When he was behind the wheel of the Confederate and Frankie was beside him, he waited until the first mosquito landed on his arm and then he plucked it off and placed it on his tongue and swallowed it. It didn't taste like anything—a bit of bark, ash, nothing. This is what his parents had done. His father would say, "Oh, look, the first mosquito!" and he would pinch it between his thumb and forefinger and place it on his tongue and swallow. "There," he said, "now they won't bother you." The thinking was that if the parent ate the first mosquito of the season, the rest of the mosquitoes would attack the parent instead of the child. It wasn't true. His father did it all the same. And Felix did it for Frankie. But he didn't say anything, didn't draw Frankie's attention to the act. He wouldn't be able to explain it. Not to Frankie. Not to Emma. So he said nothing. He leaned back against the wall of the boathouse and sipped his tea.

The boathouse wasn't much more than a shack—walls of rough-cut pine and a metal roof. He had been born in a wigwam. Bent poles covered with bark and tin and canvas, whatever they could find. They had a dirt floor and a fire pit in the center until his father had salvaged a small stove from an abandoned lumber camp. They hung all their possessions from the poles with cord, or *wiigoob*, so they wouldn't get stepped on or mildewed. An old wool blanket served as a door flap, which they weighted down with canoe paddles or logs during the wintertime. When he visited his parents after the war, he was surprised to notice how everything—their clothes and blankets and cooking utensils and hats, even the pots—smelled like wood smoke. And though his mother swept the place out and cleaned everything all the time—she was a small, precise, fastidious woman—there was a sheen to everything, as if the whole place was covered in grease. He tried, after he was grown, to find in his memory the discomfort of growing up there, but he couldn't. Just him and his brothers and parents, and the low light of kerosene, and the murmur of his brothers' voices as they told jokes before going to sleep, his parents moving around the wigwam silently in the morning and evening.

Felix and his brothers traveled a lot in those years. When they were in their teens they worked the lumber camps as far away as Orr and Big Falls. In the summer they guided for the tourists who came up to fish for pike. When he was sixteen, in 1915, he and his family were at rice camp on the Bowstring, where many Indians from farther north had come down to rice because their own had been rained out. He saw a girl from across the border there with her family. She was short and plump and she worked hard around her parents' camp.

She yelled at her younger sisters and brothers in a cheerful, ringing voice and got them, somehow, to help her jig the rice, put up wood, and haul pails of water from the lake for dishes and laundry. Felix didn't say much to her. She had quick, deft hands. Her hair, in its tight braids, was very shiny. He tried not to look at her. But when her family laughed loudly at something, he couldn't help himself and peeked over the rice sacks he was packing and caught her pretending she was fiddle-dancing in the rice pit, her dress held high in her hands, her jigging moccasins tied high just below her knees. He saw her thighs, which were thick and strong and smooth. And then the joke was over and she dropped her hands and got back to work.

That night he lay awake till very late. The wind was blowing hard across the lake and he thought about how much rice was being blown from the stalks into the water and he thought, too, of her legs—how quickly they had appeared and then disappeared—and how he would give a lot to see more of them.

The next morning, while his parents were out knocking rice, he walked over to the girl's camp bearing his mother's cooking pot filled with three yards of red flannel. "I thought you could use these," he said. And not knowing what else to say, he turned and walked back to his family's camp. When his mother and father came back and discovered Felix had given away their best pot and all their cloth, they didn't say anything to Felix, not directly. But as he was going to sleep that night they talked back and forth to one another. "I'd like some soup," his father said. "Yes," said his mother, "soup would be good. Soup with rice and duck meat." "That's the thing to eat when you're ricing," said his father. "Maybe you could boil some up." "I wish I could but I've lost the cooking pot," said his mother. "It would taste so good," said his father. And this is how they let Felix know they knew he'd given away their best pot. When ricing was over and Felix and his brothers sold their share, he bought two iron kettles, one for his parents and the other for the girl. He left one in his parents' wigwam and with the other he walked all the way to Vermillion and found her and gave it to her. They were married and then they walked back to his village.

He built them a shack with slab from the sawmill and tarpaper left over from a lumber camp that had cut down the easy trees and moved on. When he had built it he worried it was too small. His older brother, Ovid, had joked that it took a man to build himself a beaver house. And that is what it had felt like—a den in which he and his wife groomed themselves and emerged into the world only to duck back in, packed tightly into the four corners of the thing, their possessions stacked in baskets and hung in bundles tied with twine and *wiigoob* and hung from the few rafters, their food stored outside in a timber-lined pit in the summer and in a cache made of poles eight feet up in the trees in the winter. But his wife had been good at preparing food. She smoked the suckers and whitefish he caught in his nets and when they were dry and hard she rubbed the fish between her hands into a fine powder she tied in bundles. She did the same with deer meat. She jigged rice and picked berries. When he closes his eyes now he can still see her with her hands on the jigging poles, her feet deep in the pit, her moccasins tied high to her knees, looking back at him.

He hadn't been there long with his wife—round, smiling, hard-working, funny—before she got pregnant. The cabin suddenly felt very small, but no one he knew lived in more than one room. Still, they needed more space. They needed money, too. He looked around and saw a desert—all the big trees had been cut and the lumber camps had moved farther north. There was no other work to be had, not for an Indian. In the fall he and his wife got in the canoe and paddled across the lake to the drum dance. The second to the second stick got up to dance his song and afterward he spoke about the war overseas. He walked back and forth and spoke loudly about how he was going on the warpath as their grandfathers had done. Felix sat along the edge in the shadows with his wife. He listened and watched. He had had no position on the drum. All doors were closed to him. So after the dance he approached the singer and said he'd go with him. Ovid, drunk on whiskey, said he'd go, too, they'd all go. They all drank and boasted to one another about how they would find the enemy and take their lives. It was the talk of young men, and Felix supposed that young men were the same everywhere. Still drunk, their heads splitting, they filled their packs, stuffed batting in their hats, drank deeply from the lake, and set off to the north across the lakes to Canada to enlist.

He returned in 1919 to an empty house. His wife and child had been killed by the flu in 1918. The house was as he had left it, but the cradleboard had been stuffed in the rafters and the old bed had been replaced with a bigger one—one big enough for his wife and child to sleep in. She had cut up his old pants and stuffed them in the walls for insulation but that was about it. Everything else was the same, except she was gone. They were gone. Maybe the old woodworker had been right—it had been too soon, too early, to make the cradleboard. He had invited his own bad luck to enter the house and reside there. The small shack seemed big, too big. Too big anyway, for him and his grief, which sat—hard, compact, uncomprehending—on his chest. He felt as an animal must feel in its pain.

So he took their prized kerosene lantern and tipped it in the center of the wooden floor and struck a match to it. He stood outside and watched the shack burn. And when it was nothing more than a few charred logs, hissing against the snow, he shouldered his pack and left to find work in the lumber camps.

He took another sip of tea. It was cooling but not cool—almost the same temperature as the air. He leaned forward in his chair and stood and peered around the side of the boathouse. Emma no longer stood in the window gazing out at the camp. She must have gone back into the kitchen. It would be good to clean out the dock but he'd have to walk back toward the kitchen garden to get the rake, and Emma would see him and there would be a new round of requests and reconsiderations and second thoughts. He turned around and looked down at the dock. It really would be good to clean it. It was almost eleven and the train was due in at noon and he wanted as much as Emma did for Frankie's return to be grand. But now, with the missing German, the Chris-Craft was gone and Frankie had no way to get across the river, so cleaning the dock wasn't really the best thing to do, even if he could get the rake without Emma seeing him.

He looked down at the dock. It seemed empty, expectant, without the Chris-Craft bobbing alongside it. The rowboat and two canoes were turtled over on the grass next to it. The boys would have to use a canoe. There was no other option. Felix set down his tea on the chair behind the boathouse and made his way along the riverside. He took one of the paddles from where it leaned against the boathouse and walked quickly across the lawn in front of the house. Emma wouldn't be able to see him if she was in the kitchen or even if she had gone out the back door toward the kitchen garden looking for him.

If Billy had been there he could have raked the dock and helped Felix deal with Emma. But Billy hadn't come that morning. Felix had hinted that Billy would be needed but he had stayed in the village. Most likely he wanted to get ready in his own way for Frankie's arrival. Felix could tell that Billy was excited from the way he had worked the past week. He started every chore in a frenzy, throwing the dirt like a badger as he dug a new hole for the outhouse, chopping wood shirtless and stopping to swat the deerflies from his back before he attacked the wood again. Emma had them move all the furniture out onto the lawn so that they could wax the floors in the big house, and at every pass Felix had seen Billy stop before the mirror in the lobby and look at himself. Now he was probably taking a bath and trying on that new coat he got at Niesen's, along with his new hat.

Felix walked across the lawn and down to the canoes. He flipped them both over and pushed them down the bank into the river. He looped the painter from the second canoe through the wicker seat of the first canoe and got in. He didn't know how to paddle while sitting, so he knelt on the cedar ribs and pushed out into the slow current. He headed upriver and was soon screened by the cattails. Emma couldn't see him unless she came all the way down to the end of the dock, which she wouldn't do.

He relaxed a little. He paddled slowly. This would be the last bit of daytime he had alone for the next two weeks. Frankie most likely would want to join one of the search parties. Felix had been the same way after that drum dance long ago, anxious to get going, full of talk about the war and the honors he'd secure for himself and his family. It was all so slow, too slow for him at the time. The long walk across the border to Canada. Enlisting in Fort Frances, the train ride to Winnipeg to join the 52nd Infantry Battalion and then back east over the Great Lakes to Toronto and from there to Newfoundland for training, then Nova Scotia, and across to Ireland for more training. From the time he left his wife in November it was nine months before he saw action. It had all happened so slowly.

Frankie would be just as anxious, of course. Just as much on edge around Emma, too. Every Memorial Day when he'd been a boy, he had arrived excited and excitable. For the first few weeks he would go down to the boathouse just after first light. He never entered or knocked, but the walls were so thin, Felix could hear him scuffing his feet on the dock or throwing rocks into the lake as he waited. Felix would drink his tea and wash his face and eat a piece of bread, and the minute he emerged from the boathouse, Frankie would stop what he was doing and walk over to him and ask if he needed any help with anything. It took a week or two for the boy to learn to sleep in, to take things as they came, to shrug off the shawl of worry and anxiety that Emma seemed to place on his shoulders.

When Billy started coming to help out at the Pines, Frankie had drifted toward him, slowly at first, and then more quickly and completely. He no longer waited outside the boathouse for Felix. But that was the way with children. That was proper. Felix turned the canoe across the river toward the opposite bank. The weeds largely covered the bottom of the river this time of year, but between them, here and there, he saw the sandy bottom seven feet down, covered with so many empty snail shells it looked like it was covered in gravel. He reached the far shore and coasted down in front of the camp. Then he turned the nose of the canoe into the bank and let the stern drift downstream as he untied the painter of the second canoe and brought it alongside his own. Without getting out of his canoe, he fed the second canoe up and onto the bank, and, grabbing the stern, flipped it over. Some water dripped out. There must be a leak. The canvas ripped. Another season and he'd have to re-cover it. The leak was small in any event, and high up the side of the canoe. He turned and paddled straight across the river. It was only when he got close to the dock that he remembered he'd forgotten to bring along paddles. He beached the canoe and stepped out to fetch them when he saw Emma coming around the side of the house.

THREE

Billy waited on the raised cement platform outside the station in his new jacket and driving cap. The train was due at noon and it was past due. It was hot and the sun, pretty much straight overhead, didn't burn off the moisture so much as set the air to boil. It was sticky and there wasn't much wind. The jacket was the wrong thing for the weather. Brown wool twill. Though anything else would have been ruined in weeks, if not days. And it had to last him through the winter. It was all they had at Niesen's, anyway. The jacket had cost five dollars and the cap had cost two. Seven dollars for the getup. Through the spring, until breakup, Billy had gone out to Dick Bolton's camp down Six Mile and peeled spruce for five cents a stick. Dick got ten cents from the boss but he gave Billy and the other kids five (even his own skin, Dickie Jr.), and so it had taken him 140 sticks to get that hat and that coat, 140 eight-foot balsam and poplar logs peeled with a sharpened leaf-spring for a spud and lifted over end into a neat pile for the skidder. And then Bolton would charge them ten cents for kerosene and a rag to get the pitch off before he and the other boys walked back to the village. Still, he had saved his nickels, and by summer he had a good bankroll. He added to it by gutting and filleting fish at Lyon's Landing, a nickel a fish. On weekends he went out to the Pines and helped Felix get the place ready. There weren't as many people coming up this summer because of the war. Only Felix and Emma for all of June and July. Ernie's parents weren't coming up this year, but Ernie was supposed to arrive with Frankie.

Billy did whatever Felix and Emma asked of him: he unwrapped blankets and bedding for the cabins, beat the braided oval rug that lay in front of the split-stone fireplace with a canoe paddle, whitewashed the cabins, and knocked the swallow nests off the eaves of the big house with a broom. Emma spent her days gliding from room to room, changing the knickknacks, rearranging the chairs, making lists. Sometimes she spent the afternoons laboring under a vow of exhaustion in her room. When she moved the rugs, she didn't like how the floor in the big house had been worn down by foot traffic and beach sand. She had Billy and Felix move everything out of all the rooms on the ground floor, including the Chickering upright. They scraped down the heart pine and rubbed it with tongue oil and finished it off with Liberon paste wax that she had ordered special from New York. And then they carried everything back in and she set to arranging again. She tried to pay Billy, as she had in the old days when he started working as the dock boy in 1930, but he refused. Frankie was his friend. He was simply helping his friend's mother. The real payment, the real reward, would be Frankie himself and his reaction when he arrived and breathed in the smell—of wool and wood smoke and paste wax and cedar—of the Pines.

So the money he saved, nickel by nickel, did not come from the Washburns, and that meant something to him. Everything seemed to pay a nickel. A pint of blueberries equaled a nickel, a peeled spruce log equaled a nickel, a walleye—gutted and deheaded and filleted—a nickel. The train was coming in.

"Nice coat, Billy! Real nice!" Billy looked up and there he was. Frankie leaned out over the steps, his boater in his hand, his smile broad. Billy couldn't keep himself from smiling because that coat had cost him 100 logs peeled and piled, and he was thrilled that

Frankie had noticed. Of course he had. Billy didn't move from where he leaned against the beam of the depot's porch, in part because the coat was so hot he didn't want to soak his shirt. He willed himself to stay put, his hands in his pockets, the brim of his hat just so. Like an actor in one of the movies they showed in the town hall on Friday nights.

The train was slowing down, nearly stopped, and Frankie said something to someone behind him and jumped off and turned to bow with his hat in his hand to whoever was behind him and ran over to Billy and stretched his arm out and shook Billy's hand. Frankie's hand felt small, smaller, in his, but it had the same cool, moist feeling that excited him. It was only then that Billy unleaned himself from the post and stood tall. He had grown a lot in the last year and his work in the lumber camps had broadened his shoulders and chest and he noticed, happily, that he was just as tall as Frankie was, and heavier through the shoulders and arms.

"How you been keeping?" asked Frankie. Frankie had on some kind of suit—linen, maybe—with pleated pants and deep pressed creases down the front. He looked right at Billy, still shaking his hand, smiling, smiling, smiling, like he couldn't believe it. Frankie's hair was cut short on the sides and left long on top. He was as thin as ever but his cheeks were tanned and his eyelashes dusty-looking in that way of theirs. The sun shone through his ears and made them glow red a little. He seemed happy.

"You look great, kid. Really great," said Frankie.

"Look what else," said Billy, and he opened his jacket wide, like a flasher. He'd been rehearsing the move. Frankie's eyes went mock-wide when he saw the corked pints sticking out of the inside pockets of Billy's coat.

"I like how you think, kid," said Frankie. "I really like how you think. I appreciate your vision."

Billy was one year younger, but he was just as big as Frankie now, bigger. Stronger, for sure. The "kid" thing must be from some movie. Frankie wrote about the movies he saw at the Princeton Garden Theatre. And the lawn parties they had at Ivy—he'd buzzed one in the Piper Cub, he'd reported gleefully. His trips to New York. Worlds Billy couldn't quite imagine without Frankie's help. Frankie sent books, too: *The Iliad*, *This Side of Paradise*, *Tropic of Cancer*, *Goodbye to Berlin*. These he read and reread and kept in a wooden crate under his bed. Billy wasn't sure he understood the books but he tried, if only to understand Frankie, who had lived among the kinds of people in those books, visited houses like theirs, walked the streets of the cities they described. As for movies, the ones Billy saw were years old, not even current, just whatever the movie man brought in the circular tins on the back of his Model A. The man went from town to town throughout the summer—a little old man in a Model A in an antique suit—and projected the movies on the back wall of the town hall. Once the projector had broken and the movie couldn't be shown, but the man had quieted the villagers with his hands and told the movie to them instead, and he'd done a pretty good job, with all the voices and the action and suspense and all that, but it hadn't been the same. The village didn't have a library, either, other than the long shelf in the schoolhouse. Billy had read all of those books at least once by the sixth grade. Twenty miles away, the high school library was bigger, but not by much. He'd read all those books, too.

"Hey," said Frankie over his shoulder, "look who's here."

Just then Ernie came tumbling out of the train. He had on a linen suit, too. But his was crumpled and his hair was sweaty and plastered to his head. He must have lost his hat somewhere between Chicago and Saint Paul. He had grown a small black mustache. His hands were hairy. But it was the same wide, square face; the same barrel body; the same keen, cruel, round, sharp, piggish, stubborn, sly body. Another boy filed out behind Ernie. He was slender and quiet. Davey

Gardner. His parents owned the mill and he was just done with college, too.

He nodded. "Hey, Billy."

"Dave."

Ernie looked at Billy but not with the same warmth as Frankie. Ernie rubbed his eyes and stretched, as if he had just gotten out of bed, and the train and the depot and the prospect of the Pines all constituted some chore, some duty he must submit to. He walked over to where Billy and Frankie stood gaping at each other, their handshake still thrumming up and down, slowing noticeably, but still a warm, full grip. He stood with his fists on his hips and then moved them around to push against his lower back. He seemed distracted and drunk but Billy knew that Ernie saw everything in that shrewd way small, mean people see everything. He studied Billy as though looking at something for sale.

"Look what Billy's got," said Frankie.

Billy opened his coat again the same way he had before. But it felt awkward, like he was on display. Like he was acting without an audience. The coat felt shabby now, like something he paid five dollars for at Niesen's rather than Langrock's on Palmer Square.

Ernie leaned toward Billy, his head low, and squinted. He kept one fist on his hip and reached out with his other hand and plucked one of the bottles from its pocket right there on the platform in front of everyone—in front of the loggers and the station agent and the vacationers. Ernie held it up to the sun and then cradled it in his palm.

"It's got no bond. No mark, either."

"It'll work, won't it?" asked Frankie.

"It's not for us anyway," lied Billy. "It's for girls." He'd gotten the pints from Bolton, who had charged him a dollar each. Forty sticks of balsam. Forty sticks peeled and piled for those two bottles.

"Indian girls, maybe," said Ernie. "Or other kinds, I suppose," he said, looking at Billy with that look of his. "Come on, let's see what we can do." Ernie led the way and the four of them left the station agent to manage the luggage while they crossed the street to the Wigwam. Ernie opened the door and Frankie and David followed him.

"I'll wait out here," said Billy. "On lookout," he added.

"Sure," said Ernie. "Sure, sure."

Billy felt the day going terribly wrong. It had gotten off its track. Already things seemed beyond fixing, and this was the last time Frankie would be there in a long while, who knew how long?

Five minutes later, Ernie and Frankie and David came out. Ernie held a paper bag in which two fifths clanked together. "What did you get?" asked Billy.

"Eight Roses," said Ernie, smiling to himself. "Here," he said, and he handed the bag to Billy and lit a cigarette. He didn't move to take the bag back after the cigarette was lit.

"Got the scoop from Harris," said Ernie through his cigarette smoke. "Seems some German from the camp escaped. Guess he plans on heading down the Mississippi for a rendezvous with a U-boat."

"He escaped yesterday," said Billy, grateful that he had more of the story than Ernie did.

Frankie was excited. "Maybe I'll get a German before I even leave the States," he said. "I can paint a swastika on my plane before I leave the ground."

"Those are for planes you shoot down, not for returning escaped prisoners," said Ernie.

"Still," said Frankie, "we can do our part. They're organizing search parties. How about it, Billy?"

"Sure," said Billy, "swell." But it wasn't swell. He'd been hoping for the usual ritual of the Pines—the big meal on the front porch and waterskiing behind the Chris-Craft, and a chance to go fishing with Frankie. With any luck Ernie would pass out early. They walked to the Confederate and took drinks from one of the bottles while the station agent loaded the luggage. When he was done, they all got in the cab, shoulder to shoulder. Ernie was behind the wheel and David was next to him. Next was Frankie. Billy got the window. Frankie put his arms on the backrest as though they were all members of the same club.

"We are going to have ourselves a time, boys. We are definitely going to have a time," said Frankie.

Ernie lit another cigarette and talked about the fishing tackle he had brought. Frankie talked about the USAAF and B-17s, forecasting all the daring exploits he was to have. He switched from topic to topic without completing his thoughts. His hat was pushed back on his head and his words were a little slurred with liquor or excitement or both. Frankie's arm was heavy and light across Billy's shoulders. Billy's heart felt heavy and light, too. Frankie's hand cupped Billy's shoulder and stayed there. Billy looked out over the fields and clear-cuts and scrub as Ernie drove them to the landing so they could cross the river to the Pines. The day was already half over.

They didn't get across the river to the Pines till three o'clock. The ride had taken longer than they expected because Ernie had stopped twice to piss against a tree, jiggling his whole body up and down, and then when they parked on the bluff near the camp, Frankie insisted they find the prison guards and asked them, his cheeks aflame and his arms folded importantly across his chest, about the prisoner. How old? What did he look like? Any defining physical characteristics? Was he armed? The guards had taken the cigarettes Frankie offered them, but when put to the question, they looked at one another and shrugged. He looks like a German. Sounds like one, too. Look around, they said. Billy was sweating in his coat and he took it off and waited patiently while Frankie asked his questions, and when even Ernie got impatient and started bringing their luggage down to the dock, Billy helped him.

"Wouldn't you know it," said Ernie. "No goddamn boat."

It was true. The Chris-Craft was gone. And so were the rowboats. Ernie took off his linen jacket and draped it over a red willow and stomped back up to get Frankie and Davey. Billy looked around. There was a wood-and-canvas Old Town drawn up into the brush and turtled. He flipped it over and was surprised when a fog of fish flies flew out. He batted them away and pulled the canoe out and slid it into the water. It looked sound. He tied the painter to the dock cleat and waited. Soon Frankie and Ernie came stomping down the hill, careless of their pants in the fireweed. They looked at Billy skeptically.

"You know how to paddle that thing, Chief?" asked Ernie, fanning his fat face with his hat. "Joke," he said, a beat too late.

The boys piled their luggage in. It mounded up in the middle and made the canoe very tippy. Ernie made another trip up the hill to fetch paddles from the camp. Billy and Frankie looked at each other. They smiled but said nothing as Ernie came skidding back down the riverbank. Billy took charge.

"You better get in the front, Ernie. Frankie, David, you take the middle."

The other boys did as they were told, and once they were settled, Billy let go of the gunwale and stepped in the back and knelt on the cedar ribs and stroked away from the dock. They hadn't gotten farther than ten yards when he noticed water sloshing between the ribs.

"We're taking on water!" he said.

"Paddle fast, boys, or we're going down!" cried Ernie. Frankie laughed. There was nothing for it. So paddling fiercely, the bottom slowly filling with water, the canoe canting dangerously to one side and then the other, they sprinted across the river.

"Ballast!" shouted Ernie.

"No! My uniform is in there. You can't. I don't have time to get another!"

They made it across without drowning and without drowning their luggage. Ernie jumped out when the water was still knee deep, ruining his pants. Frankie and David followed suit. But once the nose was secure next to the boathouse, Billy, using his paddle as a cane, walked down the middle of the canoe and off the bow and onto dry land.

"Well, look at him!" said Frankie in open admiration.

Felix met them on the dock. He called Frankie "Mr. Frankie," and it sounded solemn and funny at the same time. He shook Ernie's and David's and Billy's hands in turn. Within moments, Emma was fluttering across the open yard, and Jonathan sauntered out of the house with his pipe in his hand and talk turned to the German.

FOUR

The morning had been all Jonathan could bear. As he sat in the chair next to the fireplace and tried to read the papers, he could actually *hear* Emma's worry, even though she said very little from where she stood looking out the front windows across the river. When she brushed past him—flounced was more like it—her anxiety and meddlesomeness trailed after her, carried in the breeze of her skirt with those stupid little bohemian plaits of straw that made such an annoying sound. It was not a sexy sound. Not like the sound of high heels on the linoleum of his office floor or the clink of earrings hitting the metal tray he kept on his desk or the slight snap of garters slipping their stays.

The sound of Emma's skirt, as she flounced down the hall and into the kitchen, was to him the sound of sweeping, a broom sound, a broom that did little to clean but made the emotional dust she was always trailing billow up around him. In that dust was her worry about Frankie. He was, in addition to the Pines, her chief project, her principal worry.

He heard the kitchen door swing open and shut. Felix, for all his diligence, hadn't gotten around to oiling that blessed door yet. It could be heard throughout the main house, and during a busy day it groaned without stop, like the braying of an abused mule. He tried to resume his reading, but the papers were of no use. His mind had somehow been pulled along after Emma. She had been successful in capturing his consciousness even if she had not convinced him to go with the others, the yokels and Indians, after the German. He could hear Emma's voice posing questions in her high whine, and the brief, soft, self-effacing answers of the Indian girls at work around the table: *yes, ma'am* and *no, ma'am* and *almost finished, ma'am.*

It was sad, really, that they shrank to such small size when Emma was in the room. Usually, after she left, Jonathan heard them erupt into excited talk, which would continue until Emma came back to the kitchen. Even if he had heard what they were saying, he could not have understood it; they spoke in their language, a concatenated glide of syllables with precious few consonants as far as Jonathan could tell. But it was nice, how they spoke to one another. They sounded like the family of otters that had collected at the dock for a summer years back, most likely trying to break into the bait cage. Jonathan had liked the otters, and he had, for the two weeks he'd been there that year, brought a folding canvas chair down to the dock to read. No one spoke to him down there. Not the otters. Not Felix. It had been pleasant. Those kitchen girls would be good company in bed. That's how they seemed anyway. Sure, they wilted when Emma came into the kitchen to scold them and make a great show of how advanced she was, but the girls knew the score. In bed . . . now, that would be different. Jonathan imagined their true nature would show; they would become as sexually sleek as their skin looked; as glossy, as liquid, as sure, cavorting like otters around his supine body.

Not that he had tried to get any of them to give it up to him. Not that he had made any advances to any of them, even after Emma caught that one—was it Betty, the older one, or Stella, the youngest?—with Ernie and Frankie in one of the guest cabins. Ernie was a robust drinking, card-playing college boy. He was the kind of son Jonathan had always imagined having, with grass stains on his chinos and skinned elbows and mischief in his heart. Emma had been outraged, but Jonathan couldn't see the harm in it. That's what it was to be young, and the girls weren't complaining. A little whiskey and a warm room and attention were all they really required. And why not? What was the harm? Where was the hurt in finding some pleasure between the smooth, stout, clasping legs of an Indian girl?

Or masturbating, for that matter. He was a man of science. And in all his years he had never seen a male patient who was blind or had hair on his palms, or warts. He himself, when he wasn't on with one of the nurses or other girls who worked in the building, masturbated every day, and with no ill effect. He wasn't tired, or sapped of his will, or a degenerate. He supported his family and gave to charity and all that. He was no Rockefeller, but still, he did his part. One of the many attempts to toughen Frankie up a bit had been to make him join the Boy Scouts. It was supposed to make a man of him, to introduce him to the outdoors, and to a fellowship of adventurers. Baden-Powell had been onto something. But then, in a desperate moment, with nothing else to read, Jonathan had picked up the *Boy Scout Handbook*. He'd spent the evening laughing to himself in his study. The parts about puberty were especially hilarious. *You might wake up with an erect penis*, stated the book. *Sometimes you might have funny dreams and feel a tickle and your undershorts will be damp because you've emitted a nocturnal fluid*. The manual made it seem so mysterious, so complicated. And the "nocturnal fluid" sounded occult. What had they been *thinking*? What was their *aim* in writing this stuff? The Boy Scouts were supposed to make men of boys, not to make boys afraid of their own dicks.

Frankie, however, did seem to be afraid of his cock. In all the years living at home, Jonathan never caught him in the act, never found the telltale washcloth (not that he did the laundry, but you find these things, even in a house as big as theirs), never caught him looking longingly at the women he, Jonathan, looked at as they walked down Michigan Avenue. He'd never even caught Frankie making small talk with the kitchen girls, much less making love to them. And, truth be told, he wouldn't have minded at all if Frankie had been with one, or two, or three. It would have given him a wealth of pleasure, a catalog of experiences he could draw upon. It would give them something to joke about when Frankie had a family of his own and Jonathan was old, a pleasant old grandfather. But Frankie didn't joke. He was cheerful but serious; pleasant in conversation and able to keep up, but underneath his banter, even Jonathan could sense a fearful reserve, a watchful, waiting, measuring consciousness.

He heard Emma leave the kitchen. The girls continued their work, but did not begin, at least not immediately, to speak to one another. Emma must still be close by, looking over the wretched garden, maybe. Oh, she loved that garden and went on and on about what good shape Felix kept it in, how he could get all the weeds out without even bending over; how it was simply a matter of using the hoe and using it regularly. And how they had to purchase so little—just cream and eggs and bacon, really—while the Pines was running from May through mid-September. It was nice to look at; the rows of peas and beans and carrots, turnips, radishes, and mounds of potatoes and squash (for the blossoms, since the squash themselves would come in, for the most part, too late for the Pines). And the corn, too, regal and green. The peas and beans were nice, garden-fresh beans were always nice. But the lettuce was bitter. The tomatoes were unevenly ripe. One had to wait too long for the corn. The raccoons always dug up the potatoes and bit into the melons. The vegetables, what there were of them, had too much individuality. You never knew what you were going to get. Vegetables these days—it was the 1940s, after all—should, with the help of science, be more dependable, more uniform; should ripen at the same time; should all be, more or less, of the same size.

Jonathan sighed and was just folding the papers and stacking them in the copper bin next to the fireplace when he heard shouts and the banging of a canoe against the dock. He sauntered into the front room and peered out of the southeastern-most window down the slope of the hill to the dock. Maybe it was the returning search party. Perhaps they'd found the German and were returning in triumph, having saved the north woods from a single, solitary submariner sans submarine. But no.

Frankie had arrived.

Evidently, since the Chris-Craft was still being used by the search party, Frankie, Ernest, Billy, and that other boy had found a canoe, one of those big cedar-ribbed canvas ones, and with Ernie in the front and Frankie and that other boy in the middle, and Billy paddling stern, they'd crossed the river.

Emma must have heard them, too. She stood at the foot of the dock, her silly skirt blowing in the hot wind and her hands clasped to her mouth in shocked, happy surprise.

Her surprise, even that, seemed hokey and staged. She must have heard them coming from the back by the garden and she had to catch and hold her "Oh! Frankie!" and carry it across the lawn and let it ripen while she stood and waited for the boys to quit their Ivy League guffawing and carousing and get out of the canoe so she could clasp him to her breast. It was that precious surprise and tenderness (as though one had opened the cupboard to fetch the salt and found a baby girl in there instead) that, more than anything else, made Jonathan wither. More than her constant worrying; more than her manner of dress (it would never occur to her to wear a suit, like the smart ones all the secretaries were wearing now); even more than her dripping, drooping monologue about their wonderful son; more than the occasional (and it had happened less and less over the years) day or two when she couldn't get out of bed and would cry and cry and, asked what was the matter, would only say, "Josephine, poor baby Josephine."

Jonathan sighed and shook his head. He couldn't see very well at this distance, but for the few seconds it took for Frankie to emerge from the canoe and come down the dock, Jonathan thought Emma might actually be right: he had grown into a man. Jonathan could see, even from all the way across the lawn, the white flash of his teeth, a broad, tan smile (acquired, it seemed, from a trip to Key West after graduation), and strong, level shoulders almost even with Billy's. And then Frankie was lost in his mother's hug.

Jonathan let the curtain back down. He knew he had to greet his son, though the thought of it made him irritable. He stopped by the fireplace to collect his pipe kit from next to the easy chair and filled his pipe as he walked out the front door, down the steps, and toward the dock. By the time he strolled across the lawn (Felix was good at keeping the grass down, even Jonathan had to admit that) and filled his pipe, Frankie had managed to free himself from his mother's hug, and he ducked his head as she tried to tuck his hair behind his ear.

"They'll be cutting that off soon, won't they? In the Air Force. They'll give you a haircut."

"For Christ's sake, Mother," he said, grinning sheepishly, looking back at Billy and Ernest and David (that was his name, Dave Gardner!), and then up at Jonathan, who had stopped nearby.

"I'm just saying," said Emma shyly. "I'm just saying you've got beautiful hair."

"I don't care about that," said Frankie, but his hand betrayed him and rose to re-part his hair and smooth it down, finishing his mother's gesture by tucking it behind his ear.

Ernie said something to Billy and David that made them laugh.

"Father," said Frankie, straightening. He stuck out his hand stiffly, and Jonathan, feeling a little foolish, reached out. They shook hands.

"The Air Force. That'll be exciting, won't it?"

"I hear we have a fight on the home front."

"Where are the others? Weren't there supposed to be more of you?" Jonathan felt uncomfortable, and it was all he could think to say.

"Couldn't make it. Naval cadets. They had to go right after graduation."

"Oh."

"Sounds like we've got a German submariner to find," said Frankie, smiling.

"An escaped German. Just one lonely submariner out in the woods. Not much of a fight." Jonathan turned away from the imaginary wind and lit his pipe.

"Felix, I've been looking for you all morning," said Emma, turning to where Felix stood in front of the boathouse.

"Yes, ma'am."

"Yes. Well, I expect you'll go with the boys after the German. Jonathan would go but he's got his journals, studying up on cases, you know. Anyway, you'll go after the German with the boys. We can't have him running around here doing all sorts of mischief. That's for sure. But after, before it gets dark, the beach needs to be cleaned, there must be some dead fish under the dock—the smell is getting awful, just awful. And if we're to swim here tomorrow—and you boys will want to, right, just like the old days?—well . . . it *does* need to be cleaned."

"Yes, ma'am."

Jonathan, pipe going, turned back to face the group. Frankie was different, as Emma had said. Broader, tanned.

Frankie nodded at his father and turned to look at Felix.

"Old Felix. Old Felix, it's good to see you. Really good."

"Mr. Frankie," said Felix. This was as close as he got to affection.

"You don't look any older."

Felix smiled.

"We'd best get after that German," said Frankie. "The longer we wait, the more time he has to cause trouble. Felix, is the Winchester still on top of the cupboard?"

Felix nodded.

"Hey, Pops, we'll need to use the Winchester. Nothing like a Winchester 101 to convince a German to come in quietly."

"All we have are rabbit and grouse loads," said Jonathan.

"There's double aught," said Felix.

Jonathan narrowed his eyes. He didn't like to be contradicted, especially by an Indian.

"Yes."

"We'll be loaded for bear, then, right, Felix?"

"Loaded for man," said Ernie, smiling. "You'll be loaded for man."

Jonathan couldn't bear any more of this banter, the bright chit-chat, and he wished them good hunting and said he'd see them at dinner. They continued in the same vein as he turned and walked back up to the house. He went to the kitchen for a glass, and the girls, who had been watching and listening at the window, scampered mice-like back to their chairs and resumed shelling peas and peeling potatoes.

FIVE

They took the path behind the Pines and cut up the trail till they hit the logging road and took it west, parallel to the lake. It was the same trail and the same woods in which Billy and Frankie had played and later used as a kind of refuge from the Pines itself, when they were teenagers. But it felt different to Billy now. The heat hung heavy among the basswood and maple. Funny, but there weren't really any pines behind the Pines except for the few planted as a windbreak between the property and the woods. The woods themselves were hardwoods and poplar. The horseflies droned in the air, and Billy's shirt stuck to his arms underneath his brown wool jacket. He hadn't thought to take it off. Frankie had been too excited, too eager to search for the German, and Billy had been too eager to be with Frankie, and so he was sweating heavily. The air had the feel of rain—a heavy, waiting feel—but the sky was clear and the stationmaster at the depot said that it was supposed to remain that way. Even so, the air . . . it was as though a man could swim in it.

Felix was in the lead, followed by Frankie—who had insisted on carrying the Winchester—and Billy, Ernie, and David were behind. Frankie peppered Felix with questions and Felix mumbled in reply. Billy suggested Ernie head north while Felix and David cut down by the slough to the south. Frankie finally caught on.

"Yeah, Felix. Good idea. We'll take the tote road here and meet you on the other side of the slough. I'll have a better field of fire with the Winchester on the road."

"Field of fire?" asked Ernie.

"Well," said Frankie, and he shrugged.

"Okay," said Felix. "Okay."

Ernie walked up to Billy and peered at him with bloodshot eyes, as though Billy had said something or offered some kind of challenge.

"One for the road," said Ernie, and he reached inside Billy's coat, removed one of the pints, and, without saying anything else, turned and stalked off into the brush, the branches flapping closed behind him.

Felix motioned to David and the two them turned and walked away through the trees to the south.

Frankie raised his eyebrows as if to say, "Well?" Billy smiled.

They slowed down. The deerflies hummed heavily around them. Billy wasn't sure if the humming sound came from the bugs or the blood in his ears. He could hear his own heart. They followed the tote road for a distance without saying anything. Frankie scanned the woods, the Winchester pointing up and to the left.

Frankie looked across at Billy. "Port arms," he said. Billy smiled again.

They continued down the road and then Billy steered them off into a small clearing.

"I don't think he's out here, Frankie."

"He could be anywhere."

"He's not here. Just slow down. Okay? Just slow down, Jesus. You're really worked up."

"I've been doing exercises," said Frankie, blushing.

"Yeah?"

"You know, to get ready for the Air Force."

"Oh?"

"Push-ups. Toe touches. Cherry pickers. Like that."

"I suppose you're stronger now," ventured Billy. His heart beat fast.

"Yeah. I think so. Running, too. When we went to Key West after graduation I ran on the beach every day."

"Let me feel."

Frankie turned to face him and Billy reached out and squeezed his arm.

"Geez."

"Stop it."

"No. Really. Pretty good."

Frankie looked straight into Billy's eyes.

"I missed you, Billy. I missed you an awful lot."

As he said it, he reached up and picked a twig from Billy's hair and leaned in, his eyes closed in expectation. Billy closed his eyes and let himself be kissed. How long had it been? A year? A full cycle of seasons and chores and school and all that work peeling pulp, and the letters, and the books, and his own pitiful letters back, smudged and probably misspelled. Billy kissed him back and savored the slight, ever so slight feel of Frankie's stubble on his lips. His blood rushed in his ears.

But then a sound crept through the blood. He heard something behind him and he turned to see Felix and David step out of the brush. And then Ernie came from the other direction.

Ernie said something, but Billy's head was buzzing and he couldn't hear what it was. Maybe they hadn't seen. It was possible. Maybe they saw but didn't know what they were seeing. Frankie was stammering and talking, and he had turned from Billy and was walking away.

"Come on, Billy. I said, come on."

Billy followed, stumbling.

"Goddamn Indians," said Frankie. "Come on."

Frankie forced his way through the brush, the branches slapping his face. Billy followed. They walked this way for a few minutes, maybe a minute.

"Hold on, Frankie. Just wait up. They didn't see anything. I don't think they saw anything."

"Saw what?"

"Would you stop? Just stop for a minute."

Frankie stopped but he wouldn't look at Billy.

"No one's going to say anything."

"Just drop it."

Billy had wanted to touch Frankie's arm again. He wanted to step close and hold him by both arms till he calmed down. But he didn't dare. He wanted to tell him he didn't care about push-ups or cherry pickers. He wanted to say that he liked Frankie's arms—yes, his thin arms, his thin arms unencumbered, free of dull muscle. He wanted to say he liked his wrists, his dusty eyelashes. But he didn't dare. He wanted to say, remember. Remember? Remember when they would steal time in the cabins. And how much he liked that Frankie let himself be held, let Billy curl his body around Frankie's smaller one. Remember? To let yourself be held takes a lot more courage than to do the holding. But he didn't dare. More than that. He wanted more: he wanted to retake the search for the German, back up the canoe, drive back to the station, and wait again—but he wanted to wait for Frankie, and only Frankie, to step off the train. And he wanted the train to be different. And the depot. It would be some other depot in some town neither of them knew or were known in. Some bland place no one would think of visiting. And Frankie would say, "Nice jacket, Billy!" and, "I like your style, kid."

But Billy said only, "Everyone's going to forget about it."

"I'll be gone in two weeks. In two weeks I'll be in Montgomery."

"I know."

"What are you going to do when you turn eighteen? What are you going to do, for your part?"

"I'll do something. I'll figure it out. Let's go back. We can take the long way around the slough and meet the rest at the big house. There will be a lot of people around."

"Shh."

"Frankie. Please, let's—"

"Quiet."

Frankie turned toward the thicker brush. There was movement deep in the middle of it, under a blowdown.

"Hear that?"

Billy couldn't see anything, but he heard the rustle of leaves.

SIX

Jonathan lay on his bed. The Pines was finally quiet. A man could actually hear the goddamn pines now. And though it was late afternoon (could it be five already?) the heat had not broken. The grass and each and every leaf seemed to ooze moisture, to drip with heat. And for that and the quiet that let him breathe, he was glad he hadn't gone with the others after the German. He'd almost caved when Emma asked him, and again after Frankie had arrived with Ernest, Billy, and that other boy whose name he could never remember. He almost gave in just so he wouldn't have to endure any more of Emma's nervous wing-beating. And Frankie's excitement was a little contagious. But, by God, he'd met enough Germans during the last war. They were decent enough, and he'd been sorry so many died. He'd even saved a few who had been pulled back to the trenches with their own and he had been glad to save them. It made him feel noble. The Japanese were a different matter. And as he lay on the bed and searched for a breeze by turning his head one direction and then the other, he wondered if he'd save one of those if he were still in the Army. Probably not. After what they'd done it was hard to imagine helping them, or lifting a finger if one lay bleeding below him. Let him bleed. He'd seen men stretched out on the ground many times, and it was surprising how seldom they themselves knew they were going to die. They'd turn their heads as though searching for something, something they could not find. And they'd say *please, oh, please, please* but he wasn't sure what it was they were looking for or asking for, and neither were they, and then they died.

Jonathan wished that the Pines were wired for electricity, because then he could bring one of the electric fans they had in Chicago, and have a breeze whenever he wanted. You'd think this was the tropics, not the north. That's how heavy the heat was. He turned his head again but did not lift his arms or move his body. He had not been wounded in the war. Not much more than scratches and a little trench foot, which came late and he was able to cure it by putting bandages in his boots and drying them over the Bunsen burner at the aid station. It must be a strange feeling to be shot. He turned his head quickly from side to side. "Please, oh, please, please," he said, remembering the pleas of the soldiers under his care. He even went so far as to make the small gurgling sound in his throat that the wounded often made, as though they were thirsty, or as though swallowing air might somehow ease the pain.

"Please, oh, please, please."

He felt himself stir. After a moment he reached down into his trousers. Well, why not? He shucked his pants and lay on the bed in his boxers and undershirt. He worked his penis out of his boxers. It lay long and limp on the sterile fabric, poking out of the fly as though draped and ready to be operated on. He liked it better this way. He liked not to see the angry cloud of his pubic hair and his penis rising out of it like some trunk out of the jungle canopy. It was better this way, with his underwear on. That way his penis was less like an extension of himself, with its taproot (as he knew from medical school) running deep down near his anus. With his underwear on, it was as though his penis had no origin, no ancestral soil; it emerged clean, without history, from the white cotton of his shorts.

This would have to suffice until he got back to Chicago.

"Please, oh, please, please."

He would have to wait weeks—weeks!—until he would hear those words spoken from any lips other than his own. There, after a long day with patients, he could close and lock his office door and spend some time with one of the nurses. Some of them, at least, were willing. They knew the score. Until then . . . well, he was a competent surgeon. He could operate on himself.

Emma would be of no help. She was a good woman. A good mother and a good wife. But passion was something he was sure she never felt. There was no changing that. Worry was as close as she came to passion, and the worry was nonstop. Worry about which wildflowers to stand in which vases at which tables, or whether or not to put parsley on the finger potatoes. She had the annoying habit of standing and murmuring to herself, arranging the flowers, stepping back, taking them out, putting them back in, and giving the vase another quarter turn. And then she would stand in front of the bookcase to the side of the fireplace and tap her chin and ask herself which books the various guests might appreciate finding, as though on accident, in their cabins. Usually Emma solved these crises on her own, but if he was within earshot she could not stop herself from asking him, even though she knew he found it annoying.

"Do you think Mrs. Norton would like *The Ambassadors*? It's funny when you read it from the right angle," she would say.

"Give her D. H. Lawrence, dear."

"Oh, be serious, Jonathan."

"Then ask Felix. I'm sure he has a recommendation."

"Jonathan, please."

Please, indeed.

Please, oh, please, please.

Jonathan worked more diligently with his right hand, and he snuck his left under the elastic of his boxers and skirted the forest of pubic hair on the way to worry his balls.

The phrase "ask Felix" had become a bit of a joke between them. At first it had annoyed him how she would go on and on about what Felix had done and what he had fixed and how fast. Every story or bit of news about the Pines involved what Felix had done. They weren't even safe in the winter. Felix lived in the boathouse throughout the winter doing God knows what—drinking, no doubt—and he sent regular letters, then telegrams, through Harris at the Wigwam. Harris probably composed them anyway, hewn from the raw materials of Felix's few words—*The Pines in good shape* or *Storm came through a few trees down structures fine.* Harris was a finder of things (he'd found Jonathan his scotch and gin, even during the dry years when Jonathan couldn't get what he wanted in Chicago).

Jonathan turned his head to one side and then the other and moved his left hand up to the base of his shaft to keep the blood from escaping, trickling back down into the lake of his usual calm. He tried to think of the kitchen girls again, but he had already left that station. He cast his mind back to Chicago, to his consulting room and the nurse he met there these days (except not of course *these* days, the days he wasted at the Pines).

Please, oh, please, please.

There were many new nurses now. Of course some were attached to the armed forces and would be sent overseas. But there was a need for nurses on the home front, too. He had many applicants and hired more than he really needed, or could afford. They weren't rich, after all. But he hadn't had much during the Crash and so hadn't lost much, and with a lot of hard work they were comfortable. The last nurse he had hired was one of those special ones, entrepreneurial. It having become impossible to find stockings, she had drawn a perfectly straight black line from her heel to her buttocks with an eyeliner pencil.

Jonathan had noticed the line and the absence of stockings when she'd sat down. But it was the girl, Madeline, who had drawn attention to it during the interview.

"I believe in helping others, Dr. Washburn. One of the ways we can help is by going without, even if it means being creative."

He'd asked her what she meant.

"For instance," she'd had her hands folded primly on her lap. "For instance, since we cannot buy stockings, but, you know, society demands we have some class even with a war on, you have to pretend."

"You're creative and helpful because you don't wear stockings?"

"Not just that, of course. I made sure it seemed as though I was wearing stockings."

"Pretense."

"Exactly."

"How far would you say that the pretense needs to go?"

"As far as is necessary, Doctor." And she stood and turned and showed him how she had drawn a black line down the back of her thighs and calves all the way to her ankles.

How easy it had been! And when they were finished, he had, in a fit of boyish gallantry, laid her on the desk and, with his surgeon's hand, drawn the line back in where it had been rubbed off.

Please, oh, please, please.

The house was quiet now. The girls were done with their kitchen work and were in the pump house working on the ironing and the laundry. The boys and Felix were still out looking for the German. Where was Emma? The shrill cheer of the reunion, the discomfort that lurked beneath it, continued to ring in his ears. It had been no different when they were being transported to the lines during the previous war. The same stiff joking and sing-alongs. "Tipperary" and "Be Kind to Your Web-footed Friends," which had made them laugh and laugh and laugh. And most of them had died. The only time during the war Jonathan had felt like himself was when he found time and enough money to see one of the prostitutes down behind the cook tents, where they had set up business. With French whores one could say anything, could do anything. And he had. He could move their bodies any way he pleased and they cooperated, whereas the dead and dying bodies at the front were awkward, stiff, smelly, and broken. And with the whores he could say what he pleased. *Let me fuck your mouth. Turn over.* And he closed his eyes, and with them shut he could see the girl under him, thin, with dark hair, and dark hair marking her legs and her armpits, and small breasts with tiny, very tiny pink nipples accentuated by two or three long dark hairs on each. And with his eyes closed he could picture this and not imagine and not have to see the wound that was her pussy, filled and filled again by so many men.

Please, oh, please. God, oh, please.

That was blessedly enough, as he lay on the iron frame bed in his room at the Pines, as the afternoon limped toward evening and everything lay still—the lake, the house, the pines themselves, and finally, thank God, finally, his own penis, spent and ragged, gasping itself smaller and smaller, retreating, eel-like, into its hiding place, having fed on his hand and his spit and his thoughts. Jonathan tucked it back in his boxers and lay on the bed for a long time. It was a long time gone before he remembered how much he hated it at the Pines and how angry Emma made him and how Frankie was his son but didn't feel like his son. And just when he remembered this, he was roused by the voices of the search party, which had returned amid much shouting and yelling.

Could it be? Could they really have done it, found the German? He stood and looked out the window that faced the forest and saw them. Ernie and David came stumbling out of the woods. They were calling his name. *Dr. Washburn, Dr. Washburn.* As they approached out of the gloom he could see the alarm on their faces. The look of boys who had seen something profound and terrible. He knew it. He knew that look and had all but forgotten it.

Dr. Washburn! Dr. Washburn!

Jonathan opened the window to call down and then, as they drew closer, he saw blood on Ernie's shirt. But where were Felix and Billy? And where was Frankie?

"Mr. Washburn! Please! Mr. Washburn!"

Oh, God, please. Please, God.

Jonathan ran down the stairs and through the kitchen. He was halfway past the garden when he realized he was wearing only his undershirt and underwear. He felt the semen drying on the fabric of his boxers.

Please, oh, please. Please!

Jonathan rounded the garden just as Felix emerged from the woods with Billy in his shadow. He sensed Emma coming up around the front of the house and turned. She held a cutting of dahlias and hollyhocks in her arms.

Felix held a body in his arms, the arms and legs dangling, the face hidden against Felix's shoulder.

Please, oh, please. Please!

He sprinted toward Felix. So slow, so slowly, slowgoing. It wasn't until Felix stood next to him that Jonathan registered that the body was not Frankie's, nor was it the German's. Felix held a girl in his arms, a girl who stirred and moaned and then whimpered. An Indian girl. A teenager, from the look of it, but not a girl he knew. She wore a white blouse, which was soiled and covered in blood, and a gray jumper and black shoes—as if she had been dressed for school or church.

Jonathan looked up at Felix and Billy, confused.

"What the hell? Felix? Where's—"

Frankie emerged from the woods at last. He, too, was covered in blood. He did not look at the girl or at Jonathan. His hands were shoved deep in his pockets.

Jonathan looked back at Felix.

"Take her," Felix said.

Jonathan did as he was told. He held out his arms to receive her.

"She's okay," said Felix. "She'll be okay."

When the girl was in Jonathan's arms, he was shocked at how light, how thin she was. Her hair was matted and tangled and studded with burrs and bark chips. Her face was dirty. But her legs and torso, where his hands clasped her, were strong and smooth. It took nothing at all to hold her. Nothing.

Felix put his hand on her head and said something to her in Indian, something low and smooth and quick. Then he turned and brushed past Frankie, heading back out into the woods. Billy stepped closer to Frankie and Felix, his eyes on the ground, his Adam's apple jumping up and down as he swallowed hard.

"Where are you going?" asked Jonathan. "Where do you think you are going?" He was surprised at the desperation in his voice, the dependence.

"To get the other one," said Felix. He stopped and turned to face Jonathan.

"Is she okay? The other one? Is she like this?"

"No."

Jonathan tried to search Frankie's eyes, but Frankie wouldn't look at him.

"Frank. Frank! What the hell happened? What happened to the other one?" He turned in despair to Felix. "Felix. What happened? Felix! Answer me."

Felix looked at Jonathan coolly.

Billy stepped forward, his eyes on the ground.

"I shot her," he said.

Jonathan looked at Billy and then at his son. "Frankie?"

"I said I shot her, Dr. Washburn," said Billy again.

Frankie looked up at his father and then to the girl in Jonathan's arms.

"I'm so sorry. I can't believe it. I'm so sorry," he mumbled.

Felix looked at the girl and at Frankie and Billy in turn but said nothing. And then he turned and disappeared back into the woods to fetch the body.

It wasn't until they had the girl cleaned and washed and, thanks to an injection Jonathan had given her, asleep in the maid's bedroom downstairs off the kitchen, that Felix and Billy returned with the other girl. Frankie waited around outside the door, pacing to the kitchen and back. He knocked but Emma wouldn't let him in as she tended to the first girl.

No one got to see the other girl when Felix carried her back because Felix had taken off his long-sleeved shirt and wrapped it around her head, either to keep the world from looking at her or the dead girl from looking at them. He carried her directly to the icehouse, where he covered her in a sheet, and there she lay until the sheriff had time to come out and look at her. By then they had found the German and that discovery eclipsed everything else. He questioned them and then left. An accident. Afterward Felix had buried her behind the Pines.

PART II

THE WAR
1943–1945

SEVEN

SAN ANGELO, TEXAS—APRIL 1943

Frankie and another cadet were crammed into the seats behind the bomb bay of a Beechcraft AT-11 Kansan. A third student, the one honing his skills as a bombardier, was stuffed up in the nose of the Beechcraft under the feet of the pilot and the instructor. Frankie was in charge of the camera: he was to record their hits on the pyramidal shacks scattered over the flat, featureless Chihuahuan desert. It was April 1943 and bombs, real bombs, were falling all over the world—Tunisia, Sicily, the Ruhr. The USAAF had stepped up its campaign in Tunisia and Sicily. The RAF had developed a new bomb the papers were calling a "blockbuster," but the RAF and the USAAF referred to as a "cookie." A 4,000-pound bomb capable of leveling a whole city block.

Frankie longed to be in North Africa. He had been in the USAAF for seven months but he was still a cadet. He and his fellow cadets were halfway through their twelve-week bombardier program, though that could change at any moment, as had everything else in the Air Force. The joke was that the Air Force wasn't as good at getting planes in the air as it was at changing course, heading, altitude, and target. Instead of dropping real bombs, they dropped casings full of sand and black powder, never more than 500-pounders, to simulate bomb strikes. What would it feel like to drop a 4,000-pound bomb? What would it be like to feel the plane lift after the payload left the bomb bay and some seconds later the explosion reached you, two miles up in the sky? That would be real, while this—all this—was just training, just another bit of routine pasted over the raw wood of experience, like a yearly coat of enamel on an already over-painted door.

All the same, Frankie was enjoying himself. As he looked down over the desert, he felt he was looking with eyes very different from the ones that wouldn't look Billy, Felix, or Jonathan in the eye when he left the Pines in August of '42. Today they had live bombs on board for a change. The advantage of training with live bombs was that they weighed almost the same as the bombs they would use in combat. Not that they had so much as seen a B-24 or a B-17 or any heavy aircraft they would use in the war. Instead, they flew the Texan for gunnery practice and the Beechcraft for bombing practice. Still, it was good to be in the sky.

The camera was pointed out of a five-inch hole cut in the fuselage of the Beechcraft. They had to record their hits if they were to pass. Frankie would rather be in the nose, accessed by a hatch a single step down from the cockpit, and so narrow that the pilot had to close the hatch after the bombardier crawled in and stamp on it a few times to get it to latch. Most of the other cadets hated getting in the nose, but Frankie had discovered that he liked being a bombardier. He liked the tight space up in the nose, the cluster of instruments and the mysteries of the Norden bombsight itself, clamped to the floor. He liked watching the asphalt runway speed under the wheels of the plane and the moment when the wheels left the ground, the soft cushion of air on which the plane rode up, up, up until the harsh geometry of the desert filled his view. There was the sight and there was the target and all the calculations he had to go through to make sure his load dropped where it belonged. He had to know his instruments and how they worked, and he had to remember his physics and math (angle, altitude, airspeed, ground speed, wind speed, and direction, the weight of the aircraft and the weight of the payload). When they commenced the bombing run, and control transferred from the pilot to the bombardier, he was blissfully, fully, completely in charge. His heart lifted. Everything that bothered him—everything that had happened before—fell away below him.

On the next run it would be his turn to remove the cotter pins from the bombs and make sure they were racked properly and pull the lever at the bombardier's command. After that he would be back in the nose. And someday, who knew when (this was the Air Force, after all), he would be matched to a crew. He bent over the camera and waited patiently for the bombing run to begin.

Like the others, he'd imagined being a pilot, not a bombardier. He had finished cadet training at Princeton and qualified as a pilot. But on his second day at Maxwell, his cohort was marshaled on the parade ground and told they were going to be bombardiers and that theirs was a special job not many men could perform. Releasing bombs didn't seem special to Frankie then. It felt, rather, like a consolation. The job of a mechanic. That evening during mess, he approached his instructor, a lieutenant with a luxurious mustache, and told him that he had taken flying lessons and would be best used as a pilot. The lieutenant listened to Frankie carefully, stroking his mustache.

"I see," he said. "So you've taken flying lessons."

"Yes, sir," said Frankie.

"This was in New Jersey. While you were in college?"

"Yes, sir. That's correct, sir," said Frankie stiffly.

"And I am to understand that you were certified as a pilot?"

"Yes, sir," said Frankie. He tried his best not to smile.

"Hmmm," said his instructor. "So there's been a mistake somewhere. Right?"

"I think so, sir."

"Well, there must be. You're in the Air Force, and the Air Force is in the business of putting planes in the air. And here we have a qualified pilot."

"Single- and double-engine, sir."

"Oh? That changes everything. Or it should, correct? You are a pilot certified to fly single- or double-engine planes."

"Yes, sir."

The other cadets had gathered around.

"Except, Lieutenant Washburn, the Air Force doesn't make mistakes."

"It might have."

"So, you're saying the Air Force, commanded by Commander in Chief Franklin Delano Roosevelt, doesn't know what it's doing? You're saying the president of the United States has got it all wrong?"

"No, sir—"

"Maybe you should replace him."

"Excuse me, sir?" Frankie's palms were beginning to sweat and his collar rubbed against his neck as he swallowed.

"It seems that the president made a mistake when he put you in bombardier training. Not that you're a bombardier yet. No, you are a cadet. Cadets don't fly planes. Cadets don't navigate planes. Cadets don't drop bombs. Cadets don't shoot down enemy fighters. They don't do any of this. Do they?"

"I don't know, sir. I don't think so, sir."

"Maybe you could tell me what they do, son."

"What who do, sir?"

"Cadets. What's the job of a cadet?" The officer turned in a circle. "Everyone, listen up! Everyone, listen! Cadet Washburn is going to tell us all what the job of an aviation cadet is."

"I don't know if I can do it, sir. I don't know if I can say, sir."

"You can fly a plane. You should fly a plane. The president of the

United States evidently wants you to fly a plane. But you can't answer a simple question of mine? You want to fly planes over enemy territory and bring death to the enemy but you can't answer a question, man to man?"

Frankie knew he was being humiliated. He knew he was being maneuvered by the officer into a situation in which there was no good answer, in which there wasn't an answer at all. And he knew that the point wasn't to obtain one but rather to secure his public humiliation. Not that the humiliation served any purpose. It was humiliation for the sake of humiliation, for the pleasure of it. For the pleasure the officer found in it. Frankie knew this. It made the humiliation even worse. When Frankie didn't answer, the officer turned to the rest of the dining hall and spoke loudly over the din.

"You all are here to learn to be bombardiers. Why? Because the Air Force needs bombardiers. Why does the Air Force need bombardiers? Because getting our bombs on target, bringing death to the enemy, is our most important job. It is our sacred duty to kill the enemy with bombs. And it is one of our most dangerous jobs. Bombardiers die. You are here because too many bombardiers have died fighting the enemy, and we need more of you to do the same. There have been no mistakes. There are no other reasons. You are here because we need you here. And a cadet's job is to do whatever we ask you to do and to do it to the best of your ability. With any luck you won't wash out. You'll become bombardiers, and you will have a chance to drop our bombs on the enemy. Do you understand?"

"Yes, sir!" said the cadets, Frankie's voice among theirs.

The officer was the first in a series of professional psychopaths who made up the officer corps at Maxwell. There seemed to be some kind of secret brotherhood of jerks among the instructors and the upperclassmen, who in their own way fed the machine of stupidity. The upperclassmen took turns grinding them down. Frankie and the other cadets slept six to a room, with one desk and one chair. When an upperclassman entered the room the cadets had to jump to their feet and scream, "Attention!" Some of the upperclassmen liked to enter the room, leave, come back on the pretense of having forgotten something, leave again, come back for another item, until the freshman cadets were exhausted and hoarse from jumping to their feet and shouting. At the mess hall the cadets sat six to a table with an upperclassman seated at the head to make sure they ate correctly, which meant sitting up straight on the leading third of the chair seat, taking a forkful of food, and bringing it straight up before altering its course ninety degrees and parallel to the ground to meet their mouths. There were all sorts of petty disciplines. But Frankie quickly learned he didn't mind. He didn't mind the routine. Or the humiliation. He didn't mind the inanity of it all. The other cadets grumbled to themselves when they were sure they weren't being overheard—when the six of them were crammed into the shower room (six men, one shower, five minutes) or before inspection or when they fell out after marching practice. How the Air Force was in love with parades! It was all inane, stupid, and empty, and the cadets knew that they were being kept busy marching and parading and cleaning and rushing from one activity to the next because the Air Force had no idea what to do with them and was trying to stay one step ahead, training them on the fly, as it were. Much to Frankie's surprise, the mindlessness was fine with him.

There had been just as much inanity at Princeton, if not more. Though while the stupidity of the Air Force didn't bother him, the stupidity of the Ivy League had settled into a dull ache just behind his eyes shortly after his arrival at Princeton. It settled down and stayed there for four long years until he graduated. Oh, God, how he had hated Princeton. How glad he was to be free of it. Free of the senselessness of the place; free of the forced hilarity, bordering on hysteria, of the eating clubs. He had been encouraged to bicker Ivy (Jonathan had been in Ivy) and he had gone along with it so as not to disappoint Jonathan. There hadn't been any interviews needed to join the USAAF. But to join Ivy? He had ten rounds of interviews, formal interviews around the large dining room table, followed by two all-night sessions of deliberations and three weeks of mandatory parties. He did it all. He smiled through it all. He drank when they told him to drink and he answered their questions (What does your father do? How do you spend your summers? What do you think you can contribute to Ivy?). And every night he was reminded of Fitzgerald's assessment of Ivy as "detached and breathlessly aristocratic." He wasn't so sure about that. "Distressed and breathlessly autochthonic" was more like it: Ivy was most profoundly concerned with being of its place. He got in, nonetheless.

When Emma pressured him to try out for the Triangle Club, he had done that, too. If being a "gentleman" was Jonathan's wish for him then being "theatrical" was Emma's, and nothing would do but the oldest musical comedy group at Princeton. He auditioned by accompanying himself on the piano on an up-tempo version of Hoagy Carmichael's "Moonburn." It did the trick. Emma was "over the moon" but Frankie's soul sank a little. Ivy for Jonathan. Triangle for Emma. And what for him? He tried out for and made the Nassoons. Participating in all of these groups had been a source of constant distress. The energy with which his "pals" in Ivy faked a lack of interest—in their studies and in each other—was rivaled only by the degree to which they affected to be "jolly" and "good sports." The same was true of Triangle, which demanded a steady output of zaniness of a certain pedigreed sort, ending in the drag revue every spring. Even while simply eating at Ivy, Triangle members were expected to burst into song with spontaneity—a spontaneity that had been rehearsed late into the evening the night before. Heaven forbid if you were in a serious mood, or simply too tired to muster the requisite amount of enthusiasm. Enthusiasm—this went for all of Princeton—was an affect that one practiced, or needed to practice, in front of the mirror every day. Frankie understood himself as a blandly middle-course kind of guy, but Princeton didn't admit to that kind of thing.

During his sophomore year, a fellow Triangle member had pulled Frankie aside after practice and invited him along on a trip to New York with "some of the boys." A few of them took the Dinky to Princeton Junction and from there, the metro line to Penn Station, then the subway up to Ninety-Sixth Street and Central Park West. As they approached the city, his companions had become more and more exuberant, more excited, more *dramatic.* When the door to the apartment opened, they exploded into frivolity and made a great show of kissing their host—an old Princeton alum—on both cheeks and clapping their hands together. For his part, Frankie didn't know how to act. It was loud. There were no women, not one. He looked around the room and saw men kissing one another over drinks, dancing outrageously (funny how his mother's language came to mind to describe something his mother would never have been able to imagine). He tried to fake having a good time but was unable to do it. One of his classmates found him sipping grapefruit juice in the corner of the living room.

"Having fun?"

Frankie shrugged.

"Aren't you one of us? You are, aren't you?"

He supposed he was. But he didn't want to kiss anyone there—that would be merely an act in a series of acts that was Princeton rather than something real. Sitting there all alone, he thought of Billy. He wanted to kiss Billy, because, well . . . because he did. Because of how he felt about Billy. Because of who Billy was, not because of what kissing him meant, to him or to anyone else. When he was next to Billy it was so thrilling, so unbelievable, so gratifying. More than anything else. Ever. He wanted to spend time with Billy precisely because he didn't have to act—act happy, act sad, act shocked. He didn't have to act at all. The lack of pretense was part of the attraction. The opposite of this. The feeling of freedom attached to Billy extended beyond him to include Felix and all of the Pines—the days structured by real weather rather than social or parental weather. The woods themselves, unfolding behind the Pines, carried only possibility.

He told his friend from Triangle not to worry, truly, not to worry at all. And then he got up and walked the sixty blocks back to Penn Station. In a state of numb exhaustion he found himself walking across the campus at dawn, wishing the campus mists were the mists of the lake, that the flagstones would melt somehow into the marshes and sloughs of the woods north of the Pines, and that Billy would appear from behind an arch as though from around the boathouse. But Billy didn't appear at Princeton. He never did.

Billy had appeared, as something of a surprise, one morning when Frankie was ten. Frankie had woken early, as usual. Jonathan was still in Chicago. Frankie lay in bed and listened for Emma's voice. Light, strong already, came through his open window, diffused by the metal screen. No sound from the garden. He heard the metal grate on the cookstove being rattled by one of the kitchen girls, shifting the ash down to the pan. But if Emma had been there he would have heard her caviling, and he would have heard the girls' polite, patient responses: nothing.

He sat up and took off his pajamas and put on his T-shirt and overalls. He didn't bother with socks. At least Emma didn't hector him about socks in the summer. He rubbed his teeth with his sleeve rather than brush them with water from the pitcher on the stand in the corner. If he were getting ready for a day at Fenwick's she would have put him through a full inspection—hair, nails, teeth, face, clothes, comb, handkerchief, pocket money, satchel. And he would have had to sit there, back straight, forearms on the table, staring at the piece of liver on his plate that didn't resemble meat or nourishment so much as leather covered in sand. Meanwhile, Emma (*Oh, I'm not really feeling all that hungry, a glass of tomato juice is enough for me, thank you*) and Jonathan (a plate of eggs, three of them, and nothing else) would shake their heads at what Jonathan referred to as Frankie's "stubbornness" and Emma would coo about his "need to get his strength up" for the long school day. Frankie didn't feel stubborn, nor did he feel weak. He just hated liver. More than that, at age ten he hated how such standoffs were the only way his parents could express their fear. Fear that he—and by extension, their lives—was not turning out as expected. Their inability to address their own fears, their own failings, their own disappointments reduced the present and the future not to ash but to fog. A slow-creeping, heavy fog of sadness that hung over his childhood.

Even then he knew, he *knew*: what Emma considered love (the constant worry, the constant checking, the constant amendments, the constant admonishments) was performed with as much regard for what other people would say about him as it was about his actual well-being. At the Pines, with no one around but Felix and the kitchen girls and the occasional drop-in from Chicago, she didn't put him through all that. As for Jonathan, he wasn't there, and so much the better. Felix never bossed him around, never made him feel inadequate. Felix let him try his hand at whatever job Emma had set him to, without seeming to care one way or the other if Frankie accomplished it. As a result, Frankie knew how to fillet a fish, bait a hook, pull weeds, swing a hammer, work a jack plane, tie a painter, and split kindling; things that, if his parents had to do them, would never get done.

Frankie paused at the top of the stairs and listened. She wasn't in the front room, the "lobby," as she liked to call it, and she wasn't in the "maid's room" off the kitchen that she used as an office. She had to be outside somewhere. That meant Frankie could skip breakfast and go down to the boathouse, where Felix was working on something, and then he would be with Felix till lunch at least.

He took the stairs two at a time, his tanned feet gripping the treads. He passed through the front room at a trot and banged out the screen door into the sun at a full run. The grass on the lawn was slick with dew, and by the time he got to the boathouse his feet were covered in grass clippings and the cuffs of his overalls were wet past his ankles. He was about to peer into the boathouse to see if Felix was inside when he saw another boy standing on the dock. With his dark skin and tan dungarees, his once-white cotton duck shirt with buttons up the front, he blended in with the cattails. He was so still that Frankie hadn't seen him at first. He stopped short and stood there. He didn't know where Felix was and he didn't know who the boy was, except that he was an Indian. He hadn't moved from where he stood on the dock, except to raise his hand slightly, and when Frankie didn't wave, he let the hand drop back to his side. He was thin, almost as thin as Frankie. His wrists and anklebones stuck out, all the more so because his shirtsleeves (the cuffs brown from use, Frankie could see) were too short and his dungarees a size too small. But his hands were long and wide and his bare feet were brown and strong and he stood still but steady on the dock.

"Hi," said Frankie. Someone had to say something. "Hi, I'm Frankie."

The boy regarded him and then turned his head upriver and brought a hand up to shield his eyes, even though the sun was behind him. "There's ducks in them cattails. Close, too," he said.

"Yeah?" asked Frankie, moving closer.

"Yeah, they don't got no feathers yet. Not flying feathers."

Soon they were shoulder to shoulder, peering into the cattails. It took Frankie a minute to see what the other boy was looking at. But then there they were, like grown mallards but dun-colored and smaller, paddling slowly in the cattails, sticking their beaks down past the scrim of algae and weeds and bringing them back up again, chattering soundlessly.

"They'd be good-tasting right now," said the boy.

"You think?"

"You bet. They ain't flown yet. Them's baby ducks there."

Frankie liked the way the boy spoke.

"We could ask Felix for the gun. Maybe he'd shoot them."

The boy considered this. His hand was in his pocket and he tapped it against his thigh. Frankie could hear something hard rattling in there. A warm scent came off the boy. Frankie looked at him, at the way his black hair fell over his ears, and the light down of black hairs barely visible against his brown skin. He was probably Frankie's age, maybe a little younger.

The boy stood taller. "We don't need a gun. We got these."

He drew his hand from his pocket and showed Frankie five stones, all smooth and oval, each about half the size of an egg.

"You think you could get one with those?" asked Frankie.

"Watch me," said the boy.

Frankie didn't know what was more amazing, that the other boy was so confident or that he was willing to try.

He took a rock in his left hand and squinted, then, like a pitcher, wound up, lifted his right leg, and threw. Frankie, who had been looking at the boy's form, tried to see where the rock landed but his eyes were too slow. The ducks scattered, clucking, through the cattails, and the ripples disappeared.

"Oh, well," said Frankie, trying to be nice.

"Look and see," said the boy. "Look and see," he said again, as he dusted off his hands.

Frankie did as he was told, not sure if the other boy was playing a joke on him. He put his hands on his knees and bent forward, trying to see something in the cattails. The other boy did the same. Then Frankie saw. He saw a patch of white and what looked like two orange twigs, poking up in the air.

"That him?" asked Frankie in wonder.

"They look different on the bottom. You always got to look for the white."

"Jesus," whispered Frankie. "Will you look at that? Will you look at that."

The door of the boathouse slammed but Frankie didn't register the sound until Felix said, "Mr. Frankie."

Frankie turned and said, "We got one, Felix. We got one."

"Did you?"

"Yep," said the boy. "We did."

Felix walked to the edge of the dock and flipped the canoe over and fed it into the water. "We'll get him on the way."

Felix steadied the canoe and the boys got in, the other boy in the bow and Frankie in the middle. Felix nosed the canoe into the cattails. The boy picked up the duck by the feet and held it up for Frankie to see.

"She's a beaut," said the boy.

He still hadn't offered Frankie his name.

Felix turned upriver and the boys spent the morning pulling minnow traps out of the current and dumping the minnows into a tin pail. Then they coasted back down the river and filled the bait cage with the minnows. By the time Frankie sat down to lunch in the big house, he was starving. He told Emma excitedly about the duck, and how the boy killed it with a rock and how the ducks were good eating this time of year.

"Billy's going to help Felix out around the place," Emma said. "He's from the village."

"Oh?"

"Some things Felix can't quite manage by himself, you know. Some jobs take two people."

"Oh?" he said between mouthfuls. And then: "What a throw."

"I'm sure," said Emma. "But it's not sporting, you know. It's not sporting. They can't even fly. I'm sure your father would agree."

Frankie said nothing. But that night as he was going to sleep, he saw the little ducks skittering away in the cattails, and Billy's long lean brown arm whipping through the sunlight. He saw the bait traps rising from the depths filled with the bright coin splash of wriggling bodies—rainbows and shiners and the bronze-black warty heads of chubs—and he heard Billy saying, "She's a beaut," and the strong, calm, calming stroke of Felix's paddling and he knew he was happy.

Now all that was behind him—seven months, sure, but more than simply those months. He was a different man. He was, now, in fact, a man. The job of the bombardier was to drop bombs onto cities, rail yards, bridges, ships, factories, and troop concentrations, and he had been trained to do it efficiently. His job was to drop bombs and kill people. What was a kiss in a cabin or in the woods compared to that? What was any of it—those many years at the Pines and that one terrible day they searched for the German prisoner—compared to the clear purpose to which he was now bent? Billy's attractions weren't, at the end of the day, any more substantial than Jonathan's disappointment or Emma's worry—just a warm, silly childhood wind that blew through the cabins in the dark and was gone. He wasn't even sure any of it had happened.

His training at Montgomery, his first taste of life in the Air Force, had been encouraging. What mattered there was not how you seemed but how hard you worked and how willingly you submitted to the larger cause, no matter how mindless it struck you. That said, the first two weeks at Maxwell were confusing: there were no billets available for new cadets, so they had to sleep in canvas tents, and instead of basic or advanced training they completed "on-line training," which was what the officers called menial work. They cooked, mopped, painted, and mucked for twelve hours a day, six days a week. Frankie had wondered at first how all that would help win the war against the Germans, but it became clear that the question was hopelessly romantic, almost idiotic—as though one or two or twenty or two hundred men would have any direct effect on the outcome of the war. But he did as he was ordered. And he liked it.

He liked, also, that he had to be in uniform and that the uniforms were, by definition, all the same. At Princeton and even at Fenwick's, Frankie had felt pressed flat under the pressure to look a certain way. Three buttons or four? Shirts were tucked in of course, but the smartest among them knew how much to blouse them so as not to look too formal. And with what agony did Frankie scuff his bucks—too new-looking and you seemed desperate, too worn out and you could be mistaken for poor. Should the pants break an inch or an inch-and-a-half? What knot should he use for his tie this year, this month, this week? Was a four-in-hand too formal? Was a half-Windsor too casual? It was maddening. But in the Air Force he wore what he was given and maintained it the way he was instructed, and beyond that he didn't worry about it. That was freedom.

When a billet opened up and he and a few of the most junior cadets finally got spaces, they still didn't learn anything that could be remotely useful. Instead, they spent six weeks marching in formation, running two and a half miles at five every morning, throwing and catching logs, doing push-ups, and running an obstacle course in full gear. This, too, was fine. Everyone knew that it didn't matter if you were the fastest (so long as you weren't the slowest) or the strongest (as long as you weren't the weakest). All that mattered was that you did it, and that you did it as a group.

Finally, after six weeks of basic training, he and his class graduated to the classroom. He had studied physics and math at Princeton. He studied them again, and also fluid dynamics, the mechanics of flight, circuitry, deflection shooting, and geometry. He graduated at the top of his class. But instead of being sent to pilot school they sent him on to train as a bombardier, with the rank of second lieutenant. And after his intial disappointment, he didn't mind.

Likewise, when he was younger he hadn't minded being thin, or "anemic." His body had always done more or less what he wanted it to. He wasn't naturally inclined to worry in front of a mirror or in front of other people. But Jonathan minded. The doctor minded. Jonathan regaled Frankie with stories of the marches he'd undertaken in the First World War and boxing matches he had won when he boxed for Princeton, and his appearance at the 1928 Olympiad in Amsterdam as a member of the U.S. Modern Pentathlon Team. He made a great show of buying the Winchester in Chicago and bringing it up to the Pines, where he stood on the dock in late summer and shot at the ducks as they shuttled up and down the river at dusk. He never got one, as far as Frankie could remember. Felix had looked on, saying nothing, and when Jonathan was done, he had taken the dip net and scooped the waxed cardboard shot shells from the water.

Frankie's agony as a child had been the result of his good nature—his desire not to cause his parents any pain. For their sake, not his, he had faked interest in being "robust" as much as he later faked interest in being "artistic." God, what a relief it had been after all to end up as a bombardier—a job that didn't demand either strength or creativity, and for which his slight frame was an asset. All in all, being in the Air Force represented freedom. Freedom from senselessness, freedom from affect, freedom from humor, freedom from socializing, freedom from feeling.

Frankie adjusted the focal length of the camera, just for something to do. The desert remained the same, always the same—self-evident. Here and there the sand and creosote were broken by an outcropping, a little hump of rock not tall enough to cast a shadow. Everything that needed to be seen was seen. The plane banked to the north, climbing a few thousand feet, then dropped back down, to simulate slipping through cloud cover. Each shift in altitude and bearing was announced, and each demanded that the bombardier make adjustments. Everything that needed to be seen and known in the USAAF was seen and known, and if you didn't see it or know it, there were always more tests, more drills, more and more and more.

If only life had had a similar clarity back before training, back at the Pines. If only he had known seven months ago what he knew now. That day he got off the train and saw Billy standing on the platform in his new coat, and then Ernie and David came tumbling out after him and they stood in the heat and the humidity, smiling stupidly in the stupid sunlight. He had wanted so badly to show them all—dumb, bright Ernie and Jonathan, his sour face floating down over the lawn to the dock, and Emma, her face so contorted by rapture at his return that she looked insane—to show them that he was no longer the boy who kicked his legs under the table and grimaced at the liver on his plate, who followed Felix around or snuck into one of the cabins with Billy when everyone else was asleep. He'd wanted so much to be a man for Billy, for him most of all, in ways he never cared to be for Jonathan. That wasn't the mark of a man, though. It was the anxiety of a boy. Get the Kraut. Let's go get a Kraut. God, how stupid, after all.

If only he'd found some way to let them know—Emma and Jonathan and Felix and Billy, all of them—that he was no longer the boy he'd been. But how could he express that when the boy he'd been, really been, was submerged under the different versions of him they cherished, while the real version, the real boy, had been as unexpressed, as unable to be expressed, as the man he was now?

These days Emma seemed to feel that her job as a war mother was to give him the news, every bit of news, about what was happening on the "home front." A whiff of antic worry clung even to her letters. She told him how Chicago was finally livable again as a result of gas rationing. Lakeshore Drive and Michigan Avenue were virtually devoid of traffic and one could ride one's bike around the Loop and actually breathe the air (not that she did, not that she would). You could hear the waves and gulls at Chicago Harbor, and it took only fifteen minutes to get from Oak Park to the Loop on the wide-open streets. Chicago was quiet, but Calumet and Gary, far to the southeast across the bay, growled and glowed like "some demon in hell" because the factories were going twenty-four hours a day, seven days a week. A lot of the blacks worked there and even some women (not that Emma did, not that she could). And instead of cars, they were building tanks! Emma informed him that she had donated his old bicycle to the government. They needed all the metal they could get—old railings, wagons, even toys and typewriters (though she had saved the Underwood he used at Princeton, not to worry). It was impossible to find dried fruit, jam, butter, eggs, and especially sugar in the stores unless you knew someone, and even then you could never get as much as you would like. Jonathan had begun accepting payment from his patients in goods rather than money: silk, coffee, sugar, ink.

As for the Pines—it was as it always was, not even the war had changed it much. The camp across the way was getting bigger, more bunkhouses were being built for more prisoners, but there was no gas to be had, so the Chris-Craft was up on cribs and covered in tarps and Felix had to paddle to town, but he was an Indian, after all, and used to such things. With no one to cook for, because gas rationing forbade touring and sightseeing by automobile, the kitchen girls had been let go. Harris reported that they had all found work on farms—baling hay, milking, painting—because with so many men in service, there was no one else to work the fields. And the cripple Mary was working for Harris himself, the skinflint.

Speaking of the kitchen girls—the pretty one, Stella (did he remember her?) married Billy this past November. That was a surprise, wasn't it? But then again, the war was making everyone grow up fast, and as a married couple they would get extra rations. And now that Billy was drafted into the infantry, he would get extra pay, which they'd need for the little one that word had it was already on the way. Wouldn't it be quite the coincidence if he and Frankie ended up serving together somehow?

He tried in his own letters, to Emma and to Prudence, to sound cheerful, upbeat. Another act.

Dear Prudy (I hope I can call you that—I hear that's your nickname at the Pines and around town),

They're keeping us busy. Classes and training. Training and classes. We have parades and PT (that's physical training) and even KP (that stands for "kitchen patrol"). We get up and make our beds and march and go to class and march and eat and study and march and study and go to bed and get up and make our beds. Still, we've actually begun flying, and that's a relief. It's a relief to get up off the ground, to feel the air underneath you. To know that nothing except the air and your movement are keeping you up.

When I get back I'll take you flying. Everything looks different from up here. I imagine the Pines is even prettier from the air, with the trees and the water. I'll take you up someday.

That's a promise. I hope you're listening to Felix. He's a good egg. I'm sure it gets lonely with everyone gone. But when the war's over, everything will be different.

I hope this letter finds you happy. And that you're doing everything you're supposed to be doing. At least spring is on the way. You're in my thoughts all the time, Prudy. I hope you know that.

Your Frankie

Even a letter like that took some effort. But after what she'd been through, it cost him only some paper and a few minutes. Emma, back in Chicago, had urged Frankie to write her, care of Harris, at the Wigwam, at least a letter or two.

She had Felix, of course, to look after her, but there was no one else. She'd had no other family but her sister, and there had been no place to send her back to. She was in school and doing quite well—he really should write her, it must be dull for a girl her age with only Felix around the place, and Emma stuck in Chicago with a million little things to do.

Frankie had done that much, it was the least he could do. Not that he could say anything of real importance, but it felt good to send her letters of his days and his hopes for hers, and stories of the Pines back before everything went to hell.

What a mess. What a pointless mess, after all was said and done. He took in Emma's weekly news—the rationing, Billy's marriage, wartime Chicago—with a kind of numb amazement: not so much at the news itself but at the idea that life elsewhere continued. It was as if all the news were part of some story, some story made up by life's author that had nothing really to do with life itself. If only he could send Emma and Prudence his news, his *real* news. If only they saw what he had seen. He wasn't allowed to say anything, of course. Their mail was censored and would be until they were, officially, officers, at which point they would be expected to censor their own mail. But even uncensored, what could he say and how could he say it in such a way as to make them understand? They couldn't possibly. They couldn't possibly understand the bombardier's manual or the Norden sight or why all of it was so important. They would never get it.

Sometimes, when he let it, that day in the woods when they went after the Kraut came back to him—the heat, the heavy air, Billy's sheepish smile as he picked the twig from his hair, then the shot, and the girl's legs twitching and jerking, spending their agony in the leaves, and the awful silence afterward—but he pushed it away. Compared to what he was doing now, all those years at the Pines and that one sad, awful day vanished below him, lost in the desert.

The day the B-17 pilot training manuals were distributed, the lieutenant in charge of their instruction had said, "Read this. Memorize it. This is your code."

And he had.

Accurate and effective bombing is the ultimate purpose of your entire airplane and crew. Every other function is preparatory to hitting and destroying the target. Nothing he studied at Princeton had that clarity of purpose. The manual went further: *The success or failure of the mission depends upon what he accomplishes in that short interval of the bombing run.* He took this to heart, too. Reading further, in that hot classroom, he felt a lump rise in his throat. *When the bombardier takes over the airplane for the run on the target, he is in absolute command. He will tell you what he wants done, and until he tells you "bombs away," his word is law. A great deal, therefore, depends on the understanding between bombardier and pilot. You expect your bombardier to know his job when he takes over. He expects you to understand the problems involved in his job, and to give him full cooperation. Teamwork between pilot and bombardier is essential.*

To read those words, so dry and precise (never mind the shifting point of view and audience), was a profound experience for Frankie. No words had ever rung more true or more necessary for him. Not even the many passages of *The Iliad* he had committed to memory. Not, *Sing, O Goddess, the anger of Achilles, son of Peleus.* Not, *A dark cloud of grief fell upon Achilles as he listened. He filled both hands with dust from off the ground, and poured it over his head, disfiguring his comely face, and letting the refuse settle over his shirt so fair and new. He flung himself down all huge and hugely at full length, and tore his hair with his hands.* Those passages, among others, which had moved him so much when he first encountered them as a student at Fenwick's—and treasured again at Princeton because he had secretly cast himself as Achilles and Billy as Patroclus and had gone so far as to underline, in pencil, the passages where Achilles mourns the death of his friend—seemed secondary to these sober, clear, necessary instructions.

He took to heart the urging of the manual that "there are many things with which a bombardier must be thoroughly familiar in order to release his bombs at the right point to hit his predetermined target." The manual went on, rightly, to list those things, set off by bullet points:

- He must know and understand his bombsight, what it does, and how it does it.
- He must thoroughly understand the operation and upkeep of his bombing instruments and equipment.
- He must know that his racks, switches, controls, releases, doors, linkage, etc., are in first-class operating condition.

- He must understand the automatic pilot as it pertains to bombing.
- He must know how to set it up and make adjustments and minor repairs while in flight.
- He must know how to operate all gun positions in the airplane.
- He must know how to load and clear simple stoppages and jams of machine guns while in flight.
- He must be able to load and fuse his own bombs.
- He must understand the destructive power of bombs and must know the vulnerable spots on various types of targets.
- He must understand the bombing problem, bombing probabilities, bombing errors, etc.
- He must be thoroughly versed in target identification and in aircraft identification.

Frankie took all the directives in the manual very seriously. He studied the schematics of the B-17 from tip to tail, though he hadn't yet seen one in real life. He spent extra time at gunnery practice, and could field dress the .50-caliber machine guns almost as quickly as the waist, turret, and tail gunners. He had never been very mechanically inclined, though he always got a thrill out of helping Felix fix the big motor on the Chris-Craft. But he found that he excelled at loading and fusing the bombs in the bomb bay of the trainers. When the racks got stuck on practice missions, he and the engineer would stand over the open bomb bays at 24,000 feet and, with screwdrivers, release the payload.

At the end of their instruction, he and the rest of the bombardiers had been assembled on the hardstand at Maxwell Field, in front of their training officers, who stood on a raised wooden platform. They raised their hands and repeated after the officers in charge:

Mindful of the secret trust about to be placed in me
by my Commander in Chief,
the President of the United States, by whose
direction I have been chosen for bombardier
training . . . and mindful of the fact that I am
to become guardian of one of my country's
most priceless military assets, the American
bombsight . . . I do here, in the presence of
Almighty God, swear by the Bombardier's
Code of Honor to keep inviolate the secrecy
of any and all confidential information
revealed to me, and further to uphold
the honor and integrity of the Army
Air Forces, if need be, with my life itself.

There was a lump the size of a bread box on the dais, covered in a white sheet. After they recited the oath, the lead instructor lifted the sheet to reveal the famous Norden bombsight, which they'd studied but never actually seen. It looked like a spare car part, but it would be treated with utmost secrecy, escorted to and from the plane in a canvas bag under armed guard.

Over the intercom, the pilot announced they were commencing the bombing run. Frankie bent over the camera and began shooting pictures, one every five seconds for the five minutes until the bombardier announced, "Bombs away." The other cadet released the racks. The bomb bay doors opened and the heavy, close air inside the uninsulated body of the AT-11 Kansan was sucked out, and Frankie's skin, awash in sweat, suddenly cooled. The pilot spoke again and the student acting as bombardier answered and took over the controls. The plane was now being flown by the bombardier.

They held level. Frankie snapped pictures. Desert. More desert. He tried to remain empty of everything except the task before him. All his thoughts—about the dead girl and the live one, about Billy (Where was he now? Was he really married? And, oh, those hands of his and that smile of his . . .), had been sucked out of the plane, along with the heat. The bombardier announced, "Bombs away," and the third student pulled the lever on the rack and the bombs—all ten of them—dropped out. The plane lifted forty feet higher in the air, suddenly unencumbered. Frankie breathed in a sudden *oh!* as he was lofted along with the lumbering metal, his body suddenly weightless and empty and free. A little foretaste, a sample, of the freedom that would be his when he finished training and was matched with a real crew and a real B-17 and was shipped overseas.

The pilot announced a new bearing and the Kansan banked as they turned back to San Angelo. Frankie sat up and stretched and then rested his back against the fuselage. The pictures would tell the official story but he knew it had been a successful run. He closed his eyes and breathed deeply.

EIGHT

THE DANCE—CHRISTMAS EVE, 1944

Mary, the cripple, was literally run off her foot. Hardly had she shut the door to the Wigwam behind another group arriving for the Christmas party when Harris shouted to her from behind the bar to get more wood because the stove was going out. So she clomped out the back door, breathing through her nose because, with the temperature at minus thirty according to the alcohol thermometer, the dry, cold air threatened to singe her lungs. Then the bell tinkled again—not that Mary needed the bell with Harris yelling, "Get the door, Mary, get the door!"—and the sudden in-suck of cold air announced the arrival of yet more Indians and loggers and their families, and Mary set off for the front. No one wanted to hang their coats—not that there was any place to hang them—because it took a while to warm up. But soon the seat backs and bar stools grew great mounds of woolen fur, and the melting frost dripped in puddles on the floor. Mary went after the broom and ushered the water and clumps of snow back toward the front door around the legs of the guests. Just when that was finished, Harris said she had to find a crate of eggs because the ones he had had frozen, and if she didn't find some good ones, there'd be no Tom and Jerrys later and, goddamnit, that was tradition! Harris turned and wiped a glass with the rag over his shoulder and, drying his hands, put a new record on the player behind the bar. The first bars of the song rolled out over the drinks lined up there, barely heard over the din.

Down went the gunner, a bullet was his fate
Down went the gunner, and then the gunner's mate

Mary, her short leg clomping over the pine boards of the dance floor, was almost to the storeroom when another breath of icy air shot into the bar. The bell tinkled and Harris shouted, "Mary!" Once again she turned and headed back to the front.

This was the end of a very long year and no one was sure what to make of the year or its end. The weather, the war—everything, really—had been turned upside down. The whole country had been battered by below-zero weather for all of February, floods through April and May that brought the Mississippi as high as it had ever been, then drought in the summer, hurricane after hurricane up and down the East Coast in the fall, heavy snow in November and early December that made it nearly impossible to get about in the woods, and now, at Christmas, a deep freeze so sudden, so sharp, that it cracked harness leather, froze diesel fuel into solid blocks, and split tires (which was especially dire, since rationing made it impossible to get new ones). The war was essentially won. Was "in the bag," according to the gossip at the depot and articles in the paper. Africa was won. Italy had been liberated past the Gothic Line, D-Day had been the greatest military feat since Hannibal crossed the Alps, and the Allies had landed in southern France virtually unopposed. Everyone had said "home by Christmas," but now it was Christmas and no one was home and the Germans were pushing back in Belgium when everyone expected to see, printed in the papers, the Stars and Stripes flying over the Reichstag.

Mary, eyes down on the floor, was almost to the front door as it banged shut, opened a crack, and banged again without latching because of the accumulated frost, frozen slush, and snow rimming the frame. Prudence stood in the entryway, her coat belted tight around her waist. Her feet were clad in black suede peep-toe Mary Janes and her slender brown legs were bare, as were her hands and head. There was no way she could have walked from the Pines—six miles in the dark if it was an inch—dressed like that.

Mary moved past her. Prudence barely looked down at her, her eyes searching the crowd for something or someone else, her chin high. The rim of her nose was red and moist-looking. Mary lifted the door and put her shoulder into it to force the latch past the striker. *"Gisinaamagad ina?"* she asked, still looking down at the floor, as she moved past Prudence back to the bar.

"Sweet Christ, is it ever," said Prudence.

"Now, now," said Father Paul, who stood by the bar, a brandy in his hands, his usual vestments replaced with a sweater buttoned up to his chin, its shawl collar so stiff and plump it looked like a yoke for an ox. His cheeks were red and his hair slicked to the side with macassar.

Prudence took off her coat, folded it in her arms, and held it in front of her. She wore a black wool dress with a wide collar and ivory buttons up the front. Some of the seams were done in white thread but not all of them. The dress made her neck seem very long and her hair was pulled back from her face with a hair band.

The door opened behind her and Dick Bolton and some of the men from his lumber camp—all of them wearing scotch caps with earflaps and red-and-black-checked jackets—tried to come in, but Prudence was blocking the way.

"In or out, for Chrissake," Dick said through the crack.

"Now, now," said Father Paul again, in the same tone, as though his job were to monitor the swearing on the eve of Christ's birthday rather than to accept drink after drink from his flock as they got well on their way to massively drunk.

"How's them Tom and Jerrys?" asked Dick over Prudence's shoulder.

Prudence stepped forward into the room to let Dick past.

"Not till later, just the usual till then, Dickie. Just the usual swill till then," said Harris. He turned to put on a new record.

"Then make it whiskey and make it warm," said Dick as he shucked his coat and stowed it on the floor next to the inside door. The music started up again, Helen Forrest singing "Long Ago (And Far Away)."

I dreamed a dream one day
And now that dream is here beside me

"Ain't that the truth, Prudy?" asked Dick.

"Dream on," she said, as if coming out of a trance. She stamped her feet and walked across the bar and set her coat on top of the jukebox, which had been broken since 1941 and with the war on wasn't likely to be fixed. In any event, Harris had taken out all the 78s and stacked them behind the bar.

Prudence stood next to the darkened juke with her arms crossed in front of her. The crowd—which comprised pretty much the whole current population of the village except for some of the pregnant women or new mothers—was antic somehow. Maybe it was just that it was Christmas and a time to look back over the year. Or maybe it was the novelty of Indians being allowed in the Wigwam at all, and the absence of men. The war had changed many things. There wasn't a man here younger than twenty-seven except for Dave Gardner, who couldn't be a soldier, what with his eyes and his heart, and a few of the kids from farms outside the village, who were exempt from the draft.

The farm boys were all gathered in the corner under the deer head, sipping beer cautiously, making it last. Many of the women were gone, too—down to Austin to work in the canneries or to Minneapolis to work at General Mills. The lumber camps were full of women now. Women with spuds and picaroons. Earlier in the fall, women had been out picking potatoes and beets and corn. Everybody, it seemed, was doing something different from what they usually did, or from what they should. Even Mary, whom Prudence remembered vaguely from those first days at the Pines—now she was a barmaid? It was pitiful the way she hurried back and forth, goaded by Harris's yelling. He smiled under his black bowler, occasionally lifting his patch to dab at the eye he liked to intimate he'd lost in the Great War, though everyone knew it was to a case of shingles. There were a few women at the tables with their husbands, sipping slowly on whiskey drinks—beer just didn't go down right when it was that cold—waiting for the Tom and Jerrys so they could go home and get ready for the holiday. The land was emptying of people and matériel—all the boys gone, and all the horses, leather, gasoline, rubber, plastic, copper, lead, typewriters, toasters, sugar, corn, beets, and timber gone, too. Meanwhile, the camp across from the Pines was swelling, full to bursting with German prisoners. Unequal pressure, like you felt before a storm. That was the feeling. It had to give somewhere, it had to give. Just one more push, one more great, collective lunge, and they'd be over.

Little colored lights had been hung around the edge of the tin ceiling and someone had put a party horn in the mouth of the whitetail under which the farm kids were hiding. An empty Schlitz bottle was stuck in the open jaws of the pike above the bar. The lights were kind and it was warm in the bar, but that didn't dispel the general feeling that they were all waiting, waiting for the weather—the malign, frigid weather of the war—to break. They knew it would. It had to. Every week, Harris posted the reports he got from the draft board on the door of the Wigwam. Every week there were fewer names of the wounded, missing, and dead. The war was grinding down. Everyone knew it. But that almost made it worse—who would be the last? Who would be the last to die before it was over?

Prudence checked the list as often as she could, as often as she could get away from the Pines and into town on foot. Even if something happened, Frankie's name wouldn't be on the list. He wasn't registered up here, so any news about him would go to Chicago. But she checked when she could, anyway. She begged Felix to move to town but he wouldn't hear of it, and begged him again to buy a radio, surely he could afford a radio, but he said, "Hmmm," and that's all he said. It was so awful lonely at the Pines. The big house was boarded up and the small cabins behind were locked tight; the snow drifted across the doors. Emma had come up in the summer but only for a few weeks. She'd brought with her some clothes for Prudence and said they'd have to last the year. Frankie still wrote, or at least letters still came from Frankie, though, from the dates on them, she judged that they arrived all out of order. But they still came. And that meant that Frankie was still out there and someday, someday soon, he'd be coming home and Prudence would be waiting for him.

Prudence smoothed the dress. She'd gotten it in Grand Rapids in October. Grand Rapids was the farthest she'd traveled from the Pines since that day in August when they pulled her kicking and screaming from the leaves. The dress fit her well, she made sure of that. Emma sent her ten dollars a month and the rest she made up by picking pinecones and knocking rice with Felix in the fall. It was from Sears, but all the same it fit her well, and no one would ever see the label anyway.

That ten dollars a month, that ten dollars and Frankie's letters had to mean something. She straightened up and looked around the bar some more. Yes, it was all so clear, everyone sensed it, it was the end of something, the end of something terrifying and grand and she'd be free, they'd all be free so very soon.

You'd be so nice to come home to,
You'd be so nice by the fire

"For the love of Christ," said Dickie, as he approached Harris at the bar, "you trying to make me cry? How about playing something else?"

"Either start buying drinks or start dancing, Dickie," said Harris, with his back to him.

"Now, now," said Father Paul again, rocking back on his heels but grinning a bit. By God, he'd probably been the first one in the door.

The farm boys under the deer's head giggled, anxious to be in on the joke, till Dickie turned and fixed them with that stare of his—the one he used with surveyors and timber agents and the like, and they quickly looked down at their drinks. Two of Dickie's men, not really from the village, obliged Harris and started cavorting around the dance floor together in their boots, shaking off clumps of ice with each step. Mary, holding two flats of eggs, weaved between the dancers, her face expressionless. She held them to her chest, and ducked and then lifted them high as the loggers careened across the floor.

"Atta girl, Mary," said Harris. "Now that's what I call dancing."

Mary clomped across the dance floor and began emptying the ash pan.

"A round, then," said Dickie, "till Harris loosens up with them Tom and Jerrys."

"Need more beer, Mary. And more wood, too!" shouted Harris across the dance floor.

She looked up and then ducked as Dickie's men veered close to her and kicked the ash bucket on their way around.

"Your boys already been at the bottle?" asked Harris.

"Oh, they mighta had a nip or two on the way over. It's cold enough to freeze the balls off a brass monkey out there."

Dickie scanned the room.

"Hey, Prudy, what you drinking?"

"Nothing yet," she said.

"Well, what to start, then?"

"Brandy sour," she said.

"And so it is," he said, and nodded at Harris, who looked closely at Prudence from behind the bar.

"Felix let you outta your cage?"

"He don't got a lotta say in the matter," she said.

"Leave her be, Harris," said Dickie. "It's Christmas and all."

Harris raised his eyebrows.

"You walk here in those shoes?" asked Dickie Bolton, looking down at her feet.

"I've walked farther in worse," she said.

"Easy now, Prudy," said Harris. "Easy now. Dickie here was just paying you a compliment."

"Amen," said Dickie. "You just look nice, is all. Don't she look nice, Gardner?" Dave Gardner sat at the end of the bar. He was handsome enough, but he looked very studious in his thick glasses.

"That she does. Merry Christmas, Prudy." He raised his glass and then looked away and licked his lips and looked back at her and then away again.

Prudy raised her glass and made a study of the bottom of it.

"Merry Christmas, Dave."

A group of girls came in the front in mid-laugh. One of them mule-kicked the door shut. Everyone turned to look.

"Mind my door!" bellowed Harris. "Or you'll be fixing it."

There were three of them. Prudy had seen them around the village but didn't know their names. They had the raven hair and light olive skin of breeds. One of them laughed and her teeth flashed in the bar light. They were pretty but not as pretty as Prudence. They stood and surveyed the room. The one who kicked the door looked at the farm boys and said, "Well?" And the boys scurried over and took their coats and, not knowing what to do with them, held them in their arms. One of the boys made for the bar and ordered three beers and brought them over quickly, bent slightly at the waist with exaggerated care. The girls picked up their beers and sipped. The leader made a face.

"Flat," she said.

"How about another sour?" asked Prudy.

"How about it?"

"I've got it," said Dave Gardner from the end of the bar. "But it'll cost you a dance or two."

"Fine by me. I just got to warm up."

She drank the second as fast as the first.

Prudence had walked farther, much farther than any of them knew. All by herself, with Grace to take care of and protect. And yet she had done it. After her mother died she had taken care of Grace, and when it got too rough, she had lit out of there, and found them a place at that school in Flandreau. And when they were going to send her away to Wisconsin she didn't let that happen, either. All by herself, she got Gracie out of the school and they walked. They walked clear from Flandreau up to Crookston and over across the north of the state. They had been so close, so very close to making it, when they veered too near the Pines on that day of all days, with that goddamn escaped German. Now Gracie was gone. But it had brought her Frankie, at least.

"That brandy going to your head, Prudy?" asked Dave Gardner.

"That's where it belongs, Davey boy. That's where it belongs." Prudence felt her limbs loosen.

If Frankie could endure the war, Prudence could endure his absence. How long could it last, anyway? Another couple months? A year? How many missions did Frankie have to fly before he was done? Twenty-five? Or was it thirty-four? Anyway, he must be close by now.

"I might as well pay up," she said, shaking her head. "How about something we can dance to, Harris?"

"You gonna go easy, Prudy?" asked Harris. "I'm the one who's got to deal with Felix if you don't." He took off the record mid-song, and everyone looked up from their drinks and conversation to see what was happening. He chose another record and set the needle down abruptly.

Drinkin' beer in a cabaret and I was havin' fun!
Until one night she caught me right, and now I'm on the run

"Come on then, Davey," said Prudence, and she reached out past Dick.

Davey finished his drink and walked around Father Paul, who stood with his eyes closed and his fingers laced over his belly as though rehearsing the next day's service. He swayed on his feet.

"I'm not that good of a dancer, Prudy."

"Don't sweat it."

He took her hand in his. His hands were thin and soft. His palms felt wet.

"Nervous in the service, Davey?"

"That's just how they are. Sorry. They're always like that."

"Ahh," she said, as they found the rhythm and shuffled across the floor in an awkward two-step. They made two turns around the dance floor, everyone watching them.

"You hear from Frankie?" asked Prudence as they passed under the pike.

"Who, me? Naw, Prudy. I haven't heard from Frankie since that day. Since, you know, your sister."

"Don't sweat it, Davey."

When they turned again, Prudence saw the farm boys looking at her hips and legs. She held their gaze till she and Dave made another turn, then she moved her hand a little lower on his back, just above his belt. The farm boys stared harder. Prudy shut her eyes, wishing Davey would take the lead. Frankie, surely, was a good dancer. He must have gone to a lot of dances in college, fancy ones with real bands. He would know how to lead.

He was a gentleman. These boys weren't so bad but they weren't anything compared to Frankie. After the accident, they had put her in the maid's room off the kitchen and Jonathan had checked her over and Emma made a big fuss about chamomile tea and tucked her in and washed her face and hands with a warm washcloth and then went in and out, bringing in things (a chamber pot, a glass of water, a sweater) and removing other things (a Sears catalog, the .22 rifle they kept there behind the door). After a long while the house finally went quiet. And Frankie had appeared at her door. Prudence smiled toward the thought. He had hemmed and hawed. Didn't know what to say. Wouldn't really look at her. He said he was sorry about her sister and that he would come back. He would come back. He hadn't tried anything funny. Hadn't so much as let his eyes rest on her too long. Light. His voice and how he stood and how he didn't eat her up with his eyes or barge in the room or bang furniture around or stomp his feet. He was a gentleman, through and through. He would never try, not until it was right, what these boys would be willing to do in a car or a closet or anywhere, really, if she gave them the chance. She rested her cheek on Davey's shoulder. The brandy sours had gone to her head.

Three of Dick Bolton's boys asked the girls from the village to dance. The farm boys continued to hold the girls' coats. The loggers whooped and set off on the dance floor until Harris barked at them from behind the bar.

"You gonna chew up my floor with your hobs!"

Dick turned to look at his crew. "Boys," he said.

The men looked at one another and shucked their boots into a corner and spun the girls in their stocking feet. The song ended and Harris put on another.

You're completely unaware, dear, that my heart is in your hand
So for love's sake won't you listen and try to understand?

They'd had three good years at Flandreau Indian School. Three good years. Before that, after their mother died, they'd lived like squirrels in a shed next to the agency, eating what food they could find, scrounging blankets, enduring—oh, it was better not even to think about what had happened there. They made it through one winter, then Prudence got them into Flandreau and they traveled there by train. What a change that had been! What a delicious change. They were given clothes, the dorms were snug enough. And they were safe. Gracie was safe. Every morning began with the ringing of a metal triangle. They lined up by company—A for the oldest down to E for the youngest—though there was an "L" company for the laziest children, the ones who needed to be punished. The triangle rang and they scurried into formation and marched out in step and got their tooth powder and washed their hands and faces and combed their hair. Then the triangle rang again, and they marched into the yard where, no matter the weather, they did their exercises. The triangle rang again and they marched to the classrooms, where they spent the morning on book learning. And again the triangle, and off to dinner for a half hour. The afternoons were spent on "vocation," which meant sewing, cooking, cleaning, milking cows, currying the horses. Then, in the dimming day, the triangle would ring again and, still in their companies, they marched to chapel. As the sun ground down to the earth, they quietly, with hands clasped, practiced their devotionals.

Prudence had done her best not to end up in Company "L," and she was never once reprimanded. She didn't see Gracie much during the days except on Sundays, when they got to eat together. Other than that, Gracie was just another head of black braided hair tucked in the rectangle of her company. But that had been, barely, enough. She was there and she was safe. The summers were the best—they were sent to work on farms across South Dakota. And for two blessed months for three summers, Prudence and Grace were sent to the same farm near Vermillion. The work wasn't much different from what they did at Flandreau. They milked and picked eggs and killed chickens, mucked out the stalls, and churned butter. The farmer and his wife didn't have any children of their own and they were kind enough.

I want you so, more than you'll ever know
More than you dream I do, I dream of you

They'd had three good years at Flandreau. But then she had to leave. The superintendent called her into his office and congratulated her on graduating. They had found a place for her in New Glarus, Wisconsin, wasn't she pleased. Oh, yes, sir. There's a war on. Yes, sir, of course. You'll be working at the Swiss Miss Textile Mart and Lace Factory, they make chevrons and insignia, don't you know. I didn't, sir. Thousands of our boys will be wearing those, don't you know. I didn't, sir. You'll be doing your part, Prudence. Aren't you glad, don't you know. What will Grace be doing, sir? she had to say. But Grace wasn't ready yet, of course. Three more years. Three more years and she would graduate, too. I see, sir.

Three more years proved too long. Too long for Gracie and too long for Prudence. Prudence lasted the summer in New Glarus, then she'd packed her things and made her way back to Flandreau and taken Gracie away.

The song ended, and Davey stepped away from her and wiped his hand on his trouser leg. Prudence blinked widely and wiped her forehead with her hand.

"Well, now," she said.

Mary, doubled over, two gallon jars in her arms, stood straight and heaved them with a grunt onto the bar. One held pickles, the other pickled eggs.

"Belly up," said Harris. "Belly up, and merry Christmas."

The dancers parted. Some went back to their tables. Others, including Dickie's men, walked to the bar and accepted the pickles and eggs Harris lifted out of the brine with a ladle.

"Hungry?" asked Dave Gardner.

"Thirsty," said Prudence.

"Jesus, Prudy. You a fish or what?"

"Be a doll, Davey."

"Whiskey and Coke all right?"

"If it's all right with you."

The farm boys, looking at one another for approval, finally set down the girls' coats they were holding and brought their empty beer bottles back up to the bar.

"Thank you," said the oldest.

"Thank you," and "thanks," said the others.

Clarence Brown, the stationmaster, came in. He wore a green Mackinaw, a blue cap, deerskin choppers, and pac boots.

"Mr. Brown!" said Harris.

"I pray to God it's warmer for our boys in Belgium," said Mr. Brown, stamping his feet, though no snow stuck to his boots. He had a thick mustache, which was iced over in the middle. He combed out the frost with the back side of his glove.

"That's the right prayer," said Father Paul, with his eyes shut. "That's the right prayer."

"What's the news?" asked Dickie Bolton.

"They're holding on. They're calling them the 'Bloody Bastards of

Bastogne.'" He held up his hand in the direction of Father Paul. "No offense, Father."

"You're reporting the news."

"Skies are finally clear. They're dropping supplies."

"Finally," said Harris.

Dickie nodded.

"Funny," said Mr. Brown, "you know what the temperature is at twenty-nine thousand feet? An interesting fact. Same as it is right now, right here where we are. Minus thirty."

Prudence drank deeply from her whiskey and Coke.

The farm boys talked among themselves, sneaking looks at Prudence.

Clarence Brown took off his coat and folded it neatly in half. He handed it over the bar to Harris.

"Just a mo," said Mr. Brown. He leaned across the bar and took a sheaf of yellow telegrams from the patch pocket and brushed them dry and stowed them in his breast pocket underneath his vest. "Obliged," he said.

"What can I do you for?" asked Harris.

"Hot toddy would agree," said Mr. Brown. He set his cap on the bar and clapped his gloved hands together. He looked much like a walrus. "Don't that beat all?" he continued. "Five miles up"—he pointed past the tin ceiling—"and it's the same as right here." He pointed down. "But our boys got their ammunition now. They'll break out."

Prudence finished her drink and sighed.

"Be a gent," said Harris to Mr. Brown, pointing at the kettle on top of the stove along the far wall. Mr. Brown walked across the dance floor and lifted the teakettle off the stove with one of his gloves. "Make way," he said, though no one was dancing. Harris put another record on and turned to take the kettle in his ungloved hand. Helen Forrest came on, singing "I Had the Craziest Dream."

I never dreamt it could be
Yet there you were, in love with me.

Prudence adjusted her hair band and smoothed the front of her skirt and walked across the dance floor toward the farm boys. Only one held her gaze as she approached.

"Dance with a girl, wouldya?"

"Okay," he said. "Okay. No one's gonna mind?" He looked past Prudence to Davey Gardner.

"I don't mind," she said, and offered him her hand.

He led her around the dance floor. He was unsure where to look. He looked her in the face, and then his gaze slid over her shoulder and down at the dance floor.

"You're really pretty," he managed.

"Oh, baby," she sighed. "You're a peach."

"I ship out in two weeks," he said to the floor.

"You'll be fine," she said.

At first she and Gracie had walked at night. All they had were two of Gracie's school uniforms and a set of sheets they used to cover themselves at night, as protection against the bugs. It was warm. They slept in windbreaks and in sheds. Between Flandreau and Crookston they ate in cafés until Prudence's money ran out. In Crookston, a farmer discovered them in one of his sheds, with green potatoes in their pockets. He brought them back to the farmhouse, and his wife set a glass of milk and a piece of bread in front of each of them without saying a word. When they were done, the woman asked them if they knew how to milk cows. They nodded. Can you pluck? They nodded again. The man and woman spoke with strong accents. Show, said the man. They milked the three cows. Then the farmer brought them to the chicken coop and pointed at the door. Prudence and Grace scooped up a chicken each, tucked the heads under their wings and swung them through the air as they'd been taught, then twisted the heads off. By the time they'd finished scalding and plucking the birds, it was late. The farmer showed them to the pump house behind the main house. His wife had set up two pallets on the cement floor. And that's where they stayed till they couldn't anymore, and then they set off again.

I found your lips close to mine so I kissed you
And you didn't mind it at all.

Prudence and the boy turned and turned. He couldn't look at Prudence for very long. He had limp, sandy hair and a very large forehead that came up to Prudence's chin. She could see a faint rash of acne across his forehead. They had moved close to the stove and Prudence tried to steer them away but the boy wasn't looking. His body slid past hers. She felt his erection glide over her thigh. His face colored and he bit his lip.

"Oh, God, sorry."

Prudence looked past his shoulder and smiled to herself.

"Oh, honey. Oh, honey. Merry Christmas."

The song ended and the boy held out his hand. She shook it and he turned back to his group. The other boys said something and he said, "Stop it." One of them slapped him on the back. They all laughed.

"They've got to pay for what happened in Malmédy," Mr. Brown was saying. "That's not what civilized people do. They'll be judged for it, mark my words."

"God will be the judge," said Father Paul, pointing one chubby finger toward the ceiling. It looked as though he were pointing at the stuffed pike.

"They ever do anything like that in the Great War, Dickie?" asked Mr. Brown. "You ever hear of anything like that?"

"Worst two goddamn years of my life that was," said Dickie.

"Why's that?" asked Harris as he took a mixing bowl from Mary and began whipping the egg whites.

"Ahh," said Dickie with a shrug. "How about for you?" he asked Harris.

"Oh, you know," said Harris, staring down into the mixing bowl as the egg whites began to set.

"I hope to Christ Dickie Junior has a better go of it than I did."

"Where's he at?" asked Harris.

"Last we heard, Marseilles. But they could be anywhere. Better there than up north. Colder than a witch's tit in the Ardennes. They say it's as bad as it is here. Them flyboys have it worse. Can you imagine?"

"Can't say I can," said Harris agreeably. He glanced at Prudence.

"Army doesn't know a goddamn what it's doing," said Dickie to his beer. "It's nothing to them's in charge."

"Now, now, Dickie. Language," said Father Paul.

"Father, would you?" asked Harris. He jerked his shoulder toward the record player behind him.

"My pleasure, my absolute pleasure," said Father Paul, and he minced behind the bar and sifted through the 78s, holding each of them up to the light.

Prudence wiped her face gently with a handkerchief from her clutch and applied more lipstick. Mary walked past her, carrying two gallons of milk from the icebox.

"Johnny-on-the-spot," said Harris to Mary. He set the mixing bowl on the counter and poured in the milk and began beating the egg whites and milk together.

"Perfect," said Father Paul to the mirror behind the bar. He placed a record on the spindle and set the needle down with a fussy flourish.

Thought there's one motor gone
We can still carry on

"How about another, Davey," said Prudence.

"Jesus, Prudy, how many is that?"

"Oh, you know . . ." She waved her hand in the air.

"Same thing?"

"You only live once. Make that a rum and Coke."

"Rum and Coke, please, Harris."

"Hold your horses, Pony Boy. These Tom and Jerrys is almost done. Dickie, would you mind?"

"Not at all."

Dickie walked around behind the bar and began upending coffee cups on the counter.

"Make way," said Harris, and he carried the mixing bowl out from behind the bar across the dance floor to the woodstove. He set the mixing bowl on top. It hissed and subsided. He continued to whisk the milk and eggs.

"Ten minutes, everybody. Ten minutes."

"Dickie, be a doll," said Prudence. She took one of the coffee mugs that Dickie had filled halfway with brandy.

"Hey now."

"Can you reach the Cokes?"

Dickie set one on the bar top.

"Let me get that, Prudy," said Davey. He opened it and poured it into her mug. She drank, blinking against the fizz that popped up into her eyelashes she'd darkened with stove soot and a dab of grease.

"Ahh, that's the ticket."

"Father, you got your toast ready?" asked Harris from across the dance floor.

"It's ready right here," he said, tapping his temple as he turned sideways through the bar flap.

The radio sets were humming
They waited for a word

The song died out and Dickie set the arm of the record player back on its rest. "Ready, boss," he said. Harris took the steaming milk and egg whites back to the bar and added vanilla and nutmeg and cinnamon. He ladled it into the mugs.

"Come on now," he said.

Dickie's men were first in line, then the girls from the village. Some of the men from the tables stood and took a mug in each hand, one for themselves and one for their wives.

"Might as well grab yours," said Dickie. Prudence finished her brandy and Coke and pushed it away and blew her hair out of her eyes. She reached out and took the hot mug in her hands and blew on the top. Some foam flew off and landed on her dress.

"Cheers, Mr. Brown," she said.

The stationmaster had been lost in thought.

"Cheers, Prudy."

She eyed his breast pocket.

"You wanna dance, Mr. Brown?"

"Oh! I think I'm too old, Prudy. But you're sweet to ask." He wiped his eyes and sipped from his mug with one finger extended.

She set the mug back on the bar very slowly and walked unsteadily across the dance floor to her clutch and took out her handkerchief and brushed off the foam. Harris finished ladling out the rest of the drinks. He wiped his hands on a bar towel and nodded at Father

Paul, who was back in his spot at the end of the bar, with his eyes shut and his chin raised toward the pike.

"Father. You're on."

"Oh, already? If you say so. If you think so."

He reached out and took the mug Dickie handed him with his thumb and forefinger. He cleared his throat.

"Friends and neighbors," he began. "Yes, I think we can say that. Friends and neighbors." Mary crossed in front of him with an armful of split wood. She used a piece of it to lift the stove handle and swing the door wide. Smoke billowed out and rolled across the ceiling. The coals glowed red. She placed the wood in the firedogs, then closed the door and latched it and shook her fingers and clomped back toward the storeroom. "Friends and neighbors," resumed Father Paul. "We live in remarkable times. Fact. We live in remarkable times indeed. The last four years have been hard ones for all of us. I look out on you just as I do in the blessed confines of our holy church and there are many of us missing. Our young men have gone off to war. They are in the Pacific. They are in Italy. They are in France. Our young men are scattered all across this world. Fact. They are on boats. They are in tanks. They are on foot. And they are in the sky over our heads. Some of them won't be coming back to us. Fact. No, they won't be coming home to us. Instead they will enter the gates of heaven and sit with Jesus Christ Our Lord and Savior. They are in God's great arms in the great by-and-by. Fact. And why is it a fact? It is a fact because we know God is on our side. God is on the side of freedom. We didn't want this war but now it's up to us to finish it. And we will finish it. Yes, we will. We will finish it and bring our boys home. You might be wondering what *you* can do."

"I'm wondering if I'm gonna drink this warm," muttered one of Dickie's men.

"Now, now," continued Father Paul, with his right palm upraised.

"You might be wondering what you can do. You can toast our fighting boys and wish them a speedy return. And then you can go home to your loved ones. They are waiting for you in the here and now. You can go back to them and in the morning you can come to church and pray for the ones who are not here. You can pray and give thanks that our soldiers are out fighting for you and for our great country. They are fighting for God. They are fighting for you. You can pray for them to be strong and to finish this war and come home. Pray for them to come home to us. Amen."

As one, they raised their mugs and said, "Amen," and drank deeply.

"Now go home and get some rest and come help me celebrate the birth of Our Lord Jesus Christ tomorrow morning," concluded Father Paul. With his tongue he wiped away a bit of foam stuck on his lip.

The men at the tables collected the mugs and brought them up to the bar and thanked Harris. The village girls walked toward the farm boys, who turned and dived for the girls' coats. Dickie's men put on their boots but didn't lace them. They fished in their pockets for cigarettes and stumbled out the front door, laces trailing. Father Paul shook himself from his reverie and put on his deerstalker and his greatcoat and, still listening to some tune or a message from above, walked lightly out the door. Mary appeared with a large tray and began collecting the mugs off the bar and the empty tables. Once a tray was full, she would bring it into the kitchen and limp back out with another one. Dickie shook Harris's hand and followed his men outside.

"Well, I suppose," said Prudence to no one. "I suppose."

Davey Gardner gave her a long look and then put on his coat.

"Good night, Harris. Merry Christmas."

"Merry Christmas, Davey."

He left.

"That was a good one, Harris," said Mr. Brown. "You make a mean Tom and Jerry."

Prudence busied herself by the jukebox. She put on her coat very slowly as Harris and Clarence Brown talked at the bar. Harris handed Clarence Brown his coat. He shrugged it on slowly. Once it was on, he removed the telegrams from his breast pocket. Harris poured himself a whiskey. Clarence handed the telegrams to Harris.

"You'll see these home?"

Harris looked through them quickly. "Ahh. Damn," he said.

"You give Felix that package yesterday?"

"I did indeed." Harris sighed and drank his whiskey down and put the telegrams in the till.

"Shame. Till next year, Harris."

"In short order, Clarence."

"Merry Christmas, Harris."

"Merry Christmas, Clarence."

Mr. Brown left.

"I suppose," said Prudence. She walked slowly, one foot in front of the other, staggering a little. But it was as though Frankie's long arms found her and she steadied. His fingers would be light on her sleeve. His smile light into her shoulder. His long fingers light on her arm. She took her scarf and put it around her neck and trapped her clutch in her armpit and walked very carefully to the front door.

"Merry Christmas, Prudy."

"Yeah, Harris. Yeah. Merry Christmas." She paused and turned back to Harris and breathed in deeply. "Anything for me? Letters or anything?"

Harris studied her long and hard.

"No, girl," he said, not ungently, "nothing today."

"Oh."

"Probably because of the holiday, you know."

He glanced at the till and then wiped out the glass in front of him.

"Yeah."

"Go on home now. Felix is probably waiting for you."

"Good night, Harris."

"Good night, Prudy."

She stepped out of the Wigwam. Everyone had scattered already. The temperature had dropped even lower, and the warm, moist air spilled out of the Wigwam around her in a thin fog.

"Sweet Mary, mother of God," she whispered. The air felt sharp in her lungs. She looked up and down the street and over toward the depot. No one was out. She could see the lights—some electric, some kerosene—shining here and there between the trees, spilling over the mounds of snow. The sodium light outside the Wigwam bronzed the road. She shifted her weight and wrapped the scarf tighter around her neck. The wedges of her Mary Janes squeaked in the compacted snow. She pulled her coat to her body and began following the path through the mounded snow along the side of the Wigwam around to the back.

"Hey, Prudy, you okay?"

Prudence looked up and saw, over the lip of the snowbank, Dave Gardner leaning from the window of his Ford Eight with the headlights off. It was hard to make out his face but the sodium light flashed off his glasses and she saw a cigarette arc out of the open window.

"Davey boy, shouldn't you be home by now?"

"She wouldn't start. Not right away."

"Ahh." Prudence teetered a little and then stood straight.

"You headed home?"

"Round about," said Prudence.

"You're going the wrong way."

"If you say so, Davey."

"You must be cold."

"I've been warmer."

"She's got a heater."

"You don't say. You got another one of them smokes?"

"Yeah."

"All right, then."

Prudence held her arms out to the sides to steady herself and took a step toward the car. Her foot punched through the mounded snow up to her knee.

"God, I hate it here," she said.

"Easy, Prudence."

"I got it. I got it. Just why does it have to be so goddamn hard?"

She took another step and then another, until she stumbled onto the plowed roadbed. She got in the passenger's side and slammed the door after her.

"Wow."

"Right? Here." Dave Gardner lit two cigarettes and handed one to Prudence.

"Merry Christmas," she said.

"Merry Christmas."

They smoked.

Prudence leaned her head back against the seat rest and then pulled it forward again. Then she bent down and unbuckled her shoes and put her feet over the heater.

"Whooeee."

"Your feet must be freezing."

"Oh," said Prudence, as though noticing them for the first time.

They smoked in silence a while longer.

"This'll pass," she said, looking first at her cigarette and then out the window.

"What will?"

"This." Gesturing again. "That." Again. "All of it."

"Oh."

"It's got to. It just has to."

Dave Gardner pulled on his cigarette again and then unrolled the window and dropped it out.

"Listen, Prudy." He turned to face her. His right knee pointing toward her. "I was—"

"Okay."

"You look so—"

"I said okay. Okay?"

"Okay." He paused. "You sure?"

"You're sweet. Just not inside me, okay. All right?"

"Okay." His voice was very small.

Prudence undid the belt and unbuttoned her coat.

Dave Gardner removed his coat and unbuttoned his trousers.

"Did you take yours off?" he asked. "Did you take them off?"

"I'll just pull them to the side," she said.

"I can't see."

Prudence reached out to Dave Gardner with her eyes closed. She saw Frankie standing in the woods, his hands shaking. And then she saw Frankie standing in the door to the maid's room off the kitchen, where Emma tended to her after the shooting. And then the small lighted window of the boathouse and Felix looking out from under the curtain across the river. She opened her eyes.

"You poor boys. You poor, poor boys," she said thickly. She found him—stiff, quivering—with her hand. "Let me help you." His cock was rigid and Davey looked down on it, pink and thick, in surprise.

"Oh, God, Prudy. Oh, Jesus."

"Not on the dress!" she screamed, and released him from her hand as the first jets of cum arced out. She scooted back against the door. "Watch the dress! The dress!"

Davey Gardner turned violently and stubbed his cock out against the icy seat back.

After a moment. "I'm sorry, Prudy."

Another long pause. A car went by on the highway.

"You're sweet, Davey boy."

"Smoke?"

"I'd better push off."

"I can drive you as far as the turnoff. The Ford won't make it out to the camp."

"Naw. I'll make it."

"You sure?"

"I'll make it somehow."

"It's cold out there, Prudy."

Prudence bent low and strapped her feet back into her Mary Janes. She opened the door and tumbled out onto her feet. She reached in and found her clutch on the seat.

"Merry Christmas, Davey."

"Merry Christmas, Prudy."

She shut the door and stood there facing the car until Dave Gardner put it in gear and drove around her, out to the street and then out onto the highway. When she was sure he was gone she turned and stomped her feet back down in the holes she had made before in the snowbank, as if she were fitting pegs in a cribbage board.

She rounded the back of the Wigwam.

A small figure sat forlornly on the back steps next to the woodpile, bundled into a thick coat.

"Gracie?" Prudence, her heart beating fast, stepped closer. "Gracie?"

A match flared. Mary. She lit a short corncob pipe and drew, the bowl glowing red.

"Oh, you. What a dance, huh?" said Prudence.

Mary said nothing.

Prudence stepped closer to her. She could see the lines around Mary's mouth when she pulled on the pipe. She couldn't be older than twenty-five. Twenty-six?

"Don't tell anyone, okay?" said Prudence as she reached past Mary and took hold of a paper sack buried in the snow on top of the woodpile. She opened it quickly and shook out a pair of woolen long johns, a pair of wool socks, and a pair of galoshes. She kicked off the Mary Janes and pulled on the long johns quickly, followed by the socks and the galoshes. Then she put the Mary Janes in the bag, along with the clutch, tucked the bag into her armpit, and shoved her hands deep in her coat pockets. Mary watched her but said nothing.

"Merry Christmas, Mary."

Mary drew on her pipe.

Prudence turned and headed for the road. It was terribly cold. Her galoshes sounded like logs banging on the frozen macadam. The road was gray between the mounded snow on either side. The snow glowed between the trees. The stars were out. It must be so cold and lonely up there. So very cold. But it was the same air. It was the same air up there as down here. Prudence closed her eyes and steadied herself. She saw Gracie's little grave behind the Pines, quiet and quietly covered with snow. The same air that flowed over Gracie's grave flowed around up there, after all. Five miles up and five miles down. It made no difference. She felt her soul swoon a little. She recovered it and kept on walking.

NINE

MIDLANDS, ENGLAND—EARLY DECEMBER 1944

Frankie was suspended over a large table in a harness attached to wires strung to the roof. A bombsight was fixed to the same wires, and he had it pressed to his face. Below him were photographs of the mainland. He crept slowly along the wires, pushing himself with little taps of his feet. He finished and pulled himself back to the start and did it again. The map table was lit by four floodlights clamped to the ribs of the Nissen hut. It was cold. There was no heater in the map room. Frankie blew on his fingers. A few more runs. A few more and he'd quit. He closed his eyes and saw, once again, the man tucked into a ball, arms clasped around his knees, spinning slowly over the top of the right wing. He opened his eyes to make it stop.

There were no runs that morning because of the weather, and Molesworth was unusually quiet. No prep, no returning planes. No battle orders fluttered from the bulletin board outside the briefing room. The wind picked at the metal skin of the hut, and the light drizzle hitting the metal sounded like low radio static. It was calming. He should go back to barracks. His fellow officers—the pilot and copilot, navigator and engineer—were all in London on a four-day leave. The enlisted men were being hosted at Moulsford Manor on the Thames. Half of the squadron was gone. He should go back to barracks. He needed to work on the letter. Usually the room he shared with three other officers was too crowded for anything but reading. The enlisted men had it worse: twenty men to a barracks.

The map table was useless, really, except as a diversion. Their actual objectives were never divulged to the crew until a few hours before each mission. The crew was briefed separately from the officers, and they wanted to know mostly if it would be a milk run or not, how long the fighter escort would last, whether the objective was heavily defended. The officers got more detail but their questions were much the same: How far? How long? Where to? What kind of flak? Would they be dropping high or low? Would they have a fighter escort or not, and if so, for how long? The table maps didn't help with any of it. They showed Belgium, France, Holland, Germany, Switzerland from 30,000 feet over clear skies in flat black and white. They didn't account for any of the variables he learned about in bombardier school in Texas. Altitude. True airspeed. Bomb ballistics. Trail. Actual time of fall. Ground speed. Drift. Not to mention the reality of combat itself. Flying in box formation and bad weather, fighter attacks, flak cover. Still, Frankie spent his free time suspended over the maps, memorizing cities and rivers, fields, villages. Hoogstraten, Eksel, Astene, Rijkhoven, Borlo, Redu, Coulonges-Cohan, Nobressart, Hunawihr, Lourmarin, Coulon, Treignac, Belvès, Saint-Léon-sur-Vézère, Hunspach, Domfront, Lisieux, Fécamp. The bigger towns and cities were often the ones they studied for the actual bombing runs. Caen, Brest, Dieppe, Rouen, Paris, Lille, Antwerp, Schweinfurt, Aachen, Stuttgart, Lübeck, Bremen, Dresden. He studied these, too.

Frankie had been at Molesworth, part of the 303rd "Hell's Angels," since summer. It was only then that he understood why bombardiers were so badly needed. Only after he'd become one of the Hell's Angels and shouted "Might in flight!" along with the rest of them and fitted himself into the catbird seat and they took off to the northeast, circled into formation for an hour, and then crossed the North Sea and into Holland and the black flak bloomed around him, and he got to see it all from behind the Plexiglas bubble in which he rode. Got to see the flak to the sides and below and saw the blinking, ragged yellow lights of the 109s and 190s coming in high twelve o'clock—that he understood why: nothing but the thin Plexiglas, strong enough only to stop "birdshit and rain," according to the experienced bombardiers, separated him from the great beyond. Bombardiers died often.

In Florida, too, in the last stage of training, they'd been grounded by bad weather, and the officers and enlisted men sat in their barracks and smoked and argued about what to name the plane that was supposed to carry their crew through the war. Naming the plane was usually a pilot's honor. But Lieutenant Adams, whose family owned a furniture store in Harrisburg, had never named anything in his life but his dog, whom he'd called Blackie because she was a black Lab. Frankie was sitting quietly off to the side, the flight manual across his lap. During a lull in the argument, he recited, without looking up: "'As he spoke, the earth-encircling lord of the earthquake struck both of them with his sceptre and filled their hearts with daring. He made their legs light and active, as also their hands and their feet. Then, as the soaring falcon poises on the wing high above some sheer rock, and presently swoops down to chase some bird over the plain, even so did Neptune lord of the earthquake wing his flight into the air and leave them.'"

Sergeant Riggle, the left waist gunner, removed his cigarette from his mouth and ashed into the Coke bottle he held. "What the fuck is that supposed to mean?"

"It means: How about *Neptune's Bitch*? It's from *The Iliad.*"

"Sold to the highest bidder," said Adams. "*Neptune's Bitch*," he mused. "Very nice." When the time came they found a member of the ground crew to paint a mermaid holding a bomb overhead, her blond hair mostly, but not completely, covering her breasts.

At Molesworth, Frankie was surprised by many things. To start, on his first night there was gear scattered around the barracks and they didn't know which bunks had been claimed. The member of the ground crew who'd shown them to the barracks said, "Don't worry about it. They won't be coming back, so take your pick." The next day they were woken at 0300 and told to report for briefing. The commander lifted a sheet off an easel and showed them their objectives—the rail yards at Rouen. He covered the mission in all of ten minutes. Within half an hour they were on *Neptune's Bitch*. By 0400 they were circling Molesworth, getting into formation. At 0800 just after they reached the coastline of France, they flew into flak. The plane shuddered as the flak burst in the middle of their formation. The plane jumped and dived, and when there were flak bursts above them it rained down, pinging against the thin aluminum skin of the plane. No one—not the pilot or copilot or ball turret gunners, the waist or tail gunners or the navigator—had as good a view of those black, powdery blooms that were bursting all around them as Frankie did. And all he could do was watch. When they were ten minutes away from the target, he and the pilot commenced preparations for the bombing run. At five minutes out, control of the plane passed to Frankie.

It was as if the volume had been suddenly turned off. Everything fell away. He couldn't hear anything, not the shaking of the plane or the thrum of the four Cyclone engines. Or the explosions in the air around them. Nothing. He reached up and felt around his head to see if he hadn't gotten a piece of shrapnel stuck in his skull or in his neck. Keeping a steady level, he guided them in. Not that he even had to use the Norden: they were in the middle of the formation, and only the lead plane needed to use its sights. The rest were to release the bombs as soon as the lead plane did.

With one minute left, a plane just above and in front of them was hit in the waist by a flak burst. Pieces of the fuselage broke off and came flying by. Skin, ribs, a cowling from one of the engines. As the plane disintegrated, the crew began bailing out. The tail gunner came shooting out the back. Two more men, probably the waist gunners, stepped out of the middle of the plane. One man popped out of the hatch in the radio room. He wasn't wearing a parachute. Frankie counted six in all. Amid paper, metal, ammunition, and maps, they came tumbling down around *Neptune's Bitch.* Then one of the crew—and Frankie never knew who it was—pushed free of the doomed aircraft and tucked into a ball. He fell downward, turning slowly through the air. He held perfect form as he tumbled toward them and cleared their left wing with about three feet to spare, and was lost to sight.

Immediately after the lead plane dropped its bombs, Frankie pressed the bomb-release switch and said, "Bombs away!" into the intercom, and Lieutenant Adams banked the plane, and they turned toward home. But the image of the man, tucked, languid, rolling through the air, stayed with him.

After that first mission, and after the second and third and fourth, he had to admit to himself that he was good at his job, good at combat. He was good at filing away the fear and uncertainty. Unlike his crewmates, he didn't have to deal with it afterward by talking about how scared he had been, if only to suggest how well he had held it together. He was good at ignoring everything—his discomfort, his isolation, the dim sense that he was one small, very dispensable part of a large operation. The other crew members had come to rely on this aspect of Frankie's personality—his resolute, predictable quietude and precision. He liked to think it gave them comfort, the sober way he had of conducting the preflight check, of tending to the others when their oxygen lines got disconnected or cut, of manning the twin .50-caliber machine guns in the nose when called upon.

Being able to ignore everything that interfered with his job was something he was good at. But at Molesworth, because of crew rotation or bad weather, there were long stretches on the ground. That was when the worry crept in, when the fear settled down deep in the gut. He might be drinking at the officers' club or reading in his bunk when, for no reason, he'd feel, he'd *know*, that if he didn't run he would shit his pants. This never happened on missions, only when he had quiet time to himself. So the best thing was to work on the map table. To check and recheck *Neptune's Bitch.* But sometimes, even when he kept himself busy—he might be over the table practicing with the sights, or checking and rechecking the .50s or recalibrating the Norden—that terrible day in the woods came back to him—Billy saying, "Wait, wait," then the shot, the girl's legs kicking and slowing and stopping in the leaves.

Frankie unhooked himself from the harness that held him over the map table. He rubbed his eyes and windmilled his arms. He had been at it for two hours. It was late, but there would be no missions the next day. Neither the officers in London nor the enlisted men at Moulsford Manor would miss him. At first—at Maxwell and Midlands—the other men had tried to get him to go drinking and dancing with them and gave him a hard time when he demurred. When they came back, stumble-drunk and bruised, drunk enough to piss their own beds, they teased and heckled him. They didn't quite trust him. But at Molesworth, after the crew had completed ten missions without losing anyone, they stopped bothering him. Whatever they had formed, whatever set of skills or exercise of luck in the game of extinction they were playing, they wanted to preserve it. No one wanted to change a thing. So they were happy their bombardier stayed behind and studied maps and practiced with the map table and checked their plane and counted the pins in the bomb racks, and they made sure he had the bolts not only for his .50 but extra bolts for the rest.

Felix had been like that. Sunk in the seat of the Confederate, he'd listen to Emma start in with her Worries and Concerns: How many trees down over the winter? Was the river too high to get across? Had the dock been washed away? How bad was the fire danger, anyway? Had Felix made sure to scythe the brush and weeds around the Pines to reduce the danger? It would have been good if he had burned the grass while the snow was still deep among the trees. Could they expect a lot of bees? Had the tiger lilies come up, or had the frost gotten them finally? Frankie had despaired that, of all the things Emma could have brought with them from Chicago, she had chosen to bring herself. But Felix seemed immune to Emma's worry. He'd been still, even calm, as he responded to Emma's flurry. The dock had been fixed. He had lit the yard on fire in April, when it was still safe to do so, and the grass was coming up good. No bees yet. Billy had cleared all the mice and mouse droppings from the cabins. The girls were ready to come and do the laundry. Nothing perturbed him.

When Frankie was thirteen, he had been allowed to accompany Felix and Billy to the village to pick up supplies without Emma. He had sat next to Billy, facing Felix in the rowboat (they didn't have the Chris-Craft yet) as Felix pulled on the oars—almost lazily, it seemed—except that with each stroke the rowboat surged ahead, as if shoved along by a giant hand. When they pulled ashore, Frankie and Billy followed Felix up the steep slope to the top of the bluff where they kept the Confederate. Back then there was no camp, just a clearing on level ground pocked by small cook pits and larger depressions near the trees for jigging rice. In the fall the Indians camped there by the dozens to be nearer the rice. And in the spring they came back when the fish were spawning in the river to net them and dry them on racks lashed together in the sun.

He had been rowed across the river many times before. And he had climbed the bank. And he had gone to the village in the Confederate. None of this was new. Yet it was, somehow. Because for the first time he did all this without Emma worrying at the very texture of the life around him.

Halfway to the village, a brush wolf sprinted out of the woods. It must have been chasing something but Frankie never saw what. It crossed the ditch and streaked across the highway in front of them. Felix always drove slowly, but the creature wasn't fast enough. The pickup passed right over the top of it and Frankie could hear its body being tumbled along the undercarriage of the truck and spit out the back. He turned to look and Felix braked and stopped. The brush wolf stood woozily in the middle of the road behind them, staring at them. Frankie turned around in the seat and looked out the back windshield. He had never seen such an animal before. He was surprised at how big its ears were. Its fur was red, almost like that of a fox, along the outside of its legs and along the bridge of its nose, which was sharper and pointier than Frankie would have expected. It swayed back and forth as it looked at the truck. A trickle of blood escaped from its right ear.

"Is that a wolf?" he whispered.

"Yeah," said Billy softly. "Yeah, it is."

"Not a real wolf. Real wolf bigger," said Felix. "You call it coyote. Wait here," he said. Felix reached down and felt under the seat and came out with the length of dowel they used to prop open the hood of the truck. He opened the door and stepped out onto the highway and walked back toward the wolf. Frankie's heart was in his throat.

"What's he gonna do?" he asked Billy.

"Shhh."

The wolf didn't retreat, as Frankie thought it might. Felix approached slowly, with his hands at his sides, his feet padding from heel to toe in a narrow line. He got close, within three feet, and still the wolf didn't move. Suddenly Felix's right hand flashed out—faster than Frankie could have imagined, he had never seen Felix move fast—and he tapped the wolf on the back of the head with the stick, sharp and fast but not hard. The wolf collapsed as though its bones had been yanked out of its body. Felix dropped the stick and placed one palm on the side of the wolf's head and the other on its hind legs, which he collected together in his hand. Then he gently slid one knee over on the wolf's rib cage.

"Come," he said over his shoulder. "Come, boys. It's safe now."

The wolf was not yet dead, only stunned. It tried to lift its head but could not. It tried to lift and turn its hind legs but could not.

"Is it going to die?" asked Frankie.

"Yes. I am killing it. I am making it die." Felix's knee pressed down on the wolf's rib cage and it couldn't draw breath, couldn't expand its ribs. There was no way for it to move or escape. "You can touch," said Felix. "Touch in the middle."

Frankie knelt down and placed his hand on the wolf's fur, where the rib cage met the breastbone. He jerked his hand back: the wolf's body was very hot. Felix nodded at him reassuringly and he placed his hand back on the wolf's sternum.

He could feel its heart beating very quickly. As quickly as his. Then faster. Frankie looked at the wolf and then at Billy. Billy's hair fell across his eyes and there was a light film of sweat on his nose that Frankie liked.

"You wanna?" he asked Billy.

"Okay," he said. "Okay, I will."

Frankie removed his hand and Billy put his where Frankie's had been. Felix adjusted his grip and leaned even more weight on the wolf. Felix's expression didn't change. Then the wolf's heart slowed. The beats came in clusters. It slowed some more. The heart beat once every few seconds. Its eyes were deep amber. They didn't move or look at anything. As the heart slowed, the eyes got narrower and narrower, until they closed completely. As they did, the coyote's mouth grew slack and its lips, very black, almost inky, spread away from its teeth, which were very sharp and very white. After another minute Felix slowly removed his knee. Then he released the hind legs. Satisfied, he removed his hand from the side of the wolf's head and stood up. "Okay. Very safe now." The wolf was dead. Felix stooped and gathered its front legs in one hand and its hind legs in the other and carried it, its head lolling, its tongue escaping from between its teeth, and put it in the back of the truck. They both got in and Felix started up the truck and continued driving toward the village.

Frankie looked out the window. Everything seemed very new.

"Felix. You were in the war?"

"Yes."

Billy was quiet.

"Did you kill anyone in the war?"

"Yes."

Frankie grew bolder. "How many? Do you know how many men you killed?" He didn't look at Felix when he asked his question.

Felix didn't answer right away. Frankie was worried. He shouldn't have asked. He had asked his father that question, and Jonathan had spoken at great length without really answering it.

"I killed seventeen. Seventeen men I killed."

Frankie thought about this a moment.

"Did you use your gun? Did you shoot them?"

Again Felix paused.

"Some I shoot. Some I not shoot."

"How—"

"We are at village, Mr. Frankie."

They were. It was the only time Frankie could remember Felix interrupting him. They got their supplies at the general store and some of the men gathered there came outside with Felix to look at the coyote. They weren't as impressed as Frankie and Billy were. After they got the supplies, they stopped in at the Wigwam. Felix spoke to Harris for a few minutes in Indian, and then Harris came out with them to look at the wolf. They spoke some more, then Felix carried the wolf into the icehouse, and they all went back in the bar. Harris opened the till and gave Felix a dollar, which he folded carefully and tucked into his shirt pocket. Harris looked at Frankie and Billy and said, "I got Bernick's. Howdy Orange or Eskimo Pop?" Frankie, unsure, looked up at Felix. "You choose," Felix said. "Orange, please," said Frankie. "Orange, too," said Billy. "Orange it is," said Harris. He disappeared under the bar and emerged with three bottles. He pried off the tops and handed them to Felix.

They looked like toys, like baby bottles, in Felix's hands. He gave one to Frankie and one to Billy and kept the other, and they walked out into the sun and sat on the bench in front of the bar and drank their sodas. Afterward they drove back to the Pines.

Later he and Billy had snuck out to one of the cabins. They kissed. And then grew bolder. Finally he reached inside Billy's underwear and drew him out. He stroked hard and Billy's cock jumped and danced in his hand. "Slower," said Billy. "Do it slower. Softer, maybe." Frankie did as he was told. Billy closed his eyes and said, "Oh," and Frankie felt Billy beating in his hand like a live heart, slowing, slower, until he grew soft.

The base was dark, blacked out. It was raining again. The paths between the barracks were lined with white-painted rocks, and Frankie used these to guide himself back to his bunk.

How many people had he killed so far? There was no way to know. He knew of only one. He would never know how many in total, although he knew that he killed more with one bomb on one run than Felix had killed during the entire four years he spent in France. Multiply that one bomb by eight per payload, and multiply that by ten missions. Or maybe his bombs never killed anyone. Theirs was a strategic bombing campaign conducted in daylight, and their objectives were rail yards, manufacturing plants, bridges, dams, supply dumps. But surely he had missed. It turned out the Norden sights weren't nearly as accurate in combat as they were in practice, or as all the secrecy and oath taking suggested. They missed their targets more often than they hit them.

He entered the barracks. It was the same, always the same. Their four beds and footlockers. The white-painted desk shoved against the narrow half-moon of the far wall. He put his hand on the stove. Cold. They received only enough coal to run the stove four nights out of the week. It could be worse. The enlisted men got the same ration for a space twice as big. He considered lighting it but he didn't want to hear about it from the others when they came back from London.

Instead, he retrieved the letter he had been working on from his footlocker. He got in bed fully dressed and pulled the wool blanket up over his lap. He took the pilot's training manual off the ammo crate he used as a nightstand and put the paper on it and uncapped his fountain pen. He read over what he had written so far.

Dearest,

I've been in Europe for four months. Some of the other guys have been here just as long but they already got their twenty-five missions and so they are going home. I've only had ten. I spoke to the chief intelligence officer a few times and asked him to put me on the roster more often. To give me more opportunities. Even if I'm not with my own crew, I told him. It's fine with me. There's lots of switching around, as it turns out. You don't always fly with the same crew on every mission, or even the same plane, the one you think of as yours. I'll keep trying. I like it, if you can believe that. But I want to come home. There were so many things left unfinished when I left. I did the best I could, I suppose. I hope this letter finds you and finds you well. I've tried to write many times. Really I have. But I never knew what to say or how to say it.

You must be wondering what it's like over here, and so I'll do my best to try and explain it. We fly at least once a week, usually twice a week. The math is pretty easy. At that rate I should have been home by now. Two missions a week means I should have been here about three months. The ground crews have it worse. They are regular Army, so they have to stay for the duration of the war, plus six months. It doesn't matter how many missions we fly, they are stuck here no matter what. Anyway, you only get credit for a mission if you drop your bombs on either the main target, the secondary target, or a "target of opportunity," but often you get blasted out of formation, or all the targets are socked in. Sometimes you can't get in formation because the clouds are too heavy over here and you have to return to base. Other times something happens with the engines, one or two give out. (That's not as dangerous as it sounds, because all it means is you lose altitude and you have to return before bombing. Since there are no mountains between here and Berlin we're not in danger of running into them—though if you lose altitude over the mainland, then it makes you more vulnerable to flak and to enemy fighters.) And so, even though we fly twice a week, we don't get credit if we don't drop our bombs on something. Sometimes we have to drop them in the ocean, and some crews try and fudge it and say they bombed a secondary target or a target of opportunity but it always comes out during the post-mission debrief. These meetings are a lot longer than the briefings before the missions, which is kind of funny, depending on how you look at it. They want to know exactly what happened—where we dropped, how many, in what order, what happened next, how many fighters intercepted us, that kind of thing. And if you lie, they usually catch you. They always find out. It's no secret where the bombs fall or where we want them to fall. The Germans know and the civilians know. Everyone knows what we are after: railroads, refineries, factories. We are responsible for trying to kill the German war machine, not the Germans themselves. Hopefully what we do makes things easier for the boys on the ground.

When we're not flying, we sit around and play cards. A lot of the guys try to get the girls around here interested in them. Usually it doesn't work. They try anyway. Since we don't have any way to get anywhere, they have to walk or bicycle. It's kind of funny that we fly hundreds and hundreds of miles every week over France and Belgium and Holland and Germany and yet we can't get to the next town over except by walking or pedaling. Some of the towns have funny names. Willingham, Cottingham, Bozeat, Kings Cliffe, Mepal. There's even a town called Warboys, which sounds pretty funny to my ears. We should be based there. But the girls aren't much interested. Here today and gone tomorrow. That's us.

All of the guys here with me, the other officers and even the enlisted men, write a lot. Every day. It's one of the few things we have in common. We all write letters home and we all keep journals of our flights and missions and who bought it and who was wounded and what kind of reception the Germans gave us.

He looked up from the letter but there was nothing to see. Just the bent metal of the Nissen, the other empty cots, the desk. He was disgusted with himself. The letter was like all the others written on base. The same jokey tone, the same in-creep of aviation jargon. He searched for himself in the words and found nothing. What would he really say? What could he *really* say—either about the war or about what had happened before? And what did Billy need to hear? He could talk about his fear, but he wasn't really scared. Not in the way most people used the word. He wasn't any more scared in the nose of the B-17 than he was after that day in the woods behind the Pines. And what was there to say about that? It wouldn't come undone. It wouldn't change no matter what he said. He kept reading.

> *They show movies on the base sometimes. In the time I've been here we've seen* The Philadelphia Story, His Girl Friday, Irene, Night Train to Munich, Boom Town, Pinocchio, The Palm Beach Story, This Gun for Hire, *and* Fantasia. *You should see the other guys after there's a hot scene! They go berserk and usually there are fights. No one really gets hurt. But especially if the movie is a frisky one there will be bikes up and down the road between here and Cambridge—there are more girls in Cambridge than anywhere else around here, but it's eighteen miles one way. By the time they come back they've cooled down a lot. The movies are a welcome break from the waiting. We wait all the time. We wait for our next mission to be posted. We wait on the hardtack for the flares to go up, and then we line up and wait for our turn to lift off. We wait while we get into formation and we wait while the pilot flies us toward our drop zone. The only times we're not waiting is when the German fighters come in, and after they leave the flak starts, and then we make the bomb run and pull out and the flak comes again, and after that the German fighters, who've been circling the whole time, take another stab at our formation. You never want to be the last one, what we call "Tail End Charlie." If you're flying "Tail End Charlie," then the fighters really come after you. Anyway, the only time things get interesting over here is*

when someone is trying to kill us or we're trying to kill someone else.

But this wasn't what he wanted to say, either. Sure, it was funny to imagine a bunch of guys watching a movie and then getting in a big brawl and hopping on their bicycles to pedal nearly twenty miles just to see a girl and talk to her. It was funny, in a way. But it was sad, too. It was sad because, while Frankie's fellow airmen might fight and shout and pedal like hell and drink themselves stupid, most of them had never been with a woman, with anyone. Or if they had, it was a fleeting thing gone too soon. So when they talked about "tits and ass," what they were really saying was that they wanted a chance. They wanted a chance to grab. They wanted a chance to grab and hold and keep holding and holding and holding. Frankie supposed this was love. Or some version of it. But even that was denied him. If only he'd listened. "Wait, Frankie. Frankie, wait!" That's what Billy had said, but he didn't wait. He'd been impatient, as though whatever he had in life, whatever had been given him, would be given over and over; that the life he had had till then didn't exist as a onetime thing, never to be had again. Even if he survived the war, and that was saying a lot, how could he ever go back to the Pines? How could he ever look at Billy again? Or Prudence? Or Felix? What could he say to any of them when nothing anyone could say could make time flow in the other direction: back from England to Florida to Texas; back east to Montgomery, and then straight north, following the Mississippi, a fat brown worm in Louisiana, as it shrank, shed tributaries, spit earth and trees back up on the banks, shed cities like a snake shaking off fleas, till the river ran clear and cool, weeds waving in the current, shallow enough for herons to wade along its edges in search of minnows; and Frankie touched down at the Pines. And then the shot would move back up the barrel of the shotgun and the gun would fall to his side, useless, ridiculous, silly, really, some silly toy his father bought to have in the house. And then Billy's hand would reach out to take it from him. And his own hands would rise to hold Billy's dear face, his eyes would rise to Billy's (Billy was taller than he was now—who could have known?), eyes that always reminded him of that poor coyote they had run over when he was a boy. And whatever Ernie said would fly back into his fucking mouth and stay there. No one took him seriously anyway. He was a stock character, the kind of loudmouth who always hung around to make things more difficult for everyone. But who really cared about him? How did he really matter? So what if he saw anything. So what?

The war had changed that much, at least. It had managed to put some things in perspective even as it tore other things apart. Nothing had the same weight. It wasn't that nothing mattered. The war didn't mean that. It meant *everything* did, everything mattered, not least what he would do when he got out. What he felt, what he had felt all those years—all those years at the Pines that, when he lived them, felt filled with empty longing and fear—had been full. They had been full, completely and utterly full. What mass, what earth-tethered mass, did those years and all those feelings have, compared to the bombs he dropped every week? Much more. He had been living as a fake thing, a copy, but there was no reason to continue living that way. None at all. He had been nothing more than a wooden puppet. That's why he liked that silly cartoon so much and watched it a few times before the reels were sent on to some other base. He had been a wooden puppet suspended by the strings held by Ernie and Emma and Jonathan, and himself, too: he had held his own strings and made himself dance all those ugly dances. And what a mistake! What a mistake it had been to want to be a man! His wish should have been the same as Pinocchio's: Make me into a boy. Make me into a *real* boy. And he might have gotten that wish if only he had been "brave, truthful, and unselfish."

Instead he'd been a coward, a liar. He'd been selfish. When they had left the woods that awful day, he was not able to look at his father or the others. It had taken all his nerve to lift his head and mumble something to Prudence. "Sorry," he'd said. That was it. That was all he could manage. Not "sorry for what I did" or anything even remotely like it. Instead, he'd collapsed gratefully into the embrace of Billy's lie.

After. The lie hung there in the air—as humid and cloying as the air itself. He felt as if he couldn't breathe. Emma and Jonathan had carried Prudence into the maid's room. Jonathan checked her for injuries while Emma bustled about, heating water and stacking clean towels. She had the good sense to get some clean clothes from one of the kitchen girls, and after Prudence was checked and bathed, Emma helped her dress and took the bloody clothes away and burned them so that no one, least of all Prudence herself, would have to look at the blood. Frankie had hung around the kitchen, useless, as his father and mother tended to her. He wanted to speak to her, to say something to her, but didn't know how and didn't know what to say. After a while he went upstairs and sat in his room. He sat in the chair in the corner and looked over the room itself: just the bed, with its white sheets and the wool blanket and quilt folded down at the foot of his bed. His suitcases, stacked to the right of the door. His uniform in its bag, hanging in the wardrobe. The nightstand, on which stood a windup alarm clock and the kerosene lantern. An empty bedroom. A stupid bedroom. Nothing seemed to provide any kind of answer, much less any relief. Eventually he shucked his shoes and took off his pants and got into bed.

Sleep didn't come. Not even when it grew dark. He turned first to one side and then to the other.

Billy came and then left. He'd offered to go get some books for Frankie. As if that would do any good. What he wanted from Billy he couldn't have. When Billy came back he feigned sleep.

At some point he got up. The Pines was quiet. Billy had left for the night. Ernie and David were either drunk or asleep in their cabin. Frankie listened at the top of the stairs. He could hear nothing. He tiptoed down the stairs and turned into the hallway and entered the kitchen. The windows were open. The temperature had dropped and a breeze came through the open windows. He walked the few short steps to the maid's room, his heart in his throat. A sliver of light showed under the door. Frankie knocked. No answer. He knocked again. No answer.

He turned the brass knob and pushed the door open. The maid's room was tiny. Just large enough for a washstand, a small desk, and an iron-framed twin bed. Prudence sat on the bed, her knees drawn up to her chest. Her arms were wrapped around her legs and her chin rested on her knees. Her hair had been washed and combed and braided. A kerosene lantern, its wick smoking and in need of a trim, stood on the washstand next to the pitcher and bowl. Prudence was looking but not looking, her eyes unfocused. Her skin was shockingly dark against the white nightgown she wore.

Frankie didn't know what to say.

"Hi," he finally managed.

Prudence's eyes flickered over to him, then back to whatever it was they were actually seeing.

"Are you okay?"

She still said nothing.

"Do you speak English? Can you understand me?"

She looked back at him quickly.

He didn't move into the room. He leaned on the jamb, his arms folded across his chest. He rubbed his own arms as though he were cold, though he wasn't.

Everything he had meant to say left his head. Standing there, looking at her, he had no idea what to do or say.

"I've got to go to the Air Force."

Silence.

"I've got to go to the war."

More silence.

"But I'll come back. I'll come back, okay? I'll come back and help you. I'll make this better. I swear. I'll come back and we'll fix this. I'll fix this. Do you understand?"

He thought he saw her nod, ever so slightly.

"You understand, okay? I'm so sorry. I'm so sorry this happened to you, to your sister. I'm just so awfully sorry. I'll write you when I'm gone. Promise. I'll make it up to you."

She didn't move or say anything in response. He closed the door and went back to his room, not sure at all if she had understood him.

What he had really wanted was to apologize to Billy. Billy came back the next day. And the day after that. He tried to hold Frankie's hand, but Frankie wouldn't let him. He wanted a chance to apologize for that. Why hadn't Billy just held his hand anyway? Why had he become a coward, too? It was bad enough that Frankie had gone down to Prudence's room and hadn't managed to tell her the truth. That had been his chance to be a man—not by shooting so blindly and so quickly. Not by "getting the Kraut!" That's not what men did. He'd had his chance down there on the threshold of the maid's room, but with each tick, tick, tick of the Westclox, the chance to tell the truth had grown more and more remote. And Billy. Billy had been awkward and tentative. He should have crawled into bed with Frankie. Billy should have held him, forced his body around him. Billy should have ignored Frankie's words and just held him anyway, the way Felix had held Prudence despite her protests. But Billy had chickened out. They'd all been puppets jerking on their little strings of guilt and shame.

Frankie put the pages next to him and got out a fresh sheet and placed it flat on the training manual.

My Dearest,

One of the problems I never expected to have over here is that I've got too much time to think. And the best thing, the easiest thing, is to try and spend all that time finding ways not to think at all. I never succeed, of course. I always end up going over that day in my mind, thinking how it could have, how it should have, turned out differently. But it didn't. No matter how often I return to that afternoon in my mind, it always turns out the same. That poor girl. That poor, poor girl.

Up till very recently I always added "and poor poor me" to the end of that. But that's not really fair, and it's not really true, either. There were many who suffered that day.

I worry about you most of all. And that's the truth. I worry about what happened to you. You had to stay there, at least for a while. I got out of there so quickly and then everything happened so fast with my training and my deployment. I'm sorry I haven't written you till now. Truly sorry. I just didn't know what to say or how to say it, and so I thought it best not to say anything. But that's not right, either. That's not the right thing to do. I didn't think about how what happened affected you. Really affected you most of all.

So let me fix the record while I can. I am so sorry for what happened. Nothing I can do can change it, I know. But I am sorry. I'm sorry, too, for how I acted. You needed me and I wasn't there for you. I shouldn't have pushed anyone away, least of all you. I should have gone to you then and told you how sorry I was and tried as best I could to make things better. I didn't.

The whole world is at war. They call this WWII, and they are right. So I know you are in it somehow doing your part. Hopefully you're still up north and not someplace else. It's safe up there—when Germans aren't escaping from that damn camp—and so I hope you stay there. Because when this is all done, all over and done, I'm going to come back and take you out of there. Neither you nor I will be reminded, or have to be reminded, of the mistakes we've made or the things we've done or the things we've endured. It's so simple. We could leave and never go back. One thing I've learned over here in England is that the world is a really big place. It sounds so silly to put it that way, but it is. I think about this every time I get up in the nose and we fly out over England and across the North Sea and out over the Continent: it's a big world. And it's beautiful, too. Beautiful in ways I can't begin to describe. I think about that every time I fly. The rest of the guys are stuck in different parts of the plane. They have these little windows to look out of and can only see small parts of everything, little bits of the countryside, little bits of the other planes around us, the fights and the flak and the ground. But I can see everything up in the nose. I watch the runway speeding up underneath us and then, when the wheels leave the ground and we go faster and faster, we fly over fences and hedgerows and walls. And in between them I see the gardens and fields and streams and the forest. All of this gets smaller and smaller underneath us, and then the whole world is spread out. I see the villages and towns and roads. The factories and trains and rail yards and everything in between. And then we're off over the sea. If it isn't cloudy I can see the waves and the light blue of shallow water and the dark, deep blue of the depths. It's hard to focus on all this once we've passed the coast over the mainland, but it's there for me to see anyway. All those little towns and villages and orchards and fields and roads. It is so green, so full of life, despite the war. So green and so full of life and so large. When all this is done I will come back, I promise. I'll come back and take you out of there. There's no limit on us. Not like we think there is. There's no reason why we can't make our own decisions. I don't know what I will do or what you will do. Right now the only thing I am qualified to do is to use the Norden bombsight to kill people. I don't imagine that skill will be much in demand after the war. But I'll find something. Even over here. We could come over here. They'll need people to rebuild this place when the war's over. We could come to England. Or France. It's funny. I've spent so much time over France in the plane but I've never touched it. Never put my feet there. Never put my hands in her earth. It looks very beautiful. A lot of the small towns and villages we fly over haven't been bombed. The bigger cities are a mess, but the war has passed some of the smaller places by. The houses are there. The fields are there. Everything is there. And it's waiting for us. And it's not so far off. It's almost Christmas. The Germans can't hold on much longer. We have destroyed their air force. Even now, every time we cross over the French coast there are fewer and fewer German planes waiting for us. Of course, the Army has pushed the Germans out of France by now. Still—the same is true when we cross over into Germany. Fewer and fewer planes. They don't have any oil and they don't have any fuel. They don't have any parts for their planes and tanks and guns. I'm not sure if they even have any men left. The Russians are rolling them up to the east, and we're rolling them up from the west, and pretty soon we'll meet in the middle and the war will be over.

We could come over here together then, far away from the sad past, and start where no one knows us. I mean really start. They make their houses—in the villages, I mean—out of stone. They cluster together down in these little valleys, all those little stone houses. We could make one of them ours. A little snug place where nothing bad could ever happen. And we could spend the days reading or out cutting our own firewood. When it gets cold we will start a fire. There won't be anyone else around except for us. I'll read to you. You could lie down and put your head on my lap while I read, if you don't feel like reading. With the shutters closed and the fire going we'll be snug and warm, snug and safe, and it'll be as though there's no one else in the world but us. Just you and me. No one will know us. They won't even know our names. They won't know where we're from or what we've done or what we've seen.

After everything that's happened—to you, to me, to the whole damn world—I'm ready for that now. It won't be long and I'll be in your arms. I'm getting tired and I'm ready to go to sleep. Before I do, I just want to say, "I love you." I know that's a bold thing to say, especially after everything else. I should have said those words before I left. I hope it's not too late to say them now. I hope that when this letter reaches you, you are far away from harm, that you're safe and sound and happy to hear from me.

Your (if you'll have me) Frankie

It was time to be a man. He would find Billy after the war was done. How much longer could it last? Satisfied, he placed the new pages on top of the other ones and put them all in a large envelope. He put the necklace he had gotten for Prudence on top. He would mail them all together the next day. He felt light, very much lighter. As an afterthought he jotted a note for the postmaster to explain to Felix that the necklace was for Prudence and the letter was for Billy. Then he took off his boots and socks and padded over to shut off the light switch and crawled into his cot, fully clothed. The other guys would be back the next day. He missed them a little. They would, no doubt, have a lot to say about what they had done in London.

He closed his eyes. Sleep didn't come right away. First, he thought ahead to the future he would have with Billy. It was pleasant to do so, a long-deferred dream. But then, as he was drifting off, he again saw the man who'd bailed out in front of him. He saw the body in its tucked position, turning slowly through the air toward the nose of Frankie's plane, and then up and over the props, and over the wing and out into space. Only this time Frankie was that man. Maybe he was dreaming. He crossed his arms over his legs and brought his knees to his chin to begin his rotation. The plane loomed, coming at him upside down and then right side up, and then he was past, and the plane grew smaller above him. He made the calculations in his head. He bailed out at 25,000 feet. At that altitude his time to impact—not counting friction, cross winds, and humidity—was 40.52 seconds. His speed upon impact would be 888.27 mph, without calculating the drag coefficient, so he'd most likely fall more slowly than that. Energy upon impact (calculating his weight at 147 pounds) would measure 0.000000883 kilotons. Hardly anything at all. Barely measurable, really. He continued to fall, moving faster and faster. He picked out shapes on the ground now. Roads. Individual trees. The trees looked soft, even cushiony. The ground was closer now. He saw individual trees, and also bushes and stalks of wheat. It must be late in the summer, the harvest was about to be brought in.

When he'd fallen to 1,500 feet he began to slow down drastically. He left the comfort of the tuck and spread his arms and legs to slow himself. It helped. By the end, he wasn't falling so much as drifting, as a leaf would. He brought his knees forward and assumed a standing position, and as if by magic—but it wasn't magic really, it couldn't be—his feet touched the ground first, so gently, so softly as not even to make a sound, and he walked ahead, didn't even break stride, because, really, now it was time to go home.

TEN

THE PINES—CHRISTMAS 1944

Felix didn't lift the curtains again. Not the one on the small window facing the river, and not the one on the back side of the boathouse. It was early yet, not even nine thirty. He knew he would not see Prudence until much later, staggering across the river ice in her shoes, her nice ones, on her way back from the Christmas Eve party at the Wigwam, her coat pulled tight around her waist, her shawl clamped tight over her hair, her eyes bleary with booze and her breath carrying the shared smoke of some boy, a different boy, all different, and all the same somehow.

The way she took to the ice! Felix preferred not to see, not even to think about it; how she stomped across without a thought about how thin it was at the mouth of the river, how strong and deep the current. She must know, she wasn't a white girl, after all. She must have known and not cared. If she were to break through, who would come? Would he have made it in time to save her? Or would someone from the camp across the river have noticed and come running? One of the Germans. Would they have saved her? They should. In a way they owed her a life.

As for the view out the other window, it never changed, had not changed since he carried Prudence from the woods, both of them covered in her sister's blood, Frankie tailing them mournfully, the Winchester cast off in the brush. Some days later, Felix had gone back for the gun. He'd pulled it from the ferns and cleaned it, but it had already begun to rust. No one except Felix took it down from its pegs above the mantelpiece anymore. For the past two years, there'd been no one else to do it anyway.

The big house hadn't changed in that time, except to settle lower in the ground. Its face had always looked expectant to him as he waited for the ice to break up and for Emma to send a telegram for him at the Wigwam (even though he had no need for a telegram to tell him what the pussy willows told him, blooming, what everyone knew; that spring was coming). Now the big house didn't look expectant so much as hollowed out. The dark door and shuttered upstairs windows resembled a mouth and eyes caught in a silent moan. Jonathan hadn't come back, and neither had any of the others.

No one except Emma. She'd come back for two weeks the following year, and Felix had done his best to make the Pines the cheerful place she thought it had been. But whatever he did—painting the clapboard, installing storm windows, jacking up the porch and replacing the rotten spindles—was not enough. This past summer she hadn't come at all, even though in the spring Felix got the place ready, gassed the boats and oiled the hinges on the doors and leveled the dock and got the girls from the village to promise they'd be around, though now Prudence did some of the work—sloppy, careless, angry.

Across the river, as if to mock their loss and the slow death of the Pines, the prison camp was thriving. Now there were at least two hundred Germans, singing their way out to the woods to build corduroy roads through the swamps, to cut the white pine and skid it out. Two hundred singing Germans to fix the track. They enjoyed work, if not their captivity. They shouted and cheered during their weekly boxing matches and soccer games. The windows of their cabins glowed with warm light during the short days of winter. The whole place emitted the cheer of shared hardship. And all the while the Pines sank lower into the earth and the wind moaned across the shuttered windows.

All this in contrast to the humble cheer of the boathouse, which, with no one in the big house, was now truly Felix's place. His and Prudence's. There wasn't much to it: in the back, sectioned off from the main part by wooden shelves as high as he stood (these had replaced the hanging wool blankets, which hadn't offered enough privacy), was his bed; the front was crammed with a small table and two chairs, the barrel stove, the washbasin and sink, and Prudence's bed, covered in a quilt made from men's suits.

At the center of the table, a kerosene lantern stood lit, the wick trimmed low. Next to it lay a thick letter from Frankie, addressed to Billy. It had come in a larger envelope with a note and a silver chain with a heart-shaped locket for Prudence. Also on the table was a telegram from Emma that Felix had received along with the package from Clarence at the station. He turned from the window and adjusted the letter, the note, the telegram, and the locket so that Prudence would see them when she returned. She'd probably be too drunk to notice. He got up and moved all the mail to his bed so that the table was clear, except for the lantern. He fiddled with the wick and then moved the letter, telegram, and locket back to the table.

The water on top of the stove hissed from the heat, but even with the stove full of jack pine and some green birch on top to keep it going all night, the house would be cold soon. Even now, with the barrel stove shaking and hissing, the wind seethed through the pine-board walls of the boathouse.

Felix sat down on the edge of his bed but got up quickly. If only Prudence would come back, his agitation would ebb. If only she would come back, he would know what to do. He would be able to look at her and know what to do. And after he gave her the locket and the news, he would be able to get something done around the place. Would she cry? Would she want to be held? Would she sulk with a magazine on her bed or writing at the table or split some wood outside, at war with the ax, if not the wood? There was no telling how she would react to anything. She was weather with no pattern he could guess. He tried. In the mornings he made as little noise as possible as he restarted the stove and put the kettle on. But he knew how to make tea the way she liked. When it was ready, he'd say, "*Biish. Biish, daanis.*" And she would stir, squinting up at the light of dawn if it was summer and the gloom if it was winter. She'd drink two cups before she got out of bed. By then he was outside, mostly to give her privacy to make water in the chamber pot and wash her face. At other times he lay on his bed, his hands folded across his stomach as she read magazines by lamplight on the other side of the divider. "Hey, Felix, did you know . . ." Something or other from one of her magazines. But other nights she'd say nothing. You never knew with her. You never knew. When he had chided her for breaking the ax handle she shrugged and said, "Cheap old ax," but when they pulled nets, she'd whoop and holler if she got a big one, then huddle down in the front of the canoe as he paddled up the river, content as a stone.

If only he had done what Emma had asked and checked the dock instead of taking the boys out into the woods to look for the German, he might have had two daughters, two girls to care for, and the Pines, and all of it, would be as it was, only better. But he had not. There had been too much to do, too much to get done before Frankie and his friends arrived. He had been about to tackle the dead fish under the dock when Emma implored him with her eyes, in that way of hers, to go with Frankie and Billy and the others to look for the German.

Frankie had been anxious to look for the German. He shook Felix's hand and looked at him with that honest, boyish face, the one Felix had watched change from the soft, fleshy face of childhood into the strong face of a man. Felix had been surprised at the tan, the strong lines around Frankie's jaw, the firmness of his grip when he stepped out of the canoe onto the dock.

"We're going to get us a German. How about that, Felix?"

"Good," Felix had said. "Good, we'll get him."

"He doesn't stand a chance with us on his trail, does he?"

"No. Not with us," he'd agreed.

And he'd watched as Emma came striding from behind the house, her arms opened wide to receive Frankie.

No one had greeted Felix that way when he returned in 1919. The shack where his wife and child had died did not open its arms to him. He had left for the war and walked into death, and death was what he had come home to. His mother and father still lived in their wigwam on the trapping grounds. His father shook his hand. His mother made him sit and fed him. Later they went to the drum dance, where Felix was expected to tell the story of his kills. The old men who remembered 1862 and 1876 and 1891 listened and nodded. And when he was done they heaped blankets on his lap and pressed tobacco plugs into his palm and shook his hand. One old man gave him a knife and three silver dollars. But no one, not one person, had clutched him and held him close as Emma had hugged Frankie.

"My son, my boy," Emma had said, trying to cup Frankie's face in her hands. But Frankie had reared back and taken her hands in his and said, "Mother. Good, Mother, good." That was when he had looked up and nodded at Felix.

"Old Felix. Old Felix, it's good to see you. Really good."

"Mr. Frankie," Felix had answered. He'd felt like saying more. But he couldn't act like they did. It wouldn't feel natural. And he could see that Frankie was trying so hard to be a man, or to be thought of as one. So he'd left it at that.

"We'd best get after that German," Frankie said. "The longer we wait, the more time he has to cause trouble." And that's when he'd asked after the Winchester.

It was where it always was. Felix had no need for it. He didn't have the energy to look for grouse and there wasn't much to them anyway, not enough to spend what money he had on shells. Once in a while he'd sit at the point and wait for ducks, and if he got one or two mallards, that was plenty. He strung nets in the river and got enough ring-bills and canvasback to keep him happy, but mallards were nice to roast once in a while. Rabbits he snared. Deer he snared. Snaring was the best way to get game, not going out after it and shooting, shooting, shooting. Why Jonathan had brought the Winchester to the Pines was a mystery, as he never walked farther than the yard. Never even took the boat out on the lake. Maybe a shotgun was one of those things that white people liked to have around for show, like dogs or paintings.

Man though he'd become, Frankie hadn't seemed capable of bringing in a prisoner. But soon enough they'd been, as Ernie put it, "loaded for man," and the four boys and Felix had set out on the path behind the garden in the haze of heat, sweat dripping into their eyes.

As soon as they stepped past the windrow of spruce that bordered the yard and the first few feet of hazel brush it was as though they had stepped underwater. The brush was thick with moisture, heavy, still, hot. Sweat seeped into Felix's eyes; the brush grabbed at his long sleeves and tried to hold him fast. This was no time to go for a walk in the bush. The mosquitoes, dormant in the heat, rose from the ground and from under leaves and covered his neck and forehead. He brushed them away at first, but then he sweated so much and his skin was so hot that he ceased to notice them. They could hear nothing except the slap of brush and the drone of deerflies and mosquitoes. Felix was in front, since he knew the trails better than any of the boys, who were talking excitedly and laughing. Occasionally Frankie broke into song—cheerful, forced singing that seemed out of place in the woods.

The trail ended at the old tote road that ran along the northern edge of the reservation. Since the highway had been built, parallel to the railroad tracks to the south, no one used this older road much anymore, except as a skid trail in winter, for the last of the old growth and pulp from the second- and third-growth cuttings. In summer, the road disappeared under the leaf-heavy branches of basswood, maple, and ironwood. Grass and weeds waved high between the ruts, and the ruts themselves baked in the August sun until the clay hardened, shrank, and cracked. Here and there Felix saw the prints of deer that had been set during or shortly after the last rain. It looked as if the earth had been made with those tracks already in place, the deer just a rumor of life.

Felix stopped on the road, turned, and waited for the boys to catch up. They seemed so out of place, noisy and heavy-footed. Frankie kept forcing his voice louder and louder, making jokes, laughing when he tripped on deadfall, the gun waving back and forth. Maybe the double-aught hadn't been a good idea.

The boys emerged from the brush and stood around Felix expectantly. It felt good to be looked at like that. Like he had the right answers.

"So what's the plan, Felix? How are we going to bring him in?"

"If we find him, Mr. Frankie."

"We will. We'll find him, right, Billy?"

"Okay."

"I won't be home for a long time. And this is how I want the last time to be. It should be memorable."

"We split up," said Felix. "Mr. Frankie and Billy and Ernest go that way. Me and David will go this way behind the swamp."

"Hey, Felix, is there any sign? Can you tell if there's any sign? What can you see, Felix?"

Felix could only see the cracked ruts, the weeds and brush bent and crushed and browning in the heat.

He shrugged. "He might have gone this way. But maybe not. It's the wrong season for tracking. Wrong time." It was a long speech for him.

"Let's split up, then." Frankie looked at Billy when he said this, and Billy nodded.

Felix was anxious to get going, too, if only to get the search over with so he could finish his work at the Pines and give himself some peace. He began walking down the tote road, making a show of searching the weeds for sign. David followed behind him, doing the same. Frankie was saying, "Okay, if you want to cut up the middle, right off the trail here, Billy and I will follow the trail and turn off when it comes up to the lake." Ernie must have agreed, because Felix could hear him step off the trail, the leaves and underbrush crackling under his feet. Frankie said something low and Billy laughed.

"Anything, Felix? See anything?"

Felix shook his head and picked up the pace. David struggled to keep up. He followed too close and the bent branches and hazel brush slapped him in the face. Felix said nothing. If David couldn't figure out how to walk a few feet farther behind, then there was no point in telling him. He walked a few hundred yards down the tote road and then turned south into the woods. All the small sloughs and depressions in the ground were dry. Not even the clay could hold what little moisture there was. Here and there in the leaves Felix saw birch-bark baskets overturned at the base of sugar maples. Sugaring was a long way off. No one used the woods anymore. Not for sugar. Even with rationing, barely any families did it. He walked fast. If he could collect all the boys soon, then he could get back and check on the dock. The important thing was to have the place in order; that way Emma would stop clucking so much, like a partridge right before flight.

The land began to dip and the maples gave way to ash and elm. It rose again into stands of poplar and birch. There wasn't any breeze and the paper hung motionless from the birch boles in the heat. Felix turned to look at David. He was sweating fiercely and batting mosquitoes and gnats from their lazy orbits. Felix kept veering right until they struck the tote road again. Frankie and Billy must be close. He slowed and let David catch his breath.

They ambled down the center of the tote road, staying clear of the ruts. The brush grew closer here. The filberts were still cased tightly in their prickly green purses, the leaves heavy with heat. Felix heard a short laugh, he couldn't tell whose, up ahead, behind a screen of brush. He slowed. There was no need to rush. Through the brush he saw someone. At first he wasn't sure if it was Frankie or Billy, and then the single figure resolved itself into two: Frankie and Billy stood close together. Billy had his hand on Frankie's arm. Frankie said something and Billy smiled. And then Billy touched Frankie's arm and they kissed, the Winchester dangling from Frankie's left hand. He reached up with his right and removed bark or a twig or a piece of grass from Billy's hair. They smiled at each other again and this time Billy said something and Frankie laughed.

Felix stopped and edged back down the road so the boys wouldn't see him and so David wouldn't see them. But Ernie came out of the woods on the other side. Frankie and Billy dropped their hands and stepped back.

Ernie said something, and Felix could see a sneer on his face.

Billy looked down at the ground. Felix couldn't see the expression on Frankie's face, but Felix heard him say, "Come on, Billy."

And then, "I said, come on."

There was something hard in Frankie's voice.

Felix could see the expression on Ernie's face as Frankie stalked away. Ernie was smiling.

And as Frankie disappeared from view, he could hear him say, yet again, "I said, *come* on. Billy, come *on*, I said."

Felix shrank back and splayed his hand out behind him, signaling David to be quiet. But Billy's head turned their way. When he saw Felix, he dropped his gaze and disappeared into the brush after Ernie.

Then they heard the blast. Felix and David jumped.

"Let's go," said Felix. His heart beat in his chest as it hadn't since he first met his wife and again many times during the Great War. But perhaps it was something he had learned then: When some people shoot, you immediately feel better. And when some others do, you know nothing good will come of it.

He was through the brush in a few strides. Billy held the Winchester, with the barrel pointed down at the ground. "Where?"

"There," said Frankie, pointing ahead into a deep pocket of brush around a blown-down basswood. His hands were shaking.

Ernie came huffing behind them. Felix could smell whiskey on his breath.

"You see that, Ernie?" said Frankie. "You see that? We got him. We got the bastard good."

He sounded fine, but his hands were shaking.

"Where?" asked Ernie, wiping the sweat from his forehead.

"Right there. Can't you see the Kraut? Can't you see him at all?"

"I don't see anything."

Felix did. In the darkest section of the deadfall he could see some kind of agony spending itself, a flurry of leaves, the shaking of branches. Animals died that way. He halted.

"Let's go get him," said Ernie. "Let's drag him out of there."

"Wait," said Felix. "Just wait. It's easier if you wait."

After a few minutes he crept forward. The brush was thicker here and he had to bend down and, finally, get on all fours, in order to work his way to the center of the deadfall. He was halfway there when he saw movement ahead. He stopped. He could see something moving. Could hear something rustling in the leaves. Maybe, thought Felix, maybe it's not a German, after all, but a deer. A doe, perhaps, with a fawn. The fawn wouldn't know to leave. They are born stupid. Felix stopped and searched deeper into the tangle of branches with his eyes. His question resolved itself. He saw an eye. And then black hair. And then a dirty white blouse and gray woolen jumper. He saw her: a girl, huddled with her knees to her chest, looking at him through the tunnel of leaves.

Felix rushed forward. The girl didn't move. Felix was on his hands and knees, the girl was curled away from him and wouldn't look him in the eye. At her feet lay another girl—smaller, younger. She couldn't be older than thirteen. Her body was rigid, her neck arched, one arm outflung, the other curled like a wing against her chest. The wound was easy to see—a jagged tear across her neck. Her blouse was dyed red.

"Oh," said Felix. "Oh. What happened?"

The girl said nothing.

"What are you doing here? What are you doing in here?"

But still she didn't respond.

"Aaniin dana enikamigak?"

The girl shrugged. She wouldn't look at him and she wouldn't look at the girl at her feet. When her feet drifted close to the other girl's matted hair, she jerked them back as if the body of the other girl were some deadly deep pool, some drowning place.

"Awenen wiin?" asked Felix. *"Awenen?"*

The girl shook her head.

"Nakwetawishin. Nakwetawishin bina."

The girl spoke. In the coming weeks, she would answer no questions. She would make no account of herself, claim no place, ask for nothing. Not food. Not fresh clothing. Nothing. By the time she did speak, it was clear she wasn't going to leave the Pines, and no one was going to ask her to. But there, in the woods, afraid to fall into the blood at her feet, she said in English:

"My sister."

"Hmmm," said Felix. "Hmmm." Nothing else came to him and he thought, for a moment, how stupid it must sound to the white people behind him; just like the Indians in the books they read. "Hmmm. Ugh."

He reached out and turned the head of the one on the ground. Her head lolled. The buckshot must have broken her neck. The other girl scooted farther back in the leaves, trying to get away from the blood. She was shaking.

"Felix!" shouted Frankie. "Hey, Felix! Drag him out. We all want to see the bastard."

No one else said anything, and then Felix heard Frankie say something low to Ernie and he heard Ernie scoff noncommittally.

"You're coming with me," Felix said to the girl.

She looked at him blankly.

"Giga-bi-wijiw. Wiijiiwishin goda. Akawe iidog. Akawe."

"Gaawiin," she said softly. *"Gaawiin ganage giga-wiijiiwisinoon dana."* She spoke with a lilt Felix associated with Indians much farther to the north.

He grabbed her wrist. She kicked him in the face. "Sonofabitch. You damn sonofabitch. Let go."

But he didn't. He had one hand around her wrist, and she reared back and kicked him again. He turned his cheek. Then he took her by the ankle and dragged her out of the deadfall as one would drag a dead deer, the girl screaming in English and Indian and lashing out with her free foot.

"What the hell?" cried Frankie. "What the hell is that?"

Ernie said, "Don't you know what a girl looks like? Oh? I guess not. I guess—"

"You. Shut up," said Felix.

"Can't you tell a girl from a boy? Can't you—" Felix took two steps and with his free hand open, he struck Ernie across the face. Ernie rocked back on his heels. He looked at each of them in surprise. No words came, but his cheeks flooded with color and his eyes teared.

"You," Felix said to Billy, "go over there and wait."

Billy nodded at the girl, still struggling in Felix's grip. "She hurt?"

"Not this one. No."

"Sonofabitch," she cried. "Damn sonofabitch. Let go, I said. I said let go!"

"In there," said Felix, with a nod of his chin. "Back there."

"What the hell was she doing back there?" asked Frankie. "She's got no business back there."

"You shut up, too," said Felix. "Stay with me, Frankie. Understand?"

Frankie looked back into the brush where the other girl lay and took a step in that direction.

"Boy!" shouted Felix. "Boy, you come with me. And you," to Ernie. "And you, too," he said to David. He took the girl and hauled her to her feet, then picked her up and carried her back to the Pines. Gradually she stopped struggling, and by the time Felix cleared the windrow and Emma came running and behind her Jonathan in just his undershorts, she was quiet, her head against his shoulder. Then Billy and David and Ernie emerged from the woods, and last of all came Frankie.

"What happened?" asked Jonathan, his life wild in his eyes. "What happened?"

"Accident," said Felix. "There was an accident."

Frankie wouldn't look at anyone.

"What kind of accident?"

"I shot. I shot her," said Billy quietly.

Felix turned and looked hard at Billy. Billy kept his eyes level and stared back at Felix for one, two seconds, before looking at Frankie and then away, over the trees.

"This one?" asked Jonathan.

"No," said Felix. "The other one. Another one. This one is okay."

He handed her to Jonathan. She had a few scratches from the struggle, but that was it. All the blood on her belonged to the other one.

"The other one? What other one? Who is this? What other one?"

"Her sister," said Felix. "Her sister."

"You shot her, Billy?" asked Emma, her hands on her cheeks in surprise and shock. "Oh, Billy. Oh, how could that happen?"

"I don't know, ma'am," said Billy. "I don't know."

And then Felix turned and disappeared into the woods. He moved very quickly and soon he was gone, and all sound and trace of him was gone, too.

Frankie wouldn't leave his room the next day. Billy came but wasn't fit for chores. He avoided Emma and Ernie and even Felix. Search parties still formed across the way at the camp and trolled the shoreline and walked the swamps. But no one at the Pines was all that interested in helping anymore, so, not having anything else to do, Felix took the metal garden rake and at last began to clear out the weeds and trash and dead fish from under the dock. It was something to do while they held their breath.

He expected to find whitefish or red horse or tullibee, which often died off in late summer, starved for oxygen. But as he reached under the dock he snagged something much larger. When he pulled hard on the rake, the corpse floated out. The German had tried to swim the river. Most likely he had hoped to steal one of the rowboats, or even the Chris-Craft. But he didn't make it. His body was wedged halfway inside one of the cribs. It had been in the water for three days and it was bloated and rotten in the heat. The tines of the rake had punctured the skin on the German's back. Leeches clung to the meat of his belly and face. Everyone gathered around and gazed mutely at the body, except for Prudence, who wouldn't leave the maid's room, and Frankie, who wouldn't leave his bed.

If only they had known. There would have been no need for the Winchester. No need at all.

Prudence told them nothing more, beyond her name. Not where she'd come from or what school she and her sister ran from, or even her sister's name. None of Emma's inquiries produced any information, nor did the investigation that the sheriff conducted. A couple of Indian runaways and a hunting accident, and it was all very sad. They stored the body in the icehouse for a few days while the sheriff did his work, and then they laid it in the ground. Frankie was bedbound, and Billy was nowhere to be found. Not even Prudence came. She stayed in the big house, staring out the window, as Felix put the body of her sister in the wheelbarrow (there was no other way to do it alone) and wheeled her up the hill and buried her beneath a pine. Emma and Jonathan came and stood silently as they watched the Indians bury another Indian. For once neither had anything to say.

Within a week of Prudence's bloody arrival and the discovery of the German under the dock, everyone had left. Jonathan and Frankie went back to Chicago, and Emma followed them. Ernie and David stayed a little while longer, drinking together in Ernie's cabin, and then they left, too. All the food that had been purchased and prepared for the celebration was left to rot. Felix piled it in the corner of the garden and at night the raccoons and skunks gathered there to feast. That fall Billy came by to see Felix a few times, but it wasn't the same. They didn't say much to each other. And then Billy got married to Stella around Thanksgiving. He'd enlisted shortly thereafter and was gone by Christmas.

One more look out the window. Nothing moved on the ice. Plenty moved below. Maybe tomorrow Felix would cut a hole and, with a blanket over his shoulders and another under his body, he'd decoy for muskie. He had a few of the decoys, painted wooden minnows with metal fins. And he could use one of the sucker spears. If only he had watched his father more closely. He remembered that he'd carved his lures out of poplar and scraped them until the wood glowed white and then wrapped beaver fat around the bit of wood, but he hadn't watched closely enough. He remembered, though, that they'd set lines in the evening and by morning, northern or muskie, big enough to feed the whole family, would be dead on the line, the stick caught in their jaws. And if no fish came, his father sometimes took a bit of root from his pouch and, with his back turned, did something to their sets. It was some kind of medicine. He'd asked about it and his father had said, *"Migizi-mashkiki,"* and that was all. He'd hidden his medicine from his son, that's how secret it was. Felix wished he had it now. He wished he knew what his father had known, that he had some power to bring the big fish in.

The camp across the mouth of the river was dark. The lights went off at ten. Felix took another look at the items on the table, sent all the way from England. He leaned over and picked up the envelope addressed to Billy. It was heavy. A long letter. Billy was in the infantry, somewhere in France. Why would Frankie send it here?

The kerosene lantern on the table guttered. Felix sat down and took the letter between his hands, and then he took his pocketknife and sliced it open. "Dearest," it began. He read slowly, mouthing the words.

My Dearest,

One of the problems I never expected to have over here is that I've got too much time to think. And the best thing, the easiest thing, is to try and spend all that time finding ways not to think at all. I never succeed, of course. I always end up going over that day in my mind, thinking how it could have, how it should have, turned out differently. But it didn't. No matter how often I return to that afternoon in my mind, it always turns out the same. That poor girl. That poor, poor girl.

Up till very recently I always added "and poor poor me" to the end of that. But that's not really fair, and it's not really true, either. There were many who suffered that day.

I worry about you most of all. And that's the truth. I worry about what happened to you. You had to stay there, at least for a while. I got out of there so quickly and then everything happened so fast with my training and my deployment. I'm sorry I haven't written you till now. Truly sorry. I just didn't know what to say or how to say it, and so I thought it best not to say anything. But that's not right, either. That's not the right thing to do. I didn't think about how what happened affected you. Really affected you most of all.

It took him the better part of an hour to read it. "Hmmm," he said aloud when he was done. And again, "Hmmm."

He took the letter and put it back in the envelope addressed to Billy. He took it and the telegram and put them both between his mattress and the mattress boards.

The wick could be trimmed tomorrow. And maybe if the wind wasn't too strong and the temperature held and the sun was out, he really would try and spear a nice muskie. The flesh was so firm and flaky and clean this time of year.

Felix cupped his hand over the mantle of the lantern and blew out the flame. He raked the coals in the barrel stove and added two more sticks of green birch. The bark caught and crackled and the light jumped around the cabin, but only for a moment, and then it dulled. He closed the door but left the grate open, and then he changed into his sleeping clothes by the firelight and closed the curtain that separated his bed from Prudence's. It got cold near the wall, with the curtain between him and the stove, but he was used to it. And Prudence deserved the heat. She liked it hot. He smiled a bit at the thought of her under her blankets, nested there, her knees drawn to her chest.

In his narrow bed, with the wool blankets pulled up daintily to his chin and his eyes closed, he couldn't sleep. When would she be back? When would she come staggering through the door, and what would her mood be? It was so hard to guess when she would be cruel and when she would be a girl, just a girl. God, she could be terrible, her silences as cruel as her words. The hours and even days when she wouldn't speak to him. And the nights she stayed out and drank. Didn't she know what that did to him, to his peace of mind? She must know and not care. But then she'd say something and smile and all those dark times would burn up and float away. Or he'd coax her out on the trails behind the Pines to check snares with him and she'd complain. She'd complain about her boots and the cold and the unevenness of the trail. But then she'd dart ahead and pull a snare from under the snow, a dead rabbit dangling there, and she'd shout, "Well, lookee here!" And she'd grab him by the shoulder and spin him around so she could, on tiptoe, put the rabbit in his pack basket.

And then, some mornings, he'd hear her moving about the cabin while he was still in bed, and then the door would open, cold gushing in, and she'd be gone, outside in the predawn. He'd rise and creep to the window and see her over the burn barrel, putting in her bloody underthings, dripping kerosene on them and setting them on fire, burning the evidence of her monthly blood. Why would she bother with that? At these times, he'd know she could not stay there, and yet she could not leave.

Maybe all she needed was more time. Another year or two, maybe three. Enough time for the hate to rust away and for the love to shine through. What else could you call his feelings for her, the care he showed her? Someday she'd see it. Someday she'd see. Frankie would come back and she'd see the truth for herself.

He closed his eyes and tried to see her walking across the ice—so vulnerable in her dancing shoes, her arms wrapped around her own waist, hugging her jacket to her body. Heedless. Heedless of the ice and the current underneath. Heedless of the wind. She had no idea how frail she looked, how thin, how unsteady she seemed when she crossed the ice.

The door opened and slammed shut. Felix could smell the alcohol before she even had time to trip over the fire rake and curse. She shucked her coat and sat down on her bed. "Jesus," she said, and she sighed and said again, "Jesus, I hate . . ." but didn't finish the thought.

Felix stiffened with nervousness (could it be called fear?) when Prudence came back to the cabin in such rough shape. The next day, after a few cups of tea, she would be manageable, and she wouldn't be sorry for what she'd said to him. But she'd do her chores, fighting her headache and the bruises. She'd stagger around with the ax and curse the log rounds she was supposed to reduce to kindling. At war. Fighting. Fighting everything.

"There's something for you," said Felix finally. "There's something from Frankie, in that box there."

Prudence didn't say anything, but Felix heard her suck in her breath and get up from her bed, so slender, so light, that the bedsprings didn't even notice.

"Oh," she said. The cabin was suddenly still. "Oh, look."

He sat up and saw her turning the locket in the lamplight.

"There's a letter, too," he said.

"Yeah?"

"Bekaa," he said. *"Bekaa, daanis."* He reached under his mattress and removed the letter from the envelope with Billy's name on it and stuffed the envelope and the telegram back under the mattress. He rose and handed her the letter and then let the curtain fall back in place and sat quietly on the edge of his bed. "It's for you."

"Of course it is," she said dreamily. "Of course."

She took it and sat at the table, her back turned from him, her face toward the light. A few minutes passed.

"He's coming back."

"He could."

"Is. He is. He's gonna come back and get me out of this shithole."

"This place has been good to us. The Washburns have been good to us." Oh, he couldn't help it, there it was, the memory of her head on his shoulder. Her smile when, once, she lifted a bass into the boat. And then, when he'd been seated as the belt man on the drum, she had helped him sew all those blankets and even come with him to the drum dance. That wasn't nothing. Felix placed his hand over his heart to make sure it was still beating.

"Did you read this? Did you?"

"No," he said toward the ceiling.

"You'd know if you did. You'd know like I know."

"Maybe he will," murmured Felix, just to close down the conversation, just to quiet whatever storm always raged inside this girl.

He watched her raise her arm over her head in the firelight.

"He's gonna come and get me away from this place," she said, slurring.

"Maybe he won't."

"Why wouldn't he? Why wouldn't he come for me? See? No reason. None at all. No reason. I can give him what he wants. And I will, too. It don't matter what anyone says about it. I don't care what they say."

"He's all the way in England. And there's a war. Lots could happen."

"It won't stop him. He said so." She pushed the curtain aside, holding on to it for support. If it fell down, he'd have to fix it immediately, because otherwise he'd have to sleep without anything between them, and if he woke in the night he'd see her, sleeping hot next to the stove, her blankets thrown off, her mouth open.

"He's never coming back here," said Felix, and he turned away from her and faced the wall.

"You don't know anything. You don't know anything at all. Especially about him. He saved me. Understand?" She stepped closer. "He saved me."

The girl was so blind. But he had helped make her that way. He didn't know how to undo it.

"You know what?" She moved closer. Her voice was low and close to his ear. "You know what? You're just jealous. You're just jealous because you don't got anything. Even this. This. This place isn't even yours." Her whiskey breath was close. "You're jealous of him. Of all of them."

"No. Please, Prudence. Please stop, Prudy."

"Yeah, you are. You want this. That's all you've ever wanted. That's why I'm stuck here."

"No."

"So that's not what you want? It's not?" He could feel her weight on the bed. Her hand slid under the wool blanket.

"No."

"No?"

She pushed the blanket aside and straddled him. He was hard already, and that was as much a surprise as everything else. It had been so long, so many long years. She reached down and, with her hand around the base of it, put him inside her.

Her dress was still buttoned to the top. Her sleeves reached to just above her elbows, and Felix was surprised at how slender her forearms were. How slender and strong.

"Prudence. No."

But she was moving anyway. As was he, anyway.

She put her hands on his chest to steady herself. "This is what you want, isn't it?"

It wasn't. It wasn't. But it was.

"Prudence."

She closed her eyes. He felt what seemed like drops of cold water on his chest, and then he saw what it was. A necklace, the chain doubled, hung from her slender wrist. A small heart dangled from it. Even in the low light, Felix could tell it wasn't gold. Just silver.

"Prudence."

She moved her hips against his a few more times, and he came.

"Merry Christmas, Felix."

"Niin dash wiin, mii eta go aano-wii-ayaamaan da-odaanisiminaan. Iw sa eta." He turned his face toward the wall in shame. He felt the cold seeping through the boards.

"Oh? Well, you're a *great* dad."

And suddenly she was off him. His penis, slick and cold and startled in the cold cabin, was already shrinking, retreating back inside his underwear, which hadn't even come off. Prudence staggered back to her bed and lay down heavily. She was asleep within minutes.

After everything that had been done and everything that wasn't, Frankie sent a silver heart? That was all? In a few months her sweat would corrode it. It wouldn't last any longer than the lie could. The layers of metal were just like the bones in the head of the pike. There was a small bone in there—inside their skulls. It got bigger every year, a layer of new bone for every year it lived. When they had fish-head soup when he was a boy (his mother, for once not shy and proper, would slurp it down), whoever got the pearl, the lobe of bone, was lucky. He'd forgotten that. But for all of them—Felix and Emma and Frankie and Jonathan and Billy and Prudence—life seemed to have the opposite effect. With each and every year, everything got smaller, another layer was worn away. Soon there would be nothing left.

He waited to make sure she was asleep before taking the envelope and the telegram from under his bed. He moved to the stove and squatted down. He opened the door and put the envelope with Billy's name on it on the coals. One second. Two. It flared up and then died. He read the telegram from Emma again.

> FOR FELIX STOP FROM THE AIR FORCE STOP DEEPLY REGRET
> TO INFORM YOU THAT YOUR SON 674448 FRANK CONRAD
> WASHBURN IS MISSING AS THE RESULT OF AIR OPERATION ON
> THE NIGHT OF 21/22TH DEC 44 STOP LETTER FOLLOWS STOP ANY
> FURTHER INFORMATION RECEIVED WILL BE COMMUNICATED
> TO YOU IMMEDIATELY STOP PENDING RECEIPT OF WRITTEN
> NOTIFICATION NO INFORMATION SHOULD BE GIVEN TO
> THE PRESS

He placed it on the coals, on top of the remains of the envelope. It too flared up and died. And then he went back to bed. He turned once again to face the wall and pulled the blankets around his body. Maybe tomorrow. Prudence would sleep late. Maybe tomorrow, early, if it was sunny, he'd go out on the ice and chop a hole and use the white man's lures to draw the muskie close. It would come and he'd stab it and bring it up, huge and glistening and uncomprehending, onto the ice. They'd have fish tomorrow night. Just the two of them. Just the two of them, and she would be kind and he would be kind, and the past would crawl back where it belonged. They'd have fish, and with their bellies full they'd think back to the good days they'd had and would have once more.

PART III

THE RESERVATION

1952

ELEVEN

THE RESERVATION—AUGUST 1, 1952

So it must have been past midnight and there was some cunt walking down the side of the road. She was swinging this black purse in her left hand and holding her shoes in her right and putting her feet down on the white line but her feet missed now and then, and when she did, she stepped into the road and then back the other way into the gravel and ditch grass before finding the line again.

Billy slowed the truck and downshifted. What was left of the whiskey he got at the VFW in Grand Rapids sloshed in the bottle between his legs. His eyes itched and he rubbed them and then rubbed his forehead and pushed his hair back across his head. He felt greasy and low and dragged out, as though at the end of another march through the bocage. But those days were well behind him. The truck he was driving was proof of that, if not the day spent at the VA for another visit with the doctor about his shoulder, which just wouldn't stop hurting. His right arm felt like some useless thing, not good enough to green-chain and stack lumber at the mill any longer, barely good enough to lift Margaret and Junior into the back of the truck on the rare day they went to the lake. His arm's only purpose was to hang from his body.

He took a drink and slowed down even more and flashed his high beams at the bitch but she didn't look back, so he flashed them again. She could be killed. She knew he was there because her feet were a little more cautious, stuck to the line a little more carefully, and her shoulders were extra even and level and her head was held high and she didn't look back. She had on a floral-print dress, some kind of flowers that weren't exactly accurate, and the black purse didn't match up but it was probably the only purse she had. Only dress, too. She was darker than Billy but she had a glow to her skin and she didn't have any stockings on and her shoes—little slip-on things—were in her right hand. When she lifted her feet Billy saw they were strong feet, narrow, dirty on the bottom from the road. She had a good body, slender but strong. The dress was fitted tight around her hips and the muscles in her ass bunched and swayed with each determined step. A cloud of moths and mosquitoes trailed along behind her, lit up by the headlights.

Billy flashed the lights again, but even when he got right behind her, the cunt still didn't look back, so he pulled alongside her, and with the truck still rolling leaned across the packages on the seat and cranked down the passenger window.

"I ain't the sheriff's deputy, for Chrissake," he said.

"I know what you're not."

"Well, what the fuck? You just out for a stroll, Prudy?"

"If it ain't Billy Cochran."

"The one and only."

"Yeah, there's only one of you." She walked faster, not looking at him or the truck.

The truck's tires crunched in the gravel. "You want a ride or not?"

Prudence stopped and Billy put the truck in park. Prudence leaned back and then leaned in and rested her head on the bottom of the open window, the necklace clinking against the inside of the door.

"Sweet Christ, that feels good," she said.

"Sure enough. You're gonna get run over out here. Where you coming from?"

"Oh, you know," she said, waving back down the dark road with her purse, which dropped from her hand. "Damn it," she moaned, and bent out of view to retrieve it. "There was a little something happening over at Judd's," she said when she stood up. "Some dancing going on over there." Billy smelled the gin coming off her.

"Is that what they call it."

"A big bunch up from Chicago to do some fishing."

"I bet. You gonna tell me your life story or you gonna get in? I'll bring you home."

"Oh, I don't know." Prudence looked down the road toward the village. "It ain't far now."

"It's three miles yet."

"I gone further than that, Billy Cochran. A lot further."

"Not drunk you haven't."

"If you say so."

Prudence grabbed the door handle and pulled, dropped her purse again, picked it up and pulled again, and dropped her shoes. "Lord love a duck," she said.

"Gotta pull harder than that—she's stuck," said Billy.

"Your truck here is a piece of shit."

"Better than the truck you don't got."

Prudence threw her shoes and purse in through the open window, put her foot against the truck, and pulled. The door swung open and she staggered back, and with a little shriek fell down in the ditch. All Billy could see from the driver's seat was Prudence disappearing from view and then her feet arcing up through the air.

"Jesus, girl," said Billy, and he got out and went around the front of the truck and down the slope of the ditch, his leather-soled shoes slipping in the dew-slick grass. Prudence was on her hands and knees, feeling around for her shoes. "That must have been some party over to Judd's," he said as he helped her stand. Her dress was soaked and the backside was caked with mud and bits of grass. Her knees were dirty.

"Life's always some party, isn't it," said Prudence, and she leaned on him as he walked her up the ditch and got her into the truck. He slammed her door twice before it caught.

By the time he slid himself behind the wheel, Prudence had the bottle raised to her lips, her head thrown back. When she was done, she wiped her lips with the back of her hand and settled into the bench seat with her legs tucked underneath her, her head against the door frame, face into the oncoming wind.

"Jesus, Prudy, you drink like a man," said Billy.

"I drink like I got to," she said lazily, her throat thick with booze.

"Gimme that," he said. She stretched her arm out without looking, and Billy took the bottle and did his own drinking as the truck picked up speed. Prudence shifted in her seat and lifted her dress up past her thighs. She picked some grass off the fabric and let the wind take it. "Ruined," she murmured.

Billy watched the road and he watched Prudence, too. When they pulled her screaming from the brush ten years earlier she hadn't looked all that different; her legs bare and covered in grass and blood, her eyes wild and blank, not settling on any one thing. At first she'd been hysterical, wild; and then, with Felix's arms wrapped around her, she had calmed down and he had talked to her in Indian and she calmed down even more; and by the time Felix had carried her out of the woods she was quiet. She wouldn't or couldn't say anything at all when Dr. Washburn checked her out and they put her in the big house. When the sheriff arrived, she still wouldn't talk. They all wondered where she'd come from, where she'd been, whom she belonged to, and how she ended up on the run.

And Frankie. He couldn't look at her, not that day and not for a long time after. He wrote her, sent her things. But he'd never looked her in the face. That day he couldn't raise his eyes off the ground, could barely move one foot in front of the other. It had been old

Felix who took charge till they got back to the Pines. Billy had wanted to help him, to go to him, as Emma swooped in, clucking and crying, asking him if he was okay, but even back then Billy had known that sometimes what a man needed was to be left the fuck alone.

"What are you looking at?" she said now. Billy didn't say anything but looked away from her long legs, from the sleek skin. The truck smelled of peat and grass and whiskey.

The Wigwam was dark. A lone light lit the street in front of the town hall. A dog crossed the street. The town was silent.

"We're here," said Billy. Those days with Frankie, those long summer days and the life they held, seemed long gone. Forever gone. On the other side of some other thing that was hard for Billy to name.

"Oh?" Prudence lifted her head from the door frame and uncurled her legs, knocking Billy's packages to the floor of the truck.

"Easy, Jesus Christ. I just bought those," said Billy as he bent to retrieve them. His shoulder seized and he had to sit up, straighten his arm, and try again. "Goddamn."

"Got any more juice?" Prudence asked.

"Some." Billy handed her the bottle from where he had stashed it again between his legs. "Richard waiting for you up there?" he asked, peering over at the blank upstairs windows of the Wigwam. Billy and Richard had worked the green chain at the mill together. Richard was cheerful in a plain, unthinking way. He had joined the merchant marine and ridden back and forth across the Atlantic for the duration of the war. Probably just as happy doing that as he was sizing and sorting the lumber off the green chain. Since Billy had reinjured his shoulder at the mill and had taken the job as a spotter in the fire tower, he hadn't seen Richard all that much. When he did, he was surprised to see him with Prudence, of all people—and acting like he was the luckiest guy in the world. Amazing a man could be that dumb.

Prudence finished the bottle and looked at it curiously, as though she didn't understand it.

"Well, I suppose," said Billy.

"Richard's at his place," said Prudence.

"I suppose he is."

She looked up at the dark windows of the Wigwam.

"That's just my place, just for me. I'm not going to live with a man who's not ready to make a commitment, you know?"

"You got principles, Prudy. Morals."

"Unlike some."

"You mean me."

"If the shoe fits, Billy."

"You ain't wearing any, Prudy."

"I never hurt no one." She looked at the bottle again. "You got any more?"

Somewhere, in the direction the dog went, was his house, one among the few that made up the village. It was small but solid enough. And in it, Stella and Margaret and Junior all curled up in the same bed. Sometimes when he came back late he would stand over them, wondering how he would fit in there. He would remove his green U.S. Forest Service shirt and somehow, with his pants on, find his way into the tangled brush of their limbs. The mattress sank lower. When he turned, the whole bed rocked and pitched and the springs bounced, but they never woke, just tossed on the bed as though on the wave of some new dream. They slept the same whether he was there or not.

The truck idled in front of the Wigwam.

"I don't keep it around."

"You always were smart."

"You think?"

"No," said Prudence. "No, not really." But then she laughed.

It felt as though they were just starting some kind of conversation they were always meant to have.

"Let's go," she said. "Let's just go."

"You think?"

"Yeah," she said. "Yeah. Let's just go."

"Richard gonna care?"

"He won't unless I do. Stella gonna care?"

"What she don't know."

"Yeah, yeah, Billy."

Billy put the truck in gear and they rolled out of the village.

"Turn left," she said. And he did, and they were once again on the blacktop.

In a few minutes they passed the place where he had first seen her that night. That, too, seemed so long ago, of another age. She had been a different girl then, walking along the road, and he had been a different man.

They passed the turnoff to Judd's Resort and the Big Winnie Supper Club, and Prudence pointed at a mailbox set back from the highway. Billy turned and followed the long driveway south through a small potato field and up to a small log house.

"I can't ask Gephardt," said Billy. "I just can't."

"You don't have to," said Prudence. "He'll sell to me."

"Germans will sell to anyone."

"You complaining about that?"

"Does he sleep hard?"

"He never has before. But I guess we'll find out. You got money?"

"Do you?"

"What do I look like to you? Just hand it over. I'll take care of it."

The booze was losing its grip on Billy. He never went to Gephardt's if he could help it. When he did—to sell rice, or get something welded or fixed—he ground his jaw and looked down, though Gephardt was always friendly enough. It was strange to think about, but Gephardt had been at the camp that day—he had to have been, when the other prisoner went missing. Germans sure enough fucked everything up. His shoulder hurt.

He dug in his trouser pocket and found four dollars left over from his stop at J. C. Penney in Grand Rapids. He had walked around the racks for a long time, through the women's clothes and kids' clothes, over to the men's and back again. He had no idea what to buy. Too many choices. Too many things he didn't understand. He didn't read anymore for the same reason. But how he had once loved the books Frankie sent. The sight of those packages wrapped in brown paper was really something. But there were too many choices now, and no one who could help him make them. Too many changes to everything.

It was summer, and Margaret and Junior usually wore the same thing—overalls and T-shirts. But Billy had wanted to get them something nice. For Margaret especially. He didn't really know what to say to her most of the time. What does one say to a ten-year-old girl anyway? As it was, she went to school and she did well and she listened to Stella and did her chores. In the summer, on Sundays, he'd put his chair outside the front door and sit there in the sun, and he could see her with her hands on her hips, surrounded by a group of boys, or squatting down in the center of them, all their heads bent low as they listened to some story or instruction. She was in charge of all of them. But around him she didn't say much. She just studied him, watched him, did what he said, and disappeared.

Just that summer he had added a new chore to her list: she had to bring him lunch every day. Stella would pack it in an old lard pail and tie flour-sacking around the top, and Margaret had to carry it out to the fire tower at noon and climb the two hundred feet up the stairs with the pail banging against her legs, and then the remaining twenty feet straight up the ladder and through the trapdoor. He made her wait while he inspected the contents and ate the first few bites. She never looked out over the edge or made conversation or gave any sign, really, that she wanted to stay.

He could have brought the pail himself in the morning when he left. It would have been easy enough. And he had eaten enough bad food in the Army, so a stale sandwich or a warm jar of milk was no big thing. But he hoped—well, he wasn't sure what he hoped—but he hoped something would happen between them in the fire tower, swaying two hundred feet over the trees. He might say something. Or she might. But neither did. And then he'd say, "Go on now," and down the ladder she'd go, to walk the three miles back to the village and resume doing whatever it was that ten-year-old girls did and thinking whatever it was they thought.

Junior was different. He was quiet but in a different way. Obsessive about his games or absorbed in whatever he was constructing out of sticks or bark or whatever was at hand in the yard. That's how Frankie had been when they were boys. Billy understood that.

He hadn't been sure what to get Margaret. But the school year was coming around, and her overalls were wearing out at the knees, so he circled back to the dresses. He was still out of sorts from his visit to the VA. Being around all the uniforms, even being around the other servicemen—the older ones and the ones coming back from Korea—made him edgy. He'd stopped at a bar in Royalton and they had served him without saying anything or acting funny about it. He had stopped again at the VFW in Grand Rapids—they'd serve him, even though he was Indian, and let him buy a pint. Then he moved on to the J. C. Penney. A dress would do, both for Margaret and for Stella. A dress for the new school year. And something for Stella to wear to church. Junior was six, so he got more overalls, big enough to last the year.

Prudence had gotten out of the truck and was knocking on Gephardt's door. Her dress was still wet and caked with dirt from when she'd fallen in the ditch, but she held herself as though she didn't notice it. The one he had gotten for Stella was much nicer, he thought, a little longer. But Prudence looked good in hers. It was all about how you carried yourself.

The cripple, Mary, answered after a minute or two and then retreated into the house. God, she was a sight. How she made it around on that leg, Billy would never understand. A minute later Gephardt himself appeared at the door. He handed Prudence a mason jar with a zinc lid, filled with clear fluid. He said something—Billy could see his lips moving and his head nodding, all smiles—but Billy couldn't hear him, which was just as well. Prudence handed him the money and he shook her hand and then closed the door, and Prudence turned and held up the jar in one hand and made the "V for Victory" sign with the other on the stage of Gephardt's front steps.

Billy had seen only one dead German before the war, and after three days in the water he didn't look like much, didn't look dangerous at all. Billy was there when Felix pulled him from under the dock. He came to the Pines every day after the shooting to check on Frankie. At first Frankie wouldn't leave the house, and Emma spent her days flowing up and down the stairs with trays of food, bowls of soup, towels, tonic, even whiskey, which had been Jonathan's idea, and when that didn't work, he'd prescribed Veronal. Ernie said there was nothing to do except to go fishing, which he did. But Billy came and sat by Frankie's bed on the first day. On the second, Frankie seemed a little better and Billy asked him if he'd like some books. Frankie said, "Sure," so Billy went all the way back to the village and got from under his bed some of the ones Frankie had sent him. By the time he got back, Frankie was asleep again, so Billy left them by his bed. On the third day, they remained unopened.

Late that afternoon, Felix finally got around to cleaning the dock, and that's when he found the body. He said nothing about his discovery, in his usual dumb way. He'd used the rake to snag the German's shirt and float him out from under the dock. Then he'd tied a rope under the corpse's armpits and pulled it onto the riprapped bank.

It wasn't long before Emma and Jonathan came out of the big house, and the kitchen girls stopped what they were doing and came and stood around the body as well, and then the news of the discovery carried over the water and the super from the prison camp rowed over. Within a couple hours, the sheriff and constables and members of the search party were there, too. No one moved the body. Billy was there, and he saw that the German was missing some of his fingers, chewed off by turtles, and that the parts of his skin that had been submerged were white, and strings of white tissue like the tentacles of a jellyfish trailed off his face, whereas the skin that had been exposed to air was black and stretched so tight from bloating that it had ruptured, leaking here and there what looked like jelly.

Everyone was so absorbed in the spectacle of the body that no one noticed Frankie until he spoke. He had gotten out of bed and come downstairs, and he couldn't stop saying, "He was there? He was there all along? Right there? Right there?" He said this over and over until Billy and Emma led him back to bed.

Around sunset the sheriff and his deputies lifted the German into their boat and brought him back across the river. The other prisoners buried him outside the fence that night and when they were done, they stood around the grave and sang, *"So nimm denn meine Hände."* The sound carried across the river and into Frankie's room, where Billy sat watching him sleep. He wasn't sure if he should reach out and touch Frankie or not. When it got dark he lit the kerosene lantern on the table next to the bed. Frankie opened his eyes.

"Hey, Frankie," said Billy softly.

Frankie turned his head away.

So nimm denn meine Hände
und führe mich
bis an mein selig Ende
und ewiglich.
Ich mag allein nicht gehen,
nicht einen Schritt:
wo du wirst gehn und stehen,
da nimm mich mit.

"You want me to read to you?"

"No."

"Who knew, Frankie. I mean, who could have known?"

"Fucking Germans."

"You couldn't have known."

"I leave tomorrow. Doctor's orders."

This wasn't how it was supposed to be. They were supposed to have two weeks. They were to go squirrel hunting and fishing. They were to have parties in the big house. Frankie was supposed to smile.

In dein Erbarmen hülle
mein schwaches Herz
und mach es gänzlich stille
in Freud und Schmerz.
Laß ruhn zu deinen Füßen
dein armes Kind:
es will die Augen schließen
Und glauben blind.

"Already?"

"When are you going to do your part in all this, Billy?"

Billy shrugged. Frankie looked away from the window open to the river, back to the woods to the north of the Pines. They went on and on. On toward Canada and north to where there were no more of them to be had.

"Are you sure I can't read something to you? Or anything else?"

Wenn ich auch gleich nichts fühle
von deiner Macht,
du führst mich doch zum Ziele
auch durch die Nacht:
so nimm denn meine Hände
und führe mich
bis an mein selig Ende
und ewiglich!

The lamp flickered. Billy listened as the singing died out over the river. He heard Ernie down at the dock tying up the rowboat and singing some mocking version of the hymn in a wobbly falsetto. Emma was in the kitchen. Judging from the smell of smoke drifting through the window, Jonathan was on the front porch with his pipe. Billy reached out and took Frankie's hand.

"Can I?" he whispered. It was the closest he'd ever come to naming whatever it was between them.

"It's not 'can I,' it's 'may I.'"

Billy's heart beat fast.

"May I?"

"We're not kids anymore, Billy. We're not children, after all."

Billy let go of his hand.

"Will you look at me, Frankie?"

"No."

"I was just trying to help. To help you. Look at me."

"No."

"Please, Frankie."

Nothing.

Billy waited a moment and then stood up. He walked to the door and opened it. Then he turned. It was just like a movie. Frankie looked at him and then looked away. And that was the last time.

A cigarette glowed under the eaves of the boathouse. "Watch out for my fish there," Ernie said without pointing. Billy looked down at his feet. There was a muskie—a big one, four, five feet—lying stiff in the grass where the German had lain. Its body glowed white in the lamplight.

"Where's Felix?"

"Up the hill, burying that girl you shot."

"Oh. Okay."

Ernie continued to look at him.

"You did, right?"

"Did what?"

"You shot her. You were the one who shot her."

"Yeah. Yeah, it was me."

"Okay."

"Okay what?"

"Okay you're telling me it was you. So, 'okay.'"

Billy didn't know what else to say. His hands flapped at his sides a couple times and he half turned toward the house, then he got into the rowboat and pushed off, watching the Pines recede into little pinpoints of light and lamp glow.

Two years later, he had advanced, one ant in a division of ants, from Normandy on D+1 across the Aure and into Trévières, up Hill 192 and down into Saint-Lô and from there to Brest. After forty days of watching bomb after bomb after bomb fall on Brest, they advanced through the streets and took the city, one building at a time. By the time Billy was done with Brest he had seen more dead Germans than he could count. In Normandy, they'd been swollen with flies in the ditches, fried black in their bunkers, but in Brest most of the dead looked fairly tame—a little blood from the mouth or nose and ears from the shock of the bombs.

By the time they pushed into Germany in October 1944, the weather had grown cold. A month later they were pushed all the way back through the snow and the cold to Elsenborn Ridge, where they held on without reinforcements against a superior German force for ten days before the Germans gave up their advance—ten days in a bunker he and Van Winckle from Arkansas had dug out of the frozen ground and covered with planks salvaged from an old barn. A week after Elsenborn they advanced into Germany near Aachen, and Van Winckle stepped on a mine. His legs disappeared in a mist of flesh and blood. Billy felt a pain in his shoulder and he sat down next to Van Winckle with a grunt. He looked and saw that his arm was hanging at a strange angle and his whole side was covered with blood.

None of it was quite real. None of it was very memorable. Not the clang of the landing-craft door opening, not the steady rolling boom of the shells overhead or the almost constant shaking of the ground. Not even killing his first German. He barely remembered that. Not the firestorms over Brest or the screaming of the horses near Saint-Lô. Not even the misery of Elsenborn or the surprise of having a piece of Van Winckle's land mine blow through his shoulder. None of it, not one bit of it stood out as sharply as the smallest thing he remembered about the Pines.

Even the weather had seemed glorious back then. The days had gone on and on and on, as though stretching themselves out to make room for the games he and Frankie had played when they were boys, the long treks down the tote road with a .22 to shoot squirrels. Sometimes moods would come over Ernie and he would go off by himself, and those times were the best. Then Frankie and Billy would go even farther. They didn't shoot many squirrels, but sometimes Billy would say, "Watch this," and he would raise his gun and take a shot at a squirrel high in the trees and it would fall, slowly, so slowly to the ground and he and Frankie would rush over and watch in that cold, cruel, curious way of boys as it died, and Frankie would bend so close that Billy could smell his hair and sometimes he'd put one hand on the squirrel's body and the other on Frankie's neck, as if to direct his attention to the animal, and he would feel the same warmth, the same animal aliveness there.

Sometimes clouds rolled in and night came on suddenly, much earlier than it usually did. Then the family would gather in the sitting room and, if the mood was right, the boys would play charades or Chinese checkers with Emma. On rare occasions when Emma had enough to drink, she would sing and Frankie would accompany her on the piano. Frankie, so shy, so tentative and thin, would come alive. His fingers became sure and strong as they pounded out the chords to "All the Things That You Are." Emma gazed down at Frankie when she sang, not at Jonathan, who sat in his chair, reading while the music fell all around him. Later, when they were older, Frankie would sing, and Ernie always did something funny toward the end, like warbling in falsetto as he came down the stairs wearing something of Emma's. Even Jonathan would laugh about it a little. And Billy would sit and watch, as immobile as Jonathan, wishing desperately that he had something to offer.

But Frankie was good at guessing his moods, and he would break into Charlie Barnet's "Cherokee," which became a kind of code. Because later they would find a way past the minefield of the adults' attention and Ernie's pranks and steal some time in one of the empty cabins. And there, in the dark, with the smell of cold ashes from the Franklin stove and the feather pillows that still held the medicinal scent of mothballs, and the wool blankets that smelled like the rain coming down outside, they would lie down side by side on a single bed. And Billy would wrap his arms around Frankie and breathe in the smell of his neck, the back of his head still damp with sweat. He'd lay his hand across Frankie's chest and feel his heart. Frankie would push his hips back against Billy's, and Billy would press back, his erection stiff against his pants. They'd keep moving this way until, slowly, hard, harder, excruciatingly, he'd come, his breath ragged, black and blowing, on Frankie's neck.

The first time, he pretended nothing had happened.

"You okay?" Frankie asked.

"Ah. Yes. Yeah, I'm okay. You?" was all he managed to say.

The next time it was much the same. But after he came he said, "That felt good."

"Yeah?" asked Frankie, his voice catching in his throat.

"Yes. Here, turn over. Turn over, okay?"

He helped Frankie lie on his back. Frankie didn't know what to do with his hands, so he folded them on his chest like a corpse. He didn't say anything, just breathed in and out excitedly while Billy unbuttoned his fly and pulled down Frankie's pants and underwear. He was hard. Billy took him in his fist, his hand moving up and down slowly. He was surprised at how long and thin and pink Frankie's was, but why was that a surprise? His dick more or less matched the rest of him. He looked on with wonder and a kind of pride in having made Frankie that hard, in making him suck in his breath and arch his back. After just a few strokes, no more than twenty, Frankie suddenly went rigid and said, "Watch out!" and he came in great looping spurts all over his own chest.

"Wow, Billy," Frankie managed to say eventually. And then they'd started to wonder—what to do? What to clean up with? This distracted them from their embarrassment, and they used Billy's socks, which they buried under the ashes in the stove.

Nights like this couldn't have been given to them more than, what, three or four times at most. It was enough. Enough then. But now?

He'd do it differently now.

Billy leaned over and took the jar from Prudence, uncapped it and took a sip. "What's he make his booze out of anyway?"

Prudence stirred. "I don't know. Potatoes, maybe. Corn? Who cares." She sat up straighter and gathered her hair behind her head. The truck's headlights shone out over the river.

"You go across much?" asked Billy.

"What do you think?"

"You ever see old Felix?"

"Not unless he comes to town."

Prudence put her feet up on the dash and let her hair fall back around her shoulders.

The truck's lights picked up the weeds and brush around the old camp. After the war, men from the village came and rolled up the fencing and removed the fence posts. The buildings were moved, one by one, over the ice on skids to a resort nearer the village. All that was left were the poured-cement pads where the bunkhouses and cookhouse and assembly building had been.

Billy turned off the lights. Across the river, the big house glowed faintly in the moonlight, like a bone tossed up on the shore. A single light shone from the boathouse.

"Old Felix has got the place to himself."

"He can have it," said Prudence. "He can have the whole goddamn thing."

"He ain't so bad, Prudy."

"Isn't he?"

"No. I don't know."

When Billy still worked at the mill, Felix had come in for this or that. He'd sort through the rough cut in that careful way of his, as if the boards had to be perfect, even though the Pines was falling into the ground and Emma and Jonathan weren't ever coming back. But Felix kept the place up anyway. Maybe it was habit. Every fall he turned the rowboat over on a tamarack crib well above the river. The Chris-Craft he winched up into the boathouse, using a come-along. He closed the shutters of the main house and made sure the cabins were shuttered and locked, too. He raked the dead leaves away from the foundation of the big house and burned them in a pile in the fire pit. And every spring he did everything in reverse. Sometimes, in the summer, Billy saw him fishing from the rowboat in the mouth of the river. In the winter he lay on the ice and decoyed muskie under a blanket in the old fashion. Once in a while, if a chore was too big for him, he called Billy, and Billy came out to the Pines. The same trees sawing in the wind. The same dock. The same cattails along the riverbank where he once killed a duck with a rock and made Frankie fall in love with him. Everything the same. But everything different. Billy couldn't look at him. Felix had killed men. He was a killer of men and so he knew too much.

He watched Prudence drink from the jar and wipe her mouth again. She wiggled her knees and brought one close to her face to inspect it. The imprint of her splayed toes was held in an outline of fog against the windshield for a minute before fading. She thought everything was as it seemed to her—Frankie's necklace, this silver one with the heart, proof of his love—as much of a fact as Felix's kindness.

Gephardt's vodka was doing its work. Billy's head was swimming. "What makes you so sure about everything, Prudy?"

Billy reached out toward the necklace. "Let me see that," he said. Prudence leaned toward Billy obligingly. The necklace dangled toward him. He held it between his fingers.

"They sell necklaces like that at J. C. Penney, you know. I was just there."

"Yeah? This one came from England," she said, and as though just saying the words exhausted her, she leaned her head on Billy's shoulder. It hurt but he didn't say anything.

"If you say so. But they got them in Grand Rapids."

"Not ones from him. Not necklaces from Frankie."

But Frankie would never send a necklace like that—so tacky, so clear that it was. And not to someone like Prudence. Why couldn't she see that? No one who sent books like the ones Frankie sent Billy, no one with that depth of feeling, could send something so tinny to someone like her. It was all so obvious. It was more like the version of Frankie who existed in Prudence's mind who had sent it, not the real Frankie. Not the Frankie whom Billy knew better than anyone else did.

Billy let the necklace drop back into its nest on Prudence's chest. He took her right hand with his left and pulled her up, mostly to relieve his shoulder. She knew all the moves, though, so there was nothing awkward about how she turned her hips and slid her right knee across his lap until she was sitting on his lap facing him, her head in his neck, her small breasts level with his chin, her arms around his shoulders. Her hip bumped the steering wheel and Billy slid the two of them over to the middle of the bench seat. He shifted his weight again and reached with his left hand and freed the packages from underneath him and pushed them over on the driver's side of the seat. Her dress was still wet and the skin on her arms was clammy.

"Aren't you cold?"

"Okay," she murmured, and then, as though conceding some point on the very far side of a long argument, "all right." Prudence leaned back and reached over her shoulders and undid the clasp at the top of her zipper, then she dropped her arms and brought them behind her back to unzip it, the way boys did when they asked you to guess what was in their hands. She crossed her arms in front of her, grasped the opposite sides of the dress, and pulled it up and over her head. Her white underthings glowed mutely against her skin; three moths, two perched over her tits, one over her pussy. She leaned forward and put her head on his shoulder. He shifted uncomfortably and she switched to the other shoulder. He looked down but didn't like the look of her underwear; so unnatural, so rude and obvious against her dark skin. Not like a moth. More like a bandage, maybe. He looked away, over her shoulder, past the windshield and over the river to where the Pines stood as expectantly as ever.

That's how it seemed. Waitful. It was waiting for him and Frankie—waiting for a time when Emma no longer came up and Jonathan had forgotten about it. Then it would be theirs. It belonged to them. It felt that way to Billy even though he'd never heard from Frankie after that day. No letters. No telegrams. No necklaces, that's for shit sure. Nothing at all. From Felix, Billy had heard about Frankie getting shot down over Aachen, just before Christmas 1944. He might have died when the plane exploded or he might have been able to bail out. If he had bailed out, he hadn't made it.

"Are we going to get this over with or what?" asked Prudence.

Having taken the first steps in the dull sequence, there seemed no reason not to finish the dance. Billy reached down and began to unbutton his pants.

"Here," she said, not unkindly, and she lifted herself off him and lay back on the bench seat with her head by the door. She pulled her knees to her chest and slipped off her underwear and put them on the floor of the truck. She picked at her knee again before extending her legs and placing them on either side of his thighs. With the glaring underwear gone, so bright and crude, it was as though the lights had been turned off and the outer dark had finally crept inside the truck, where it belonged. Billy slid his own pants and underwear down around his ankles in one motion, as if he were skinning a rat.

He felt foolish, vulnerable, with just his shirt on, and he started to unbutton it, but Prudence reached for him blindly and pulled him on top of her before he could finish. He registered, dimly, that she didn't want there to be too much distance between them—not so that he wouldn't see her nakedness, but so she wouldn't have to see his. Or maybe that was the only way she knew to do it.

He pressed himself into her and felt her hip bones grind against his, and he tried to raise himself up on his arms but couldn't manage it with his shoulder. She didn't notice. Her eyes were shut and she reached for him and stroked him a few times, to no effect.

He sat back up and Prudence sat up with him. That was better. He breathed deeply as she straddled him. She took him in her hand and, leaning forward, rubbed him back and forth a few times on her crease, as though buttering a cob of corn. With her eyes closed, she fit him inside her and flapped her hand in the air to dry it before draping both hands over his shoulders. Her parts felt swollen and a little shallow.

He wrapped his arms around her—her rib cage so narrow and her breasts so small—and moved when she moved. But he was far away, and drunk as she was, Prudence sensed it. She slowed her pace, the movement of her hips grew smaller, more disinterested. Billy took her face in his hands and she reared back in surprise. But gently he brought her face down toward his, parting her lips with his tongue. He kissed her neck, the way one dog nuzzled another, then raised his face and kissed her again. Prudence sucked in her breath, taking some of his with hers. His mouth suddenly felt cool. Her hips settled lower on his and he felt her knees squeeze tighter on either side of his buttocks. She pushed the tip of her tongue inside his mouth and he was surprised at how small it was.

It was his turn to pull back and study her face. All along he had thought of her as familiar. Not a friend, certainly. Not that. But wrapped up so closely with Frankie, so much a part of the same thoughts over the past ten years, as to be familiar. But she was not. She was a stranger to him.

"Oh, Billy," she said. "Oh, Billy, what are you doing?"

He didn't answer. Instead he moved his lips down her neck and took her nipple in his mouth. It was as hard and brown and small as his. He felt the heart necklace cold against his cheek. After a moment he left the nipple alone and proceeded to the next. But the cold metal of the necklace left some trace, some mark, on his desire. He took the heart in his mouth and bent her face down toward his again, and this time, when their lips met, he passed the little piece of metal into her mouth.

"I'm just doing my part, Prudy."

Prudence let the necklace drop and bent her head closer to his, and he could feel her hair falling around his face.

He'd done his part eventually, though it wasn't the part he thought he was going to play. For one, he thought there'd be some sense to it, some logic. But from the moment the landing-craft door clanked down on D-Day+1, he'd felt he was a bit player in a drama of overwhelming scale. Nothing had prepared him for the constant, hollow thumping of the mortars, the ripping of German artillery, the planes constantly overhead, the rumble of armor on the narrow roads. Nothing had prepared him for the sight of those French towns, skeletonized by their own aircraft and artillery, or for the stench of rotting cattle and horses. Nothing had prepared him for the ceaseless, numbing thunder of the bombs that fell on Brest for thirty-nine days until the men took it.

By the time the 2nd Division crossed into Germany, he was convinced he had seen it all, had felt it all, and that he and the other infantrymen were a walking joke. His .30 carbine wasn't even powerful enough to stop a deer. Thus far his role had been to walk and dig and cower and run forward and dig and cower some more. When the 88s hit them, they dropped into their foxholes and fortifications and waited till it was over. But things changed in the Ardennes. After pushing them back into the Belgian forest, the Germans began timing their shells to burst at tree level. Whereas before they could count on luck in their foxholes, now the explosions shredded the trees and sent kindling-sized splinters of wood flying down at them. But the wood didn't usually rain straight down. And so when they heard the shells coming, Billy and his squad jumped from their foxholes and ran to the nearest trees and hugged the boles, their eyes shut tight. They shut their eyes and waited, in the cold thunder, for luck and the trees to carry them through.

By Christmas 1944, fewer American planes were flying over Belgium. The air war had largely been won. There were no more German factories to bomb. Sometimes, though, a squadron of P-47s would dive out of the sky, or a box formation of B-17s and Liberators would pass high above them. He couldn't help but wonder if Frankie was in one of them and could see him down there. But would Frankie even recognize him anymore?

Before his unit had pushed into Germany in December, they'd had a week of rest at Vielsalm, twenty miles from the border. It was September, and the weather had not yet turned cold. He and his unit had been moving and fighting steadily since June 7; 114 days they had crawled and walked and crouched across France and Belgium. But in Vielsalm, at last, they had a week of rest.

They bivouacked in the hunting château of some Belgian lord or count of whatever it was they had for rich people over there. The château had been occupied by the Germans, but they must have liked it, because the place was clean and well cared for when Billy's company took it over. He unrolled his blanket in a room on the second story.

The village itself, unlike most of the villages Billy had fought in and marched through, had as yet been spared bombing and artillery fire. It was not much bigger than Billy's own village. The Church of Saint-Gengoux still rose next to the lakeshore. The village center, small as it was, stretched along the curved shore of the lake. The houses, made of dark local stone, stood shoulder to shoulder. But it was as if the village had been hollowed out like a pumpkin. There was nothing in it—no clothes in the shops, no coffee or tea in the cafés. No butter, bread, chocolate, chickens, horses, cows, hats, gasoline, cooking oil, rubber. Even with all the trees surrounding the village, there was a shortage of lumber, because the lumber mill had no fuel with which to run the saws, and the Germans had taken the blades away during the occupation. More strikingly, there were no young men except for the soldiers of the 2nd Division, whose shoulder patch—the Indian Head Star and motto "Second to None"—seemed to awe the villagers in a way that their gaunt bodies didn't.

Van Winckle and Billy forced themselves to walk slowly down the main road that ran parallel to the lake, so that they didn't exhaust the sights too soon. They had reached the middle of the village when a middle-aged man—bald except for a fringe of hair—stood up from the chair he was sitting on outside a shop. He shook their hands and spoke to them in Walloon. He pointed down at their feet and spoke again, this time in French, then pointed up at the painted wooden sign hanging above their heads, which depicted the outline of a shoe. When he pointed down at their feet again, they looked. The leather of their Type II Roughouts was cracked across the toe box, and the stitches holding the rubber soles to the uppers had been worn and broken through, so that gaps opened with each step.

The man pointed at their boots again, then at the sign, then jabbed himself in the chest with his finger. He stepped to the side and swept them into his shop with one hand as he held the door open with the other. He motioned them toward two chairs. Not wanting to offend the old man, they sat down, ill at ease with their M1s across their laps. Billy set his behind his chair and Van Winckle did the same. The cobbler scurried behind the counter and came back with a short wooden stool. He planted it in front of Billy and sat down. He raised both hands in front of them and, with a flourish like that of a casino dealer, turned them front to back to show that they were indeed empty, smiling broadly. Billy smiled back. The funny gesture put him at ease, because it reflected some understanding of what Billy had been through in the preceding 114 days. The man hitched up his sleeves and delicately, without touching Billy's skin, unbuckled and unlaced the boots. He did the same for Van Winckle. Then he took each pair of boots in his hands, bowed as though he were handling religious relics, and retreated to his work area behind the counter.

With a hooked awl, he first pulled out the rotten cord that held the soles on, and then ran a knife between the leather and the rubber, separating them. He lifted a section of the floorboards and reached in blindly, seeing with his hands, while smiling at Billy and Van Winckle. When he righted himself he was holding up a sheet of heavy leather. He pointed east and shook his finger as if to say "no, no, no," then held the finger to his lips. He placed the soles of their boots on the leather and scribed their outline with a curved knife, then with firm, expert pressure, he pieced out the leather. He reached under the counter and extracted a thick square of boiled wool felt from which he cut foot beds, using the leather insole as a pattern. Billy and Van Winckle, in their bare feet, watched him work, flexing their toes against the floorboards, enjoying the feeling of air on their skin. The old man opened a can of adhesive and secured the bottoms, then fitted them to the uppers, and finally, using a treadle machine, stitched the boots back together. He carried them back out to Billy and Van Winckle and motioned for them to try them on. They fit perfectly, and the felt insole provided what seemed like an extravagant amount of cushion. As a final gesture, the old man greased the boots with neat's-foot oil. He clapped his hands again and flipped them—palm and back—to show that he was done. Billy and Van Winckle moved to pay him, but the old man protested in French. So Billy reached into his pocket and handed over a pack of Luckies, and Van Winckle did the same. Then, bowing, he saw them out.

Out on the street, Billy and Van Winckle looked at each other. "Goddamn," was all Van Winckle could manage. Billy said nothing. They had nowhere to go in their refurbished boots except back up the hill to the château, where Van Winckle couldn't stop talking about his boots, describing in detail what the old cobbler had done and marveling that he didn't want any money. Still Billy said nothing. He suddenly couldn't stand the sound of Van Winckle's voice, the metallic twang of it. He got up from his bedroll and wandered out of the château through the kitchen, past the carriage house, and up the hill to the spruce that grew straight and true behind it.

These trees were much bigger than the spruce back home, and straighter. A few hundred yards in, the trees opened up, and he saw a small cottage tucked between them. It was dark. He put his thumb on his shoulder under the sling of his M1, but it wasn't there. He'd left it by his bedroll in the château. He panicked for a moment. He patted his pockets as if something in them would provide a secondary line of defense. He listened. The wind raked through the pines. One of the shutters of the cottage banged in the wind.

The cottage was small compared to the château, but it was bigger than all the shacks in Billy's village. It was made out of the same dark slate as the rest of the buildings. The windows were framed with rough-hewn spruce logs, and the rafters were squared spruce as well. Billy could see adze marks on their faces. The door was secured by a strong iron hasp and padlock. He tried the shutters on the window to the right of the door, but they were barred from the inside. He moved off the steps and tried the window to the left. The wooden bar was rotted and he was able to open them. The leaded-glass window was filthy, and he rubbed his sleeve on the glass and cupped his hands and peered in.

The stone interior was plastered over and whitewashed above walnut wainscoting. Opposite the door was a massive split-stone fireplace with a metal grate on a swivel pulled to the side. There was a low table of dark wood in front of the fireplace, surrounded by wooden chairs with wickerwork seats and backs. The chimney was almost black with soot, and behind it, above empty pegs, Billy saw the outlines of three guns painted in soot, as though the ghosts of the guns rested there. On either side of the fireplace were deep bookshelves filled with leather-bound books. Both of the far walls were covered to the wainscoting with prints of stags, boars, and birds in flight.

A plane droned overhead. Billy rested his forehead against the glass. Frankie hadn't listened to him. After Ernie saw them kissing, he'd said, "Goddamn Indians," and stalked off into the woods, and Billy had run after him. He should have taken the Winchester from Frankie then, before anything could happen. He'd known they weren't going to find any German out there. They weren't going to find anything.

What if Frankie had listened to him? "Wait for me, Frankie. Wait." And he did. He turned to face Billy, the Winchester drooping. "What is it?" "Just wait, okay?" And in two steps Billy was there, by his side. He took the gun out of Frankie's hand and raised his own and held it against Frankie's face. Frankie closed his eyes and his lashes brushed away Ernie's incredulous sneer and Felix's stoic, comprehending gaze. And they turned away from the deeper brush and blowdown because there was nothing to see there, nothing waiting for them there. Instead they turned back toward the Pines and walked up the steps to the stone cottage.

The door was unlocked and when Billy pushed it open and stepped in, still holding Frankie by the hand. A fire in the stone fireplace greeted them, radiating heat. They shucked their jackets and hung them from the rack next to the door. They removed their boots. Frankie dropped into one of the chairs near the fire while Billy hung the Winchester on the pegs and then sat down next to him. The books were funny in their old-fashioned way, so sure of their own authority. Frankie filled the teakettle from a pail of water, his gestures sure and precise, and Billy put it on the hob and swung it over the flames. After they had their tea they moved to the couch. Frankie wasn't tired, not at all, but Billy was. And so he did something he'd never dared before. He stretched out with his head in Frankie's lap. He closed his eyes against the bright glow of the fire. Frankie rested his elbow on the couch arm and read a book. His left hand rested on Billy's forehead and he absentmindedly stroked his hair. They had nothing to hide, nothing to worry about. Occasionally Frankie lifted his hand to turn the pages of the book, and Billy's forehead felt the heat of the fire until it returned. And then the hand drifted down to his chest, and his stomach, and lower still. Frankie lay down next to Billy. They had nothing to hide because no one could see. There was no rush. There was no rush this time, and it was Billy who was being held and Frankie who was doing the holding.

They had all the time in the world. So they stood and took off their clothes and lay back down again. Billy closed his eyes against the utter shock of having Frankie's full length pressed against his legs, his back. How perfect, how acceptable, it was to feel Frankie's skin against his, and what a surprise it was to feel how cold the front of Frankie's thighs were, and how warm his groin. He felt Frankie's erection pressing against him and he reached back and brought it between his legs so that it rested against his own, which was now in Frankie's hand. They had all the time in the world, and they'd use every blessed minute of it. Frankie tasted him. And he tasted Frankie back. They had all the time in the world.

Billy's mind's eye retreated until the two of them were framed by the window. Then he moved farther back still, and up, until the boys inside the cottage and the window itself were framed by the trees. Higher and higher in the sky he went, until he lost sight of them, and the firelight was a glow, a smear, then gone altogether. The slate-shingled roof was lost among the branches. At last there was only a wisp of smoke, which might have been from the chimney or, from that height, might have been from the fires of war burning brighter all around them in the dark.

Billy fit his hands in the grooves of Prudence's ribs and helped her move. His orgasm, which had felt a long way off—and was made even more notional by the whiskey and vodka—arrived suddenly, unannounced. He kept going on empty for another half minute, the way a heart-shot deer would keep running till it died. Prudence leaned back and looked at him, still galloping along on top of him, but then she slowed and stopped. His erection melted. Prudence coughed and his penis gushed out, along with a rush of semen.

"I came inside you," said Billy apologetically.

"Don't sweat it, Billy Cochran."

"I mean—"

Prudence rolled her eyes and shook her head.

She cupped her mound with her left hand and dismounted. She found the door handle with her right hand and stepped out of the truck. She squatted down and peed on the ground, her upper arms resting on her knees.

"You're a peach, Billy."

She picked something out from between her teeth with her fingers, stood, and slid back into the truck. She bent forward and rummaged on the floor of the truck for her purse. Billy could see the knobs of her spine. She sat straight and put her feet back on the dash and lit a cigarette. She stared out the windshield across the river.

He reached down and pulled up his pants, lifted his hips off the slick seat and brought them all the way on, and buttoned them and renotched his belt. He couldn't look at her.

"I didn't do it."

"Feels to me like you just did."

"No, Prudy. I mean, I didn't shoot her."

"You don't know what you're talking about, Billy Cochran."

"I was there. I was standing there. Right next to him."

"I know it. I was there, too."

"Frankie's the one who did it."

Prudence didn't look at him. She took another drag on her cigarette and looked at it as though it might tell her something before ashing out the window. He could feel her mind working.

"You were there."

"Yeah. Yeah, I was there."

He still was. Still there. Forever there. Forever walking fast after Frankie after Ernie and David and Felix had seen them kiss. The branch slapping to a standstill like the ticking of a radiator. The goddamn heat bearing down on them. The lazy sound of deerflies. And Frankie just ahead of him. "Stop, Frankie. Wait, Frankie. Just wait." He'd said that and Frankie had stopped. And he'd waited until Billy caught up. Very little sun came through the canopy. There was no wind, not a lick of it. Nothing. Frankie's hair was damp at his temples and he bit his lip.

"Just calm down, Frankie. We can circle around the back." That's all they had to do. They could just take the long way around and avoid Ernie. Felix wouldn't say anything. Davey Gardner was scared of his own shadow. And who would he tell? A mosquito landed on Billy's arm and he pinched it between his finger and thumb. It was so dripping hot, even the mosquitoes were slowing down. He reached out for Frankie's arm. Frankie waved his hand away. "Hear that?" He bent forward and peered into a blowdown in front of them. Something stirred deep in the branches. "Hear that?"

Frankie raised the gun. "Watch me," he said. Just the way Billy used to when he shot at squirrels high in the trees. Just the way he had said it when he killed that duck that first day long ago. Billy reached out and said, "Stop," but Frankie fired at the same time. Billy's ears rang. He wasn't ready for the sound. The forest absorbed it. But then, a second later, they heard something thrashing in the brush. Frankie turned toward Billy, smiling.

"You see? You see that? I got him! I got him! That's what a man does, Billy. I can't believe it. I got him." Billy took the gun from him. Frankie's hands were shaking and he fumbled for his cigarettes. "I can't believe it," he said. "Lucky or what, kid?" he said. But they'd never been lucky again.

"I was right next to him, Prudy. Next to Frankie, I mean. He's the one who did it, Prudy. I'm telling you. He was the one who did it. He wanted to get the Kraut. He wouldn't let anyone else carry the gun." Billy was crying.

"I'm tired, Billy."

"You didn't know him. You were only around him for those two days."

"You were the one holding the gun when Felix pulled me out of there."

"I took it from him, Prudy. I took it. He couldn't even hold it anymore."

"So what? But it was you. You were holding it. I saw you holding it," she said. "I saw you."

She looked very small and lost, pressed against the door across the seat from him. She seemed miles away.

"But no one told me. No one told me that."

"I'm telling you."

"I want you to stop, Billy. I just want you to stop telling me."

"You should know. It was him that did it. I'm telling you."

"And I'm telling you I'm tired. And I'm telling you I want to go. I need to go home. Let's go."

"Prudy."

"Just stop talking, Billy, and start driving. Please start driving." She drummed her feet on the floor.

Billy slid behind the wheel and moved the packages back to the middle of the bench seat.

Prudence retracted her feet and hugged her knees.

He started the truck and the sound of it was loud in his ears.

When they reached the blacktop, Prudence dropped the rest of her cigarette out the window and curled up, facing away from Billy.

"Here," said Billy, pushing the package across the seat. "You can put this on. It's new. It's brand new."

Prudence reached behind her and felt around on the seat for the package. She found it and dragged it across her hips and clutched it to her chest. Billy couldn't see her face. She stayed that way till they pulled up in front of the Wigwam. Then she gathered her things—dress, underwear, bra, purse, and the package containing the dress Billy had bought at J. C. Penney for Stella—and got out of the truck, clutching them to her chest. She turned and kicked the door shut with her bare foot, then leaned her face in the open window.

"You know what, Billy?" Her teeth were clenched and she hissed the words. "You know what? You ain't my type. You ain't even my type at all."

With that she turned and walked around the side of the Wigwam and disappeared from view.

TWELVE

THE RESERVATION—AUGUST 3, 1952

The stranger knocked on the door just after noon, sweating into his black clothes. He held his black hat in one hand, a small suitcase at his feet and a soda bottle in the other, and his lank hair stuck to his scalp. He was small, with narrow shoulders, and his suit was much too big. His eyes were dark and deep-set, framed by gold-rimmed glasses. His jaw was narrow and pointy, and his mouth was very small. He was nervous, even Mary could see that. She peered out past his shoulder to confirm that there was no car—she'd been out back hanging laundry and hadn't heard one. He must have walked from town. She looked down at his shoes. They were like the black shoes the men wore to church, with leather soles. The tops were covered in road dust.

She used to walk all the way from her parents' camp into the village and back, once a week. Six miles one way. What looked like easy walking could be hard if you weren't dressed for the heat. And her short leg—the one they said would catch up to the other but never did—ground into her hip with each step and made walking painful and difficult. Even as a young girl, by the time she'd made it to town, she was tired, a slow coal burning in her hip. But she'd have to load up her pack with flour and soda and whatever else they needed and walk back. Later, when she was a teenager, she worked in the kitchen at the Pines, and that had been hard, too: a long walk from town, the river crossing, and then all that cleaning, scrubbing, sweeping.

Now she was married. No one thought she'd ever get a husband, and they said as much. At best you'll find some drunk half-breed, they'd said, but most likely not even that. But she had found Gephardt, or he had found her. They found each other. Together they proved everyone wrong. How many times had she seen him at the camp without actually seeing him? How many times had she limped by on the other side of the fence? She searched her mind but had no recollection of him, not until after the war. He had decided to stay on when the rest of them were sent back to Germany. She first encountered him in the spring of 1946, when he saw her in the store and helped her carry her things back to her parents' sugar bush. Mary liked to think that he stayed for her. He had chosen her, though. He had chosen her and she had chosen him when everyone in the village had nothing good to say about her, but she had succeeded.

Now that she was married, she made her shopping list at her table, and then she tied on her scarf to keep her hair down in the truck, and Gephardt drove her and she didn't have to walk. Her husband. Hers. Her house. Her wash. Her kitchen. Her stove. It was all hers. She had proved them all wrong, and she was not above being a little prideful about it.

She was still shy. She hid her shopping list face-side against her aproned belly because only she understood her pencil marks, little symbols that weren't real words, not like the ones the girls who had gone to boarding school knew how to make. Oh, you're real old-time, the others would sneer. Why even use real paper, they'd ask. Why even use your hand or a pencil? You should just bite down on birch bark and make your list that way. Mary had wanted to go to school far away in the prairies in Flandreau like many of the other girls. But not even the missionaries or the agent or the superintendent at the school would have her. When she went to church as a girl, the priest didn't seem to care one way or another about her salvation. And why? Because one leg was shorter than the other? Because she wasn't pretty like the other girls? What kind of God had men like that working for him? The pastor at Trinity Lutheran in Deer River was always nice to her, almost as nice as Gephardt, whose arm she held as she climbed the steps to the church.

She wished she knew more English, though, more than the little she had to do her shopping and trading. When the stranger stood at the door and said, "I have come," his accent was so thick she couldn't follow along, and she wished she understood more. "I have come for him," he said again, and of course Mary knew that he was speaking of Gephardt. She smiled and motioned the stranger into the kitchen, and then motioned for him to sit. She held a jar under the pump and filled it with water and set it on the table. Once the stranger was seated, she went out to the shed to get Gephardt. Gephardt was so creative. He'd found a way to run a line in the house so she didn't have to pump water in the yard, which was a terrible chore in the winter, with her leg the way it was. Hard work. But with him, the hard work wasn't quite so hard as it used to be.

Gephardt was in the shed patching a canoe. She told him there was someone to see him, and he put his things down and walked past her. She turned and followed him. He opened the screen door and stopped just inside. The stranger sat at the table with the water in front of him, untouched. They stared at each other. Both afraid. Both tense. Mary wasn't sure Gephardt wanted to sit down. It was so unlike him. Lots of people came to the house. Gephardt's skills were in demand. He could make anything, really anything, out of metal. Rice threshers, saws, spuds. He had a still and made liquor out of potatoes. Who else knew how to do that? People were always coming by, especially for a jar of "Gephardt's," which is what they had come to call it. Since he couldn't always understand them very well, he made big gestures with his hands and smiled at them a lot. He served them coffee and didn't mind when they sat in the shed and watched him work, even when they drank. Once a couple of breeds from over across the line had fallen asleep while they were waiting for Gephardt to finish welding the seams of a syrup pan, and he didn't even wake them. He threw some blankets over them and let them sleep in the shed. In the morning Mary came out with biscuits and yesterday's coffee and set them on the packed earth of the shed floor. She stood over them until they stirred and since she knew the type—she knew they'd take whatever they could and wouldn't think twice about it—she said: "Eat. And then out." And she added: *"Maajaayok akawe. Giishpin igo maajaasiweg giga-basidiyeshkooninim."* Just so they'd know she wasn't joking. Gephardt was so kind, so generous, that he'd get taken advantage of if she wasn't there. But that's how it always was, wasn't it?

Gephardt wasn't so easygoing with the stranger in the kitchen. He didn't even look like he'd sit down with the man. The man didn't look like he wanted Gephardt to sit down, either. Then he reached in his pocket and took out a pistol and pointed it at Gephardt.

It couldn't be bigger than a .22. They had one, too, and it was barely strong enough to put down the pigs. Sometimes even holding it against their skulls didn't do it, and she had to shoot again.

Gephardt raised his hands like a crook in a movie and sat down.

Once the men faced each other across the table, the stranger spoke to Gephardt in German. Gephardt nodded slowly, his eyes on the stranger.

"We are in America now. I speak English now."

The stranger said something and he grew angry, and Gephardt said something back to him in the language of his country.

All the prisoners at the camp had spoken that language. During the summers she'd walked past the camp and seen them inside. One had even escaped, but he had drowned in the river. She'd seen them in the winter, too, when the Pines was closed, walking in long lines out into the tamarack swamps south of the village to cut timber. She saw them laying the corduroy and heard them singing while they worked. She didn't know what they had done. She didn't know if they were warriors or just men who got caught up in war. They were hard workers and they were cheerful, too. Nothing like the old men she knew when she was a girl—old men who had fought the Dakota and still carried scalps they'd taken and hidden from the Americans. Those old men had brought out those scalps at the drum dances back when her family still went to the dances. At the ceremonies they recounted how they'd come by the scalps—how they'd shot or stabbed or bludgeoned the enemy and then cut off his scalp. The belt man at the dance, Felix, was the most fearsome of them all. When he danced the belt, he held his war club high. Mary was just a girl and was made to sit off to the side. Her parents told her not to look at Felix, not to say anything to him. She stole looks out from under her scarf and thought she could see blood on his war club. He held it up in the air over his head when they checked the drum. It was still dirty with blood after all those years, though he certainly couldn't have used *that* in the war. When she saw him at the Pines, working on the dock or painting the house or cutting the grass, he didn't seem so fierce. Not as fierce as he did when he danced the belt or spoke for his songs. For each feather, he recounted a kill he had made in the Great War. It took a long time. There were seventeen feathers on the belt.

Gephardt was nothing like that. He laughed and sang and he worked hard, and she was sure he'd never touched blood, even though he was one of the enemy. He had wanted to stay. He liked the woods, he said. He liked the cold. He liked her. It was possible, but no: Gephardt had not touched blood. Mary knew men who had, like Felix, and he was not like them. Not like them at all.

The stranger said something to Gephardt and he shook his head. He shook his head and scowled and spoke. The stranger said something else. Gephardt raised his hands and held them up so the stranger could see. The stranger sat back and picked up the gun. He shook his head and then he looked at Mary.

"He is not who he says he is," said the stranger. He said it twice before Mary understood what he meant. "He is not who he says he is."

"He is my husband," said Mary as best she could. "He is my husband in the church."

"He is a bad man," said the stranger. "Bad things he has done."

"No," said Gephardt. "No bad man. I make things. I fix things."

A bad man. Could it be? Could a bad man have chosen her? Was that all she could hope for? Had the other girls been right?

The stranger ignored Gephardt. He kept looking at Mary. Finally he turned and spoke to Gephardt in their language again. He went on for a few minutes. While he spoke, Gephardt kept shaking his head, and once he hit the table with his fist.

"We are in America now. All that is over. We speak English now."

"My English is good. Better than yours," said the stranger. "But we don't speak it. We speak so you can understand. I speak so you understand."

"I am married. Speak for she to understand."

The stranger looked at Mary.

"I, too, was married. I have children. I tell you about your husband. What kind of man he is."

Mary narrowed her eyes. What kind of man he is? One who works. That's who. All he does is work. He spends nothing. He works and they save. The farm that had broken the Norwegians who moved there first makes a life for them. The fields were bad. Rocky and sandy. But they made the fields work for them. Gephardt was good with his hands, and if there was a job, he did it. They had a pig and chickens. Gephardt has made a small mill and cuts lumber. The roof didn't leak and the walls were packed with rock wool. The cellar dug into the side of the hill was braced and solid and cool and lined with canned pork and beans and berries. And he had, the year before, built a parcher and parched rice. Now it was only the old-timers or the very poorest who dug pits in their yards and danced their rice and ate their meager harvest full of chaff and hulls. The rest brought their rice to Gephardt, and he parched it and threshed it with his machines, and it was fine rice. He never burned it. And it never broke. Long, tan grains of rice—none of them popped. No hulls floated to the top of their pans when he finished it.

And this man, this stranger. Who was he? Who was he to come here and tell her about her husband? Gephardt took care of her. He didn't mind that when they walked through town he was a block, sometimes two, ahead of her, stomping through his errands at full speed while she lagged behind. He didn't mind and he didn't make jokes about her. He never teased her about her leg. He had even cut a block of wood and fashioned it just so and attached it to her shoe so her legs would be the same length. That's who he was.

And she worked, too. Their bedding was clean and ironed. Their pots shone. None of her canning popped in the summer. She knew Gephardt. She knew the man was better than anyone. No stranger could tell her what he was, she could see it in his life. He had chosen her when no one else would, and that meant a lot to a person—even to someone lame and marked for work and who would never bear a child.

"I speak so she understands," said the stranger. "He is not who he says he is. He is from my town, my city. You understand? We know each other."

Her hip hurt. She leaned against the sink and narrowed her eyes, trying to catch the words that flew by. They knew each other. They were from the same country. This much Mary caught, but the rest was lost. She squinted and stared at the stranger. It was the look that took over her face when she was trying to understand what people were saying. They thought she looked that way because she was mean. The kids joked that she was a witch. They were scared of her.

Gephardt scowled. Shook his head. "I know him not. I know not this man here." He gestured at the stranger across the table, his water untouched, his sweat drying on his brow.

The stranger ignored him. He spoke to Mary but he looked at Gephardt while he spoke.

"He is from my town, see? In the war we hide. I hide. My wife. My children. But this man"—he pointed at Gephardt—"he tells them where to find us. He tells them. Now I have no wife. I have no children."

Gephardt half stood. "*Nein, nein, nein*. No, no! I say nothing. I don't know you. I never see you."

"Your name is Gephardt Miller."

"Yes. No. I am not that man." He sat down. His face was crunched and concerned. "I am not that man."

Mary couldn't pronounce his name. Miller. Her name now, too. But she didn't need to. She was thirty-five years old. She'd lived with her parents until she was twenty-five and then her aunt after that. All that time—all those long years—she'd lived in shacks covered in tar paper, under roofs covered only in tar paper. She'd endured the damp summers and dry, cold winters as everyone did. She'd never felt the thrill of milled lumber under her feet except at the store, church, or post office. It never occurred to her that it was ridiculous to live in a shack with dirt floors, and to sweep them every day. Cleaning dirt. That had been her life until Gephardt, sweeping dirt on dirt. But then Gephardt had come up to her in the store and talked to her, or tried to. She bowed her head. She couldn't understand anything he said. She looked at her hands. But Gephardt smiled and gestured and smiled some more. He took the rice sack full of groceries from her hands and helped her carry the flour and the pound of nails back to her family's sugar bush. Her parents offered him tea. He held the tin cup on his lap and smiled. He came back to the sugar bush until they closed it down. He found her through the spring and summer—at fish camp and picking berries. Always her parents offered him tea. Always he accepted. Sometimes he brought them gifts. Yards of cotton twill. A pound of salt. A roll of tar paper. They were married in the fall and moved into Gephardt's cabin southwest of the village, just off the highway. She was happy. She took great pleasure in sweeping the wood floors of their cabin. She scooted the dirt into a pan and threw the dust and hair and wood chips inside the cookstove, where they crackled away into nothing. No more sweeping the dirt off a dirt floor. And so it didn't matter that she couldn't say his last name, her own last name, the *l*'s a sound she couldn't get her mouth around. It didn't matter because she had proved them all wrong. She was the one with insulation in her walls. She was the one with a husband she didn't have to pull off the road because he fell down drunk. A husband who never set foot in the Wigwam. He worked hard and he took care of her. And what could they say about that?

"Your husband's name is Gephardt Miller and he is from my city. Before the war. He was there and he was an engineer. He makes things."

It made no sense. The stranger was trying to get her to see something. But there was nothing to see. She saw everything already. Everything she needed to know. Before the war. Well, that was a long time ago. Six years? Ten? Beyond that phrase, Mary had understood nothing the stranger said. Gephardt had told her about the war—how he was in a ship, not a regular one. Not a boat like they had on the big lake. He had been in a ship that went underwater. A submarine. He'd tried to explain it to her but she'd waved away the explanation. White people were always inventing new ways of killing one another. But there were only a few ways, really: burn, drown, cut, shoot, or hit.

The gun still sat on the table, a dull thing. More like a toy. And could this stranger even use it? It was hard to tell with white people.

At the drum dance, when Felix danced his position and spoke, he was clearly a great man, a great warrior. He spoke for each feather on the belt—how he had clubbed three men to death with his rifle, had shot nine, and had stabbed five with his bayonet, all before he turned twenty. When he danced she averted her eyes and looked only at his feet, delicately stamping on the floorboards. With him, it was easy to believe he had done those things, had touched blood, because delicate as his steps were, even dainty, she felt a chill come over her whenever he walked by. But this stranger at their table, in his black suit, with the sweat cooling on his face and the empty soda bottle he must have bought at the Wigwam? It was hard to imagine he could do anything at all to them, not to them and everything they had built together.

Gephardt shook his head again. "I am not that man. I am not him. I know him. He is dead. *Er ist tot.*"

"You have his name."

"I take his name. Yes, I take it. I am not him. I am from Lübeck. I am a welder then. *Jetzt.* I join metal. The man you seek. He is dead. He drown in the river."

The stranger looked at Gephardt steadily. Mary could see he wasn't sure what to believe.

"Look!" said Gephardt and he held up his hands—pocked with scars from working with iron and steel, strong, gripping hands. He wasn't handsome. His legs were bowed, and though his back was broad, one shoulder dipped lower than the other and the muscles of his neck were bunched. In the village they called him "the crab." He couldn't understand them anyway. It didn't matter. They needed him, which was why they said such mean things. "No engineer. He is dead. That one drowned. I take only his name."

What could he mean? Whatever the stranger wanted, Gephardt couldn't give it to him. That was clear to Mary. It should be clear to the stranger. He was looking for a man, but Gephardt wasn't him, so he should just leave. He should leave and leave them alone.

"You try to trick me."

"I am no Göttingener. I am not from there. Gephardt Miller. Yes, he is from there. I am not that man. I am Herman Jünger. I am from Lübeck. That man, he tries to escape. They have a big search but no one finds him. He disappears from them and then they find his body on shore. Half in the water, rotting away. That is Gephardt Miller. I take only his name."

"You are a Nazi!"

"*Kein Nazi. Nein, nein. Kein Nazi.* Politics I don't care. War I don't care. Fighting I don't care. I wanted work. I find work, welding work, on the U-boat. I find work there welding. The Nazis never want me and I never want them."

Mary understood that word. *Nazi.* She'd heard it all during the war years—*Nazi, German, Kraut*—the men who left and the few who came back used these words. They must all mean the same thing. They must just mean the enemy. And who cared about that, anyway? When the fighting was over, it was over. When the blood price had been paid, it was all over. Her grandfather spoke of fighting the Nadisoog. They would stop fighting and be brothers. *Gii-paabiindigaadiwag owiigiwaamiwaang gaa-ishkwaa-miigaadiwaad.*

"It doesn't matter. You helped them. You helped them kill my family."

"I help no one kill."

"You lie." The man hit the table and the gun jumped. The water sloshed in the jar.

"I don't kill anyone for purpose." Gephardt looked meaningfully at Mary. And then down at the table.

"You lie. Now is the time for truth," said the man.

"I kill one man," said Gephardt mournfully. "I kill him before the war, you see. I kill him in Lübeck. It was accident."

That couldn't be true. Could it be? Mary crossed her arms. Her husband was not the man he'd said he was. And he had blood on his hands that no one had washed off. It was still there on his hands. Gephardt turned to Mary.

"I kill a man in a fight. I hit him too hard. Here"—he pushed both hands into the right side of his rib cage—"I hit him here," he explained to Mary and then to the stranger. "It was an accident."

"Liar!"

"It is true. I tell the truth. I tell the truth to you."

"Damn liar!"

"This is why I take his name. I take his name when they want to send us back to Germany. They put me back in prison. I don't go back to prison. I love America. I love freedom. My wife"—he gestured at Mary—"she does what I say. I make this house. I have life."

"You lie. You helped them. I don't care you were in prison. I don't care you join the U-boat from prison. I don't care! You helped them. So you are not Gephardt." The stranger sat lower in his chair. "So you are not him. You still must pay."

The stranger closed his eyes and reached out and took the pistol in his right hand and fired. Gephardt flinched and grabbed his left forearm. He looked in surprise at the small hole that opened up in the muscle.

"You've hit me. I am shot!" he said in surprise.

"I shoot again," said the stranger.

He aimed at Gephardt's face and shot once more. Gephardt's head snapped back.

But then once, twice, Mary hit the stranger in the head with the blunt side of the kindling ax. His chair tipped and he fell on the floor. She tried to hit him again, but he fell against the wall and his chair blocked the way.

Gephardt bent low over the table, his face in his hands. Blood dripped between his fingers and pooled on the oilcloth.

Mary set down the ax and lifted Gephardt's head in her hands. Satisfied, she lowered herself back down to the table and then took his left arm in her hands and looked at it this way and that before setting that down, too. He moaned through clenched teeth but didn't say anything. Mary righted the stranger's chair. Gephardt stayed quiet while Mary dragged the stranger's body away from the table into the middle of the kitchen floor.

"Dead?" asked Gephardt through his hands. His voice sounded strange. Thick.

"Not dead," she said. A pump knot had risen on the back of the stranger's head. He jerked a little, but that was all.

"Will he die? Is he dying?"

Mary shrugged grimly.

She set the metal handle of the ash rake in its socket and tumbled the grate and added some cedar shavings to the firebox. When that was done she opened the damper wide and put water to boil and limped out into the yard. She broke off some red willow growing near the swamp edge and took the shoots back into the house and peeled them and put the peelings in the boiling water.

She approached Gephardt again. He hadn't moved. A large puddle of blood had collected on the oilcloth and dripped to the floor. She took off his flannel and eased his head back off the table and set him straight in his chair. The first pistol shot had passed through his arm without hitting the bone. The second shot had gone through his cheek. She felt his cheekbone with her fingers. He cried out. She grimaced but said nothing. His cries were not important.

"Bad?"

"Not bad."

"Is it broken?"

Mary shrugged again.

"I can't feel it."

She soaked strips of flour sacking in the willow tea and cleaned his face. The wound in his cheek was black around the edges, as though smudged with pencil or soot. She could see a gray line running along the wound channel under the skin. Every time she pressed the wet rags to his face, dark red blood oozed down to his jaw and dropped onto his long johns.

She worked on his wound in silence. When she was satisfied, she packed his pipe for him and stuck it between his lips and lit it for him with a sliver of cedar from the wood box. He nodded in thanks and pulled at the corncob pipe, and with every suck on the pipe he winced but didn't say much. Then she bathed and dabbed at his arm until it stopped bleeding.

When the stranger woke, he saw much the same scene he had left. Gephardt sat in his chair smoking, with his back to the door. His cheek was swollen and he didn't use his arm. Mary stood with her back to the counter by the icebox, her arms crossed over her apron. The stranger sat up and scooted back until he rested against the wall. He looked at Mary. She handed him a tin cup of tea and then stepped back to observe him. He took a drink, but before the weak tea could settle in his stomach he retched and threw up on the plank floor.

"I am sorry."

Mary said nothing. With great sighs and grimaces, she mopped up the vomit with more torn rags and then retreated next to the icebox.

After a while he tried drinking the tea again. This time it stayed down.

"Thank you," he said. He reached back to feel the knot on the back of his head. His hat was on the table but he made no move to get it. Gephardt packed another pipe. He held out the tobacco pouch and papers to the stranger, but the stranger motioned them away with his hand.

"You sit in chair?" asked Mary after the stranger finished his tea.

He nodded his head yes, testing it. Mary helped him rise and walk the few steps to the chair. He sat down as he had before. His hat and his pistol rested in the middle of the table. Four .22 short cartridges glinted dully in the light of the kerosene lantern, which Mary had lit and set back on the small plank nailed to the wall above the table, next to a fillet knife and a spool of thread with a needle stuck through the outermost windings. The sun had sunk lower but the heat was still heavy on the land and in the house. The stranger took out his pocket watch. It was six thirty.

Mary stood again to the side and watched Gephardt. His wounds would heal. The boys from the village had gone off to war and come back with worse, missing legs and fingers, and they had healed. Maybe there was nothing that could kill except death.

"Mary," said Gephardt, "our guest is hungry. You are hungry, yes?"

The stranger nodded.

Mary grabbed a fistful of starter from the bowl of sourdough setting in the warming rack and mixed it with soda and lard and flour and fried it. She set the plate of steaming bread between the two men, along with the jar of lard. With her fingernail, she broke the seal on one of the precious jars of raspberry jam she'd canned the week before, then broke the wax and extracted it. A few red seeds clung to the wax, and these she licked off before she set the wax in a bowl to be melted and used again.

"We eat," said Gephardt.

The stranger said, "Yes. We eat."

Afterward, the stranger stood, and Mary helped him into his coat and handed him his hat. She wrapped the rest of the pan bread in a grease-stained bit of flour sacking and handed it to him.

"I keep the gun," she said. "We keep that but you go now. Your work here is done. You are done here." She put the gun in her apron pocket along with the shells.

"Yes," said the man, unsteady on his feet.

"No more trouble for us. You go."

"Yes," said the stranger. "Yes." He turned to face Gephardt, who stood up to face him. They shook hands.

The stranger turned out of the shack onto the road. They watched him walk slowly down the road. It wasn't long before he was gone.

Gephardt sat back down in his chair. Mary looked at him; his arm must hurt and his face, too, but they would heal. He would once again be the strong man, the man who fixed things and smiled at her. Whoever he might have been long ago and whatever he might have done in those times were not who he was now. Now and for as long as she was there he would be Mary's husband.

Out the window, there was no longer anything to see. The man had gone, and with him everything he had known and the evil he had brought into their house, as though it were any old house and not hers, not the house that she had helped build and made into a home. Not just any home, but a place where such bad things would never happen, as they did when she was a girl.

The gun was heavy in her apron. She took it out and put it on top of the icebox, and the bullets she put with the others in the old Blue Tip matchbox, which held the stray shells that turned up around the house like seeds, in their pockets and pants and coats. They had a .22 rifle but it would be nice to have the pistol. In a few months the snow would come, and with it the ice; it would be a relief to bend the stove wire into snares and set them around the weeds and willows bordering the yard and down the tote road, where the hazel brush grew close, hiding all the many living things that were out there. With the gun she could check her snares, and if there were rabbits that were not yet caught, maybe sitting in the sun, maybe just sitting there out of reach, they might as well be miles away, because even a few feet off the trail, there was no way to catch them; but with the gun it would be different, because with the gun she could take them, yes, she could, she could level off and shoot them, and when they got shot in the head, they jumped and jumped, and their blood would be on the snow—yes, it would, it would be on the snow—and would slick up the brush; their blood was something not like ours, because their blood nourished us and made a fine brown gravy when she gutted them, but she would leave the blood sopping in their rib cages and set them carefully in the water. Their blood was not like ours because theirs was life for us and ours was not. With that gun she would be able to shoot them down, and their life would spray out on the snow, the bright red life waiting, like the raspberries in the jar, which she closed now, to be eaten.

PART IV

PRUDENCE

THIRTEEN

THE WIGWAM—AUGUST 3, 1952

My dear daughter I am going to do a terrible thing. That's what they say it is, a terrible Sin, they say, but I don't think so and it's only because I love you that I am making my plans. Yes love there is no other word for it. No other way to describe it. Richard calls me Sweetums and Honeydrop but it is only the honey he is after he is such a simple man he confuses honey with the taste of honey but that's how boys are—they don't understand what it is to live in the world. They don't know how it is to live in it but I do and let me tell you it is an awful thing. It is an awful thing to be torn between wanting it and hating it and the only thing to do is to let it go and for that I am sorry so very very sorry because who knows maybe you would grow into a big good girl and a strong girl who would find everything I might have missed and could not see. But Such Is Life. I once thought I could steal life from life and have it be my own my very own. This is what I thought when me and Grace left out of _________ with nothing of our own and not a word of English to share between us. I was thirteen and this was 1938. The village was not a good place it weren't much more than a gathering of drunks and when the veterans got their checks it was a constant party everyone putting on their finest vests and their clean trousers and the whiskey would pour and if it ran out everyone would make for the nearest logging camp and if there was no whiskey for them they would drink whatever they could find even kerosene and all these Indians would be lost in the woods and many would fall asleep there and when they came back they would be covered in mosquito bites and with great knots on their heads from when they ran into tree branches and tree trunks. It would have been funny but they were a rugged bunch and me and Grace had no one to take care of us no one to look after us and so sometimes we would sleep in the church but they found us there anyway. As I say I was thirteen and that was something they wanted because when they were drunk those village men thought of nothing other than what might be hidden between my legs which was nothing special then let me tell you. Nothing special at all. I was as plain as unbroken ground but this is the thing about men—they always think there is something valuable hidden down there where they cannot see and so they will endeavor to see it no matter what. That is what happened when me and Grace were staying in that cabin next to the store right under the nose of the BIA agent, but he couldn't care less for us since we had no allotment to sell and no timber to lease and so we were beneath his notice and it was there the first time and it must have been spring because I was just thirteen and it was warm out and we had only one dress each I remember both they was dresses from the missionaries and I don't believe in God or the Spirits they never done nothing for me but I believe in a dress, a pretty one, because then people see you as respectable. There was no windows in that cabin it was more of a storeroom than anything and there were sashes but no windows and the mosquitoes had quite a time with us till I took my extra dress and tacked it over the window and took yours and chinked it around the other window so at least we wouldn't get eaten alive they were ever a nuisance and a plague and the heat was unbearable with the windows covered but it was easier to sleep in the heat that way and you complained and were still at an age when you wet the bed which is a funny thing because we didn't even have beds and had to make do with flour sacks and feed sacks and it gives me some satisfaction now that when you peed the bed it soaked down into the corn and flour and so all of the proud men of the village and all their livestock such as they were which wasn't much were eating our piss. They were awful people with no pride and no consideration for the desperate times that were our times such was our lot I remember it was around that time because our woolen dresses were thick enough to shut out the bugs and most of the light. Yes it must have been June because we would shut ourselves in the storeroom when it was still light out as I didn't dare show myself when those village men were drinking and did our best to sleep and snuck handfuls of corn from the sacks but one of those old men came in he knew where we were and he was whiskeyed up and he was one of them who had been away to the Great War and he said in the dark you girls are in here I know it and he felt around with his hands and I thought then if I was quiet enough he wouldn't find me and he stumbled over the sacks and then tripped on some iron hoops and said goddamn it all I can't see a goddamn thing though I could see him plain through the cracks in the logs but that's how whiskey works on a man it makes him blind and he said this here is a little shit shack and I'll find you I swear and of course he did. I am glad to this day he found me first because you were only about nine and were sleeping just hard even with that stinking man tripping around in the dark and his hand found my ankle and he said there you are girlie there you are now and he did what he would and then staggered out when he was done and you never woke and I thank God for that because my sweet little sister I didn't want you to be scared. I was able to clean up after he was done and in the morning I snuck out around dawn and made to burn my bloody underthings in the burn barrel behind the store but the owner was awake and he said you girls stay away from here I don't want you stealing anything and I didn't argue because I didn't want him to see my clothes so I had to bury them along the north wall of the shack and if I ever went back to that village even now if I went back I imagine those rags are still there it's funny how something rotten will always stay that way and so in the light of day I buried my underthings and I had no replacements no spares. I saw that man the next day. He had come in from the logging camps with his winter's pay that's why he was there and he was proper in his vest and his canvas pants which I saw he took a great care to mend and with you right behind me I walked up to him you wouldn't even look at him but kept looking to the side and he was standing in front of the agency with our father and they said morning girls and I could tell neither had slept and I said father I need a little money for a dress just a little money and he said now you know I got no money for you why don't you go look for some berries to sell or do what I say and go out and peel some pulp they're always looking for pulp peelers and I said Grace needs looking after and then I got up my nerve and said to him but all the while I was looking at this man I need underthings mine are all wore out and I am practically a woman now aren't I? My father were hardly a man he were more like a season, he came around once a year to do what he'd do to our mother while she was still alive and then he'd be gone again. Still if he knew what this man this friend of his had done there would have been blood and that man were quite the coward. Still our father didn't say nothing and so I repeated myself ain't I a woman now I can show you if I like. Right up there in the sun on the steps with the whole village to see. That man who came in the shack was turning red he wanted everything to stop. Well Jesus Christ ain't you a little something-something said our father. The other man said aw look I got what the girlies need but he surely meant something else with those words though my father didn't catch his meaning and he took a dollar out of his pocket and handed it over and my father says if you want to throw your money away at my kids I won't stop you. And he snatched that dollar and didn't look back but went right to the trader's and bought me some cloth they surely didn't sell underthings in the village and the peddler who came through with such items didn't come but twice a year and only when the logging outfits had just paid out their rolls we didn't have stores like you have nowadays and I figured I could make myself what I needed and with the extra I got us some lard and a bag of oranges and we ate all the oranges straight away and when everyone was good and drunk we cooked ourselves some bannock on sticks over the trash barrel and it felt good to have some fat in us there's nothing like grease to make you feel you're alive. But that man must have thought we had ourselves an arrangement because he came back two nights later and it was the same thing he was fumbling around in the dark and cursing he was even drunker than before and I didn't want you to wake up so I kicked out my foot so he could find it and he said ahh there you is girlie there you is his English wasn't any good and they say men are dogs but they aren't even that smart. They aren't any better than foxes who just follow the same paths no matter what especially when the going is hard which is why they are so easy to snare because he meant to do the same thing he done before but I wasn't about to let him ruin my underthings which I had just made because I couldn't be sure of getting any more money so I said just wait and I took them off so he wouldn't rip and tear anything and he did his thing again and he was quite satisfied and he said sure I got what you want but how would he know what I want and then he was so drunk he retched up his whiskey in the corner of the shack before he left he might have been as dumb as a fox but he more of a pig than anything else and he kept coming back and every time he did I was able to get a little more from him though I have to say he must have thought I liked what he was doing but I didn't and that's the truth though you can't tell that to anyone without them nodding like sure sure they know that's what I say but the truth is something different. It is the truth. I don't expect that bastard understood it because after the first few times he came after me I learned the more I acted like it was something I wanted the faster he finished and it got so that I put a dab of lard down there so it wouldn't hurt so bad not that he could tell the difference between pig fat and a woman's pleasure which I never felt not once in my whole life. They say it's a wonderful thing a thing that takes your breath away. Anyway this is how we got through the summer or the part of it when the bastard still had some money to throw away but so it came one night he showed up with another man and I knew what they were after and the bastard made to do like he usually did with me but then the other man was standing there and talking real loud saying so where is she then you said she'd be here and you were but you were ever a hard sleeper and you knew nothing about the hard choices life had forced me to make and I said don't you touch her don't you dare I'll scream and I'll raise such a fuss you'll never be able to walk around the village again but for your shame and the bastard laughed and said it don't matter none I don't walk around as it is but his friend was quiet and he must have been thinking about it hard I knew who he was. He had a wife and kids and put on quite the show being such an important ceremony man but he was ever a man even though he was a ceremony man the bastard made rough with me and said just open your legs and close your mouth we got ourselves an arrangement and I did as I was told and while he was at his business I looked over at his friend who couldn't take his eyes off us and I said let's see you wipe your kids' tears off while your fingers smell like my sister's pussy and he walked out. My tongue was the only weapon I had the bastard slapped me hard then and told me to mind what I was doing and I did but I knew things would only get worse. The next day we packed up our stuff and went to the church and I told the priest a sad story about how we were practically orphans and needed to go to Flandreau and he said the salvation of our souls and our education were surely the most important things and in a short while we were on a wagon over to the railhead and from there we rode the train to Flandreau. It was exciting to be moving that fast across the hills and then the prairie and over the Red River and you squealed and laughed to see everything moving by so quick and said this is how birds must feel and I think you were right I felt like the master of the sky and that nothing could touch us if only my dear that were somehow true.

The train let us off at Grand Forks and to us it was truly a big city we had never seen anything like it and we thought the grain elevators the grandest of houses because we had no idea people didn't live there and we stood in all the people until the conductor came up to us and shook his head and read the cards that had been hung around our necks on necklaces of butcher's twine to see who we were and where we were going because neither of us could speak English and couldn't read either and he sat us in his office and gave us bread with real butter and it was a delicious thing to eat that sitting in a chair like proper ladies and we were careful not to get our dresses dirty he sat there in his office himself and worked on his papers and the work and the papers seemed like the greatest of mysteries and we thought him in his uniform and with his pocket watch and his papers a great person maybe even some kind of chief we didn't know he was but a lowly stationmaster or something like it. But I want you to know that he was a great man because of his kindness. He was a kind man. All he did was treat us like the children we were but that was surely something that had never happened to us before. After some time he motioned for us to follow him and we did. He showed us another train and then we were off again this time heading south and it wasn't that long not more than a few hours and we were at Flandreau and it was impressive with all the buildings made of brick and a creamery and a power plant there were electric lights everywhere which were something we were not used to at all and showers and dormitories and beds and everything you'd expect and it was truly an amazing place and mr brophy himself came out to meet us and he was an impressive friendly man and he showed us around along with the supervisor of the girls' dormitory and they brought us in and showed us where we'd sleep. They put my things by my bed but I didn't see another for you and I thought maybe they'd put you in a different building for younger girls which they did. We had us three good years there and I did as I was told and got good marks and never once got in trouble. I was graduated and they said they had a place for me in Wisconsin far to the east. It was like a death sentence to me. I had no choice and so I went. I lasted as long as I could and then I came back for you. I had always been by your side and protected you and it broke my heart truly it did more than anything else to see you looking up at me when I was leaving and questioning me with your eyes because you understood what that girl told us but you didn't dare say anything but I would come back for you. No one knew you like I did and no one knew your fears or the things that made you laugh or anything that a mother would know because that is what I had been to you. I said in our language so the older girl wouldn't understand don't worry about any of it but be ready for when I come for you because I already got a plan. It took me a few months to get enough money. But I got it and came back for you. We left in the night because you were my life and I was yours and we would always be together come what may we knew enough about the bush to take care of ourselves we were as they said wild animals and there is safety in that wildness and I knew that we could find someplace better than the damned village someplace far from loggers and whiskey someplace that had respect for us and our girlhood and where we would be together and it was to that brighter future that happy island we directed our footsteps. It was slow going we were no longer birds skimming over this green earth but worms that burrowed into all its low places and no one wants to be something like a worm but they survive and haven't far to fall not far at all we were happy to be together and we knew we would make it. We was going to Canada because they have lots of Indians up there so many you can get lost in them. That was my plan.

But then on our way we was hiding in the brush. We had just turned around the Mississippi and were getting ready to cut north. That's where the portage trail was from the big lake Winnibegoshish they call it and from there we would find Bawaatang it's called and that would lead us north. I knew my way around and I knew the rivers and streams and lakes because I had been dragged from camp to camp while our mother was still alive and I could have been a proper woods girl one of those Indians who knows things but I never had the chance before or after because while we were waiting out the sun Felix and Davey and Billy and Ernie and Frankie came near and they shot my sister and she died there shaking and shivering in the leaves while they watched and that was the end of my dreams there was no point anymore. And that's where I stayed even after Frankie died and they closed the Pines and moved back to Chicago. I was stuck around those people and they weren't you and they weren't my people even Felix though he were always good to me. We had some good times and he was always gentle but he was a man like all the others I had known as a girl. The only one of them worth anything was Frankie and that's just how it goes the good die young. My sister and you are proof of that and so was Frankie. He was the one who came to me after you got shot the rest of them went about with their business it was only Frankie who came to me. He stood there in the door of that little room they put me in. He had too much respect too much kindness to barge in and do what he really wanted to do he was better than most men. No. No he wouldn't ever force himself on a woman or take advantage of her. He said things to me that night standing there in the doorway his arms so strong and delicate you could tell he was a gentle man and he looked at me and said he would come back. I'll come back and make this right. I'll come back and fix things he said such was his noble gentle heart. Of all the goddamn people in this world he's the only one worth anything because he's the only one who never lied to me or let me down he said he'd write and he did and he sent me that necklace which is the treasure of my heart. Only he didn't come back. He didn't come back but that was hardly his fault.

I don't care what Billy has to say he is a piece of work himself. And just tonight I saw him which is the reason for this letter I guess. I needed a ride and we all pay with what we have little did I know way back when you and I were leaving that school we would pay like we did. Not during those long days when we slept in windrows and in barns and we worked here and there for our keep it wasn't work like I've been forced to do since it was honest and it left me tired and just emptied right out not all balled up and anxious like I've felt these many years oh you could give me that kind of work forever and I would be happy mucking out horse stalls and feeding slops and picking potatoes and beets and stirring lye and plucking chickens and cleaning fish and everything the poor people between Flandreau and here needed done in the hot days of July that we spent walking our way north and east. Our plan was to get to Canada and find ourselves a home on one of the reserves up there and everyone can say what they want but those dirt farmers struggled in them days and they were by and large good people and they often put us up for a few days or a week they were simple people and they wouldn't stand us being used unfairly they come to our country to avoid all sorts of unfairness themselves but I can't say the same for those Washburns except for Frankie he was always good to me. Billy told me some things and really made me think back on the days at the Pines I'd rather forget and I tried to shut my ears but he told me anyway. But God Jesus in heaven I know that some people like poetry and all that pretty stuff but words aren't made for that all words do is tear a person apart. They are bad and are used for bad no matter what smart people say and I don't care what language it is people talk only because you can't go around shooting people all the time and that's the truth. But Frankie. He was different. That is love and make no mistake about it that is love and not that other thing. I don't believe what Billy said I know the type of breed who is always jealous of everything everyone else has so what he says against Frankie is bound to be all twisted up. After White Earth which we avoided because they were always on the lookout for runaways like us we ran out of places that would have us the farms got smaller and smaller and there were more trees and so we had to get by living the way we'd grown up it were no hardship eating grass seeds and picking leeks and catching fish here and there at the beaver dams where they got trapped but the days were so long and sometimes with the storms that come at night it was impossible to see anything we didn't know the country there so we had to travel at first light and dusk and it took us a lot of time to make any progress. That day we were hiding in the hazel brush it were so dense that no one could see in there not anything and we knew by then how to be very quiet and still but Billy was enough of an Indian to sniff us out but not enough of a man to see his enemy before he shot. We heard them coming Felix and Billy and Ernest and Frankie and the quiet one David and then they got quiet and we thought they left and since we couldn't really see them I jumped and I guess so did you when the shot came and you started shaking your arms and legs all over the place and your blood was all over me and it couldn't have been more than a few minutes before all the blood left and they dragged us out of the brush and beheld you and Billy saw what he had done and Felix was rough with your body and rough with me and with Frankie too who was sensitive and not made for such troubles. I didn't even get to say a word before Felix took me up in his arms and carried me out of the woods and I didn't want to give him or anyone else the satisfaction of anything so I wouldn't say anything when they asked me their questions and when the Doctor checked me over and even when they buried your body I wouldn't give them any satisfaction at all but then the body washed up under the dock and they knew how empty it all was and how big the mistakes they had made and then it was like they owed me something like they owed me your life and that's a joke because that was a debt they couldn't pay and when everything was settled and done they kept me because they didn't know where to send me I never did tell them where I was from because to go back to that awful place and without you by my side would have made losing you more awful than it was in the first place. So they kept me and made me sleep down in Felix's shack and after they left I had to rely on him to bring me to school and to get me back across the river and I watched his hands as they prepared our food and as they cleaned our clothes and fed the fire. I couldn't stand the sight of them those thick fingers and their dainty fine gestures that looked so strange on such a big man. I hated them and hated him and I couldn't help it because as I say Felix was good to me but there was something separate in him some watchful thing like he knew more than he was letting on. I was hard on him at times and I guess I'm sorry for that because he would just look confused and hurt like some bear that had been shot in the gut and just sat down in the leaves too ignorant to know what had happened to it but once in a while Frankie would send things back to me from overseas little letters and sometimes a present and he was forever sending things to me because I owned his heart no matter what Billy says. Though when he visited me that night and stood in the doorway and said he was sorry so so sorry what did he have to be sorry for if he didn't do it? Frankie wrote me and called me DEAREST and told me he'd take me away from this terrible place and he sent me that necklace with a heart on it from England and we know that hearts mean LOVE. I was certain Frankie would come back and take me away when the war was over and we would make happy lives together and maybe even live in the big house just me and him. But Frankie never did come back but Billy did. I just can't believe it and I can't have you in a world like that. He said that Frankie is the one who done the shooting and that he never loved me but you can't trust a man to tell the truth. I remember hearing Billy right before the shot. It was Billy I heard right before you got shot saying "wait, wait, Frankie" that much is true I remember that clear as anything but I don't know what he meant. Why would Billy be saying wait wait Frankie if Billy done it after all? And after Billy told me those terrible things and did what he did between my legs he gave me that dress the one meant for his wife though I don't care I'll wear it anyway and they will see. I only wanted my sister and you but the world won't let me keep either one it surely won't. Why after all these years would he say such a thing. All that death was behind us. All of it was gone and done with. And why did my heart beat so fast when he said it, those words I had waited for so long. The world too harsh a place for such a thing to be a lie. It must be true. It must be. So it's time for me to make some decisions for myself.

It's getting on toward mid-morning. Richard has gone out to find us some whiskey and you'd think that it'd be easy to find such a thing in a broken-down village like this but maybe it's because the only place you can be sure to find it is in an Indian's gut or a logger's gut not on the shelves. We already drank up the rest of what we had yesterday and all last night and the gin too though that's as terrible as the plants they come from all scratchy and patchy you see them and ground hemlock around the blueberry patches and they make my skin crawl and so does the gin but we drank what we had because what them loggers say is probably true that it is liquid courage and you and me need all the courage we can get to get to where we are going. I already got everything else ready yesterday they sell it right on the shelves of the store and I bought it all proper like a lady who runs her own house and the man says to me what you need that for and I said well I got some rats I gotta take care of and he said well by God you're staying over at the Wigwam why don't you let Harris worry about it and I said they don't take proper care of the upper rooms and so I will because I won't sleep with a rat and I think he got my meaning because he straightens up and he says in all his years in the village he never once saw a rat and I said well then why do you sell the stuff then and he said people use it for this and that but for mice mostly and I said oh well that's probably what I am hearing at night. Mice. And so I got it and I'm ready. I don't need anyone where I'm going. Just you. Just my Grace. People say what I am about to do is a terrible thing but the world is a terrible thing and that's the truth. And I'm doing you a favor you don't need the world and I don't need the world but we need each other and so we're going to have to stick together and you have to listen to me I'm taking you to a good place you better believe it.

The train's just come in. The passengers are getting off the usual people but there is a small man that just stepped off he has a funny way of walking and he looks very serious. He don't belong here. But neither do we my sweet, my sweetest heart. We won't be here much longer not to worry. So I am going to stop writing. I'm not alone I got you. And I'll be seeing you soon anyway in the sweet by-and-by and perhaps there I will get to hold you in my arms and when you get older you can hold me in yours and we will have quite a time and the fields will be green and wide and life will be what we make of it.

EPILOGUE

THE WIGWAM—AUGUST 3, 1952

Not long after the maid found Prudence, the sheriff came. After him, the coroner. Soon, everyone in the village, Indian and white and in between, had gathered outside the hotel, in front of the hardware store and the grocer's, on the platform that served the depot, and in the Wigwam itself.

It was, as dramatic events go, quiet. There wasn't much fuss. It wasn't that kind of village. And it was too hot, in any event, to do more than sit and wonder and shake one's head. Rat poison. And with a baby on the way. The only disruption had been when Felix barged into the Wigwam and up to Prudence's room and insisted on accompanying her body to the coroner's office off the reservation.

The sheriff, sweating through his uniform, looked dully at him.

"You family, Chief?"

"I'm her father."

"You don't look it."

Felix shrugged.

The sheriff looked at Felix and then around at the others and then at the small room itself, the dust blooming off the sills with every dry, cracked breath of the window. The room was nothing much. A narrow iron-framed bed covered with white sheets and a neatly folded gray army blanket rolled up at the foot. A three-drawer dresser with a white enameled washbasin and matching pitcher on the top. The top drawer of the dresser was slightly ajar, a pair of white cotton women's underwear hung out over the drawer front, drying. A washcloth and bar of soap rested on an enameled tray next to the basin. A dirt-stained floral-print dress lay crumpled in the corner. A black clutch stood on the dresser. A silver necklace and heart pendant lay on top of a long, neatly folded letter next to a clutch of dried flowers on the windowsill, and there was also a bottle of gin there, and a yellow cardboard box, and a single, bent spoon. A brandy bottle had been set carefully in the wastebasket on top of crumpled brown craft paper and some clothing tags. Next to the only chair, over which had been folded a short wool jacket, was a small red cardboard suitcase.

"Is that true?" asked the sheriff of no one in particular.

No one answered.

"I asked if that's true or not." This time he took the time to cast his blood-rimmed eyes at those gathered in the small room; at Felix, at Billy, then at Harris and the washing girl who had discovered the body.

"No," said Harris. "No, that ain't true."

The sheriff looked hard at Felix.

"So that ain't true."

"That's my girl," said Felix.

"So it is true."

"That's my girl," said Felix.

"Jesus Christ. Fine. Fine, fine, fine."

So her body was loaded onto a canvas stretcher, covered with a white sheet, and handed down the narrow stairs like a ham in paper. And Felix, looking very out of place, rode in the back of the cruiser, last in the caravan of official vehicles that sped off toward the county seat, though now there was no rush. Everyone watched them go. Felix sat straight in the backseat with his hands on his lap and his cap dusting the headliner. He looked for all the world like one of those cigar-store Indians; for all the world as though he'd been turned to wood. They watched until the dust and the heat and the grasshoppers—surprised, interrupted—resumed their dreary duties of marking time in a place where time didn't matter anymore.

They saw the Jew that day. And they remembered him later when they bothered to think about it. This was 1952, and no one had seen a Jew on the reservation before. Even the men who had served in the war hadn't seen any. None in Minneapolis in 1944, when they had been fed roast beef at the Milwaukee Road Depot before shipping out. And none in Europe, either. Not alive. Not dressed, anyway, as this one was, in a black suit and a black hat. They saw him step off the train and adjust his hat and wipe his forehead and then disappear into the Wigwam only to reappear a few minutes later with a small suitcase in one hand and a soda in the other and set off down the highway.

"What was that?" asked Billy Cochran.

The others looked after him as he walked out to the highway and turned west, picking his way through the uncut weeds on the shoulder of the macadam.

"Christ Almighty, I think it was a Jew," said Dickie Jr., who'd been to Mittelbau-Dora.

"A what?"

"The last of his goddamn tribe."

A NOTE ON SOURCES

Although this is entirely a work of fiction, I consulted many people and many books in the course of constructing it. Books that were particularly helpful were Anthony Beevor's *The Second World War* and *D-Day: Battle for Normandy*. Also very helpful were Jack Myers's *Shot at and Missed: Recollections of a World War II Bombardier*, Brian O'Neill's *Half a Wing, Three Engines and a Prayer*, and John Comer's *Combat Crew: The Story of 25 Combat Missions Over Europe From the Daily Journal of a B-17 Gunner*. I have also quoted from the *B-17 Pilot's Training Manual*, available at:

http://www.merkki.com/bombardiers_of_usaaf_in_world_wa.htm.

ACKNOWLEDGMENTS

I would like to thank the Lannan Foundation for its generous support. My time spent as a Lannan Resident in Marfa, Texas, saw this novel to completion. I would also like to thank Adam Eaglin and Becky Saletan. I am in debt to you both and couldn't have done it without you.

I would also like to thank Gretchen Potter and my children, Elsina, Noka, and Bine, for enduring long absences and disappearing acts into the northern woods, the deserts of West Texas, and into those even more baffling interior landscapes where novels are born. My beautiful children—you gave me all the reason to venture out and even better reasons to venture back. Thank you.